With Seduction in Mind

The moment he touched his mouth to hers, Sebastian knew he'd been wrong, terribly wrong, to think stealing a few kisses from Daisy Merrick would be a harmless seduction. Her lips were every bit as soft as he'd imagined, their taste every bit as sweet, but what he hadn't imagined was the effect her kiss would have on him.

The contact of her mouth against his brought waves of pleasure so acute it was almost like pain. His heart wrenched in his chest, and arousal instantly began coursing through his body, and he felt as if he were a green youth of sixteen, kissing a girl for the first time. The taste of her eclipsed any sensation he'd felt before, making one word hammer through his brain and pulse through his blood.

More.

By Laura Lee Guhrke

WITH SEDUCTION IN MIND
SECRET DESIRES OF A GENTLEMAN
THE WICKED WAYS OF A DUKE
AND THEN HE KISSED HER
SHE'S NO PRINCESS
THE MARRIAGE BED
HIS EVERY KISS
GUILTY PLEASURES

ATTENTION: ORGANIZATIONS AND CORPORATIONS
Most Avon Books paperbacks are available at special quantity discounts for bulk purchases for sales promotions, premiums, or fund raising. For information, please call or write:

Special Markets Department, HarperCollins Publishers, 10 East 53rd Street, New York, New York 10022-5299. Telephone: (212) 207-7528.   Fax: (212) 207-7222.

Laura Lee Guhrke

With Seduction In Mind

AVON

An Imprint of HarperCollinsPublishers

AVON BOOKS
An Imprint of HarperCollins*Publishers*
10 East 53rd Street
New York, New York 10022-5299

Copyright © 2009 by Laura Lee Guhrke
Excerpts from *With Seduction in Mind* copyright © 2009 by Laura Lee Guhrke; *The Most Wicked of Sins* copyright © 2009 by Kathryn Caskie; *Captive of Sin* copyright © 2009 by Anna Campbell; *True Confessions* copyright © 2001 by Rachel Gibson
ISBN 978-0-06-145683-1
www.avonromance.com

First Avon Books paperback printing: September 2009

Avon Trademark Reg. U.S. Pat. Off. and in Other Countries, Marca Registrada, Hecho en U.S.A.
HarperCollins® is a registered trademark of HarperCollins Publishers.

Printed in the U.S.A.

10 9 8 7 6 5 4 3 2 1

For Aaron
Because of the typewriter.
Now, where's my Steampunk?

Chapter 1

All the world's a stage, and all the men
and women merely players:
they have their exits and their entrances;
and one man in his time plays many parts.
William Shakespeare

London, May 1896

Daisy Merrick was unemployed. Such a circumstance wasn't unusual—Daisy had been in that particular pickle many times before. Some people, including her sister, were inclined to see her ever-changing job situation as her own fault, but to Daisy's mind that opinion was most unfair. Today was a perfect example.

Bristling with indignation, she marched out of the offices of Pettigrew and Finch, where she had just been informed by the matron in charge of typists that her services would no longer be required. And no, Matron had added upon her inquiry, they could not see clear to providing her with a letter of character. Given her shameless conduct, no favorable reference would be possible.

"My shameless conduct?" she muttered, pausing on the sidewalk to search for a passing omnibus amid the traffic that clogged Threadneedle Street. "Mr. Pettigrew is the one who should be ashamed!"

When that gentleman had cornered her in the supply closet, taken up her hand, and confessed to a deep and ardent passion for her, she had refused to succumb to his advances, as any respectable woman would have done. Yet, when informed by Matron Witherspoon a short time later that her employment had been terminated, Daisy's indignant explanation had not saved her job. Mr. Pettigrew, Matron had reminded her with a superior little smile, was a founding partner of an important banking firm, and Daisy Merrick was a typist of no consequence whatsoever.

An omnibus turned the corner, and Daisy waved her arms in the air to hail the horse-drawn vehicle. When it stopped, she climbed aboard and handed over the three-pence fare that would take her home. As the omnibus jerked into motion, she secured an empty seat and considered how best to explain to Lucy that she'd lost yet another job.

Though she knew the blame could not be laid at her door, she also knew her elder sister might not see things quite that way. Lucy would list all the reprimands Daisy had received from Matron for her impertinence during the three months of her employment with Pettigrew and Finch. No doubt, Lucy would remind Daisy of how Mr. Pettigrew had witnessed Matron's latest scolding a week earlier, of how he had patted her hand once the older woman had gone, of how he had called her honesty "refreshing" and assured her she had no reason to worry, of how he'd said he would "take care of her."

Lucy might even be tiresome enough to bring up the warnings she had issued regarding Mr. Pettigrew's assurances, and her own blithe disregard of these warnings.

Daisy bit her lip. In hindsight, she knew she should have followed Lucy's suggestion and informed Mr. Pettigrew that she couldn't impose upon him to intervene with Matron on her behalf. Had she done that, this mess might have been avoided. But having a sister who was always right could be so aggravating, and Daisy often felt an irresistible compulsion to fly in the face of Lucy's well-meant advice. This had been one of those times.

The employment mishaps that plagued Daisy's life never happened to her sister, of course. Lucy, Daisy thought with a hint of envy, was tact personified. If the stout, elderly, sweaty-faced Mr. Pettigrew had seized her by the hand, declared the violence of his affections, and promised her a tidy little income and a house in a "discreet" neighborhood, Lucy wouldn't have raised an eyebrow. She would have informed him in a dignified manner that she was not that sort of woman and that surely he would not wish to dishonor either of them by making unsavory assumptions about his female employee's virtue. Such a prim, maidenly speech—along with a gentle reminder to think of his wife and children—would have had Mr. Pettigrew, one of London's most important businessmen, hanging his head like a naughty schoolboy. He would have withdrawn from the supply closet thoroughly ashamed of himself, and the entire episode would have blown over.

Daisy, however, was not made of such stuff. She'd stared at Mr. Pettigrew's perspiring face in openmouthed stupefaction for only two seconds before blurting out in characteristic fashion the first thought that entered her head: "But you're so *old!*"

Her impulsive reaction had sealed her fate. Instead of withdrawing from the supply closet feeling ashamed of himself, Mr. Pettigrew had departed in a huff of injured masculine dignity, and Daisy had lost her fourth post in less than a year.

It was her outspokenness that always seemed to land her in the suds. While working for a fashionable dressmaker, she'd discovered most women did not want to hear the truth about their clothing choices. When asked for her opinion, a showroom woman did not tell the wealthy but stout client who adored silver satin that silver satin made her look fatter.

Daisy hadn't had any better success as a governess.

A baron's daughters, Lady Barrow had informed her, did not play games like rounders. They did not fill their coloring books with images of orange grass, green sky, and girls with purple hair. They didn't need to do sums and learn long division. No, a baron's daughters sewed perfect samplers, painted perfect replicas of the Italian Masters, and made useless—but perfect—falderal for their friends. When Daisy said that was just plain silly, she'd been shipped home from Kent in disgrace.

As a typist for the legal firm of Ledbetter and Ghent, she'd learned the hard way that Mr. Ledbetter did not appreciate having the errors in his legal briefs pointed out to him by a mere typist.

And now, there was Mr. Pettigrew—powerful, influential banker and lecherous cad. Another lesson learned, she thought with a sigh. A woman who earned her living needed tactful ways to contend with dishonorable propositions from the sterner sex.

Ah, well. Daisy tried to adopt a philosophical attitude. She gave a shrug and tucked a loose strand of her fiery red hair behind her ear. Everything would turn out all right, she told herself as she leaned back in her seat and stared through the window at the brick-fronted publishing houses that lined Fleet Street. It wasn't as if she would be tossed into the street. Lucy was the proprietress of an employment agency, and after an inevitable round of "I-told-you-so's," her sister would insist upon finding her yet another post.

Daisy didn't want to seem ungrateful, but she couldn't greet the prospect of Lucy's help with much enthusiasm. Her sister had the tendency to think only of the practical aspects of a position, never considering whether the tasks were interesting. Daisy thought of Lady Barrow, Mr. Ledbetter, and Mr. Pettigrew and thought perhaps this time she should find her own job. She might have better luck that way.

How delightful, she thought, if she could announce to her sister that yes, she'd lost her place at Pettigrew and Finch, but she'd found another post straightaway. Lucy wouldn't be able to give her that exasperated look and heavy, disappointed sigh if her next employment situation was a fait accompli.

The omnibus passed Saxton and Company, a book publisher, reminding Daisy of the half dozen manuscripts crammed into the drawers of her desk at home. She smiled to herself. What she ought to do was stop dabbling and become a real writer. After all, her friend, Emma, had done that very thing with much success.

Lucy wouldn't like it. Despite Emma's example, Lucy had always discouraged Daisy's literary ambitions. It was a most uncertain sort of job, she'd often pointed out, filled with rejection and criticism. And the pay, if there was any at all, was sporadic and often dismally low. That wasn't a consideration for Emma, who had married her publisher, a wealthy viscount, but it was of vital importance to Daisy and her sister.

Girl-bachelors, alone in the world, they had to earn their living.

The omnibus halted at Bouverie Street to take on a new passenger, and as Daisy stared at the street name painted on the corner building, she felt a jolt of recognition. Bouverie Street was where Emma's husband, Viscount Marlowe, had his publishing offices. How extraordinary that someone should have hailed this omnibus one block from Marlowe Publishing at the very moment she'd been thinking about becoming a writer.

This, she realized, could not be mere coincidence. This was Fate.

The omnibus began moving again, and Daisy jumped to her feet. She leaned over the passenger beside her to give the bell wire a hard yank, causing the other passengers to groan at the further delay. The vehicle lurched as the driver applied the braking mechanism, and Daisy grabbed for the brass handlebar overhead with one gloved hand to stay on her feet, flattening her other palm atop her straw boater hat to keep it in place. Once the vehicle had come to a full stop, she moved toward the front, ignoring the hostile glances of her fellow passengers.

She disembarked and paused on the sidewalk, looking up Bouverie Street to the brick building on the next corner. The chance of ever becoming a published writer was somewhere between slim and nonexistent, but Daisy waved aside any consideration of the odds and began walking toward Marlowe Publishing. Becoming a writer was, she felt certain, her destiny.

Daisy was not only rash-tongued and impulsive. She was also an incurable optimist.

Opening nights were always hell.

Sebastian Grant, the Earl of Avermore, paced across the oak floorboards backstage at the Old Vic, too agitated to sit down. It had been so long since he'd had a play on, he'd forgotten what opening night was like.

"It's bound to fail, of course," he muttered as he paced. "My last play was a disaster, and this one is worse. God, why didn't I burn the stupid thing when I had the chance?"

Most people would have been shocked to hear England's most famous novelist and playwright disparaging his work in this manner, but his friend, Phillip Hawthorne, Marquess of Kayne, listened to Sebastian's condemnation of his latest play with the forbearance of one who had heard it all before. "You don't believe a single word you're saying."

"Oh, yes, I do. The play is shit." Sebastian reached one end of the stage and turned to start back in the opposite direction. "Utter shit."

"You always say that."

"I know, but this time, it's true."

Phillip did not seem impressed. He leaned one shoulder against a supporting pillar and folded his arms, watching his friend pace back and forth. "Some things never change."

"You'd best go home before the thing starts," he advised darkly, ignoring Phillip's murmured comment. "Spare yourself the torture of watching it."

"Is there nothing worthy in it?"

"Oh, it opens well enough," he conceded with reluctance. "But in the second act, the whole story falls apart."

"Mm-hmm."

"The dark moment is so anticlimactic it might as well not be there at all."

"Mm-hmm."

"And as for the plot—" Sebastian broke off and raked a hand through his dark hair with a sound of derision. "The entire plot rests on a silly misunderstanding."

"You're in good company, then. Dozens of Shakespeare's plays are based on misunderstandings."

"Which is why Shakespeare is overrated."

Phillip's shout of laughter caused him to give his friend a puzzled glance as he passed by. "What's so amusing?"

"Only you would have the arrogance to deem Shakespeare overrated."

Sebastian failed to see the humor. "I need a drink."

He walked to a table offstage, where a variety of refreshments had been laid out for the actors. He chose a bottle and held it up with an inquiring glance, but Phillip shook his head, and Sebastian poured gin into only one tumbler.

"There is no reason for Wesley not to tell Cecilia the truth," he went on, resuming discussion of his new play as he set down the bottle and picked up his glass. "Except that if he did, there would be no reason for the letter in the handbag, everything would be resolved before the end of Act Two, and the play would be over."

"The audience won't notice."

"Of course they won't." Sebastian downed the gin in one draught. "They'll be asleep."

Phillip chuckled at that. "I doubt it."

"I don't. I've seen the rehearsals. I give it a week before it closes."

His friend's silence caused him to glance over his shoulder. "No protest of that for friendship's sake?"

"Sebastian, the play is probably fine."

"No, it's not. It's not good enough." He paused, for he could hear his father's voice echoing back to him from childhood, a voice that had uttered those same words about nearly everything he'd done as a boy. "Never, ever good enough," he muttered, pressing the cool glass to his forehead.

"That's not true," Phillip's voice overrode the past. "You are a fine writer, and you damn well know it. That is," he amended at once, "when you're not torturing yourself over how awful you are."

Sebastian took a deep breath and turned around. "What if the critics slaughter me?"

"You'll do what you always do. You'll tell them to sod off and you'll write something else."

Sebastian could not be so sanguine. "What if they're right? Remember my last novel? When that was published four years ago, everyone hated it. Even you admitted it wasn't any good."

"That is not what I said. You demanded my opinion, and in my answering letter, I said it was not one of my personal favorites, and that was all I said."

"You're so polite, Phillip." Sebastian took a swallow of gin and grimaced. "It was garbage. I haven't written a thing in half a dozen years that's been worth a damn. The critics know it. You know it. I know it. I shall be slaughtered tomorrow."

There was a long silence, and then Phillip spoke. "Sebastian, I've known you since we were boys. I watched you on the fields at Eton twenty-five years ago, cursing yourself every time you missed a goal, yet swaggering around like God's gift to football every time you made one. I watched you agonize over every single word of the novel you wrote when we were at Oxford, yet when it was published, you accepted the praise heaped on you with a complacence that made me want to throttle you for your conceit."

"Do you have a point?"

"I have never ceased to be amazed by this dichotomy of your character. You possess an unsurpassed arrogance about your work, and yet at the same time, you battle these agonizing uncertainties. How can two such opposing traits exist in one man? Are all writers like this, or only you?"

These days, he felt none of the arrogance his friend spoke of, but he felt all of the uncertainty. "It's been eight years since I last saw you. Living abroad changed me. I can't—" Sebastian broke off, unable to voice the truth, though it echoed through his mind as an inalterable fact. He couldn't write anymore, but he couldn't say that out loud. "I'm not the same man you knew," he said instead.

"You are exactly the same. Pacing back and forth like a cat on hot bricks, disparaging your latest work in the worst way and telling anyone who'll listen that it's rubbish. You've already made your usual dire predictions that everyone will hate it and it will fail miserably. I'm waiting for the part where you announce your career is over and the cycle will be complete." Phillip shook his head. "No, no, Sebastian, you may think you've changed, but you haven't. Not one bit."

Phillip was dead wrong, of course. He had changed, and in ways his friend couldn't possibly understand. Still, there was no point in telling Phillip what havoc the past eight years had wrought. There was no point in informing his friend that there wasn't ever going to be another book or another play. He was finished.

Weariness came over him suddenly, smothering his bout of nervous energy. He lowered his head, pinching the bridge of his nose between his thumb and forefinger, and he couldn't help a wave of longing for the cocaine. Three years since he'd last taken the stuff, but God, he still craved it. With cocaine to silence his crippling creative doubts, writing had been so easy. He hadn't cared if the work was good or not, because for the first time in his life, it was good enough. Cocaine had made him feel as if he could do anything, ward off any adversity, triumph over any obstacle. The cocaine had made him feel invincible.

Until it had almost killed him.

"Sebastian?" Phillip's voice intruded on his thoughts. "Are you all right?"

He lifted his head, forcing a smile. "Of course. You know how moody I am on an opening night."

A bell sounded, indicating that the play would begin in five minutes' time, and Phillip straightened away from the pillar. "I'd best take my seat. My wife will be wondering what's become of me."

"You shouldn't have come."

"Yes, well, I'm a glutton for punishment."

"You must be. The play is rubbish."

"You always say that." Unperturbed, his friend moved toward stage right.

"I know," Sebastian called after him. "But this time, it's true."

"Rubbish?" Sebastian stared in disbelief at the folded-back newspaper he was holding. "The *Social Gazette* is calling my play rubbish?"

Abercrombie, assuming this to be a rhetorical question, made no reply. Instead, the valet lifted the tray of shaving implements, gave Sebastian an inquiring look, and waited. Saunders, the footman who had brought the morning papers, also stood by without replying, waiting to be dismissed.

Sebastian ignored them both. He read again the opening line of the review printed in that morning's edition of the *Social Gazette*: " 'Sebastian Grant, once considered to be among the most brilliant writers of the nineteenth century, stumbles in his first attempt at comedy, *Girl with a Red Handbag*. The plot is rubbish—' "

He broke off in the same place he'd stopped before and glanced at the byline. "George Lindsay," he muttered, lifting his head with a scowl. "Who the devil is George Lindsay?"

Abercrombie did not answer, once again ascertaining that a reply from him was not expected. He continued to wait by the shaving chair for his master to sit down.

Instead, Sebastian resumed reading. " 'The plot is rubbish,' " he repeated, his ire rising, " 'with an unbearably trite theme and an utterly implausible story line. As a comedy, it might be forgiven these flaws if it were actually amusing. Alas, this reviewer found these three hours at the Old Vic as amusing as a visit to the dentist.' "

Thoroughly nettled by what he had read so far, he moved to toss the newspaper aside, but then he changed his mind, his curiosity overriding his disdain. He resumed reading.

" 'Everyone knows that Sebastian Grant possesses the aristocratic title of Earl of Avermore, and that estates are expensive to maintain in these times of agricultural depression. Theatrical comedy, however, is not only fashionable, but also quite lucrative. This reviewer can only conclude that in the writing of this play, the author was motivated by monetary rather than literary concerns.' " He paused and looked at Abercrombie. "Well, yes," he said in mock apology, "I do like to be paid for my work. Shocking, isn't it?"

He didn't bother to wait for his valet to attempt a reply. " 'The result is unfortunate,' " he went on. " 'Instead of returning to London theatre as a first-rate Sebastian Grant, he has chosen to return as a second-rate Oscar Wilde.' "

With a sound of outrage, he hurled the newspaper through the air, sending its pages flying in all directions. "A second-rate Oscar Wilde?" he roared. "Unbearably trite? Utterly implausible? Damn the impudence! How dare this critic . . . this blatherskite . . . this . . . this nobody who uses adverbs with such abandon . . . how dare he shred my play in this manner?"

As Saunders moved to gather up the pages of the newspaper, Abercrombie spoke at last. "Mr. Lindsay must be a man of no breeding, sir. Do you wish to shave now?"

"Yes, Abercrombie, thank you," he said, glad for the distraction. "This critic calls my play rubbish, but his review is what belongs in the dustbin. Saunders," he added, "put that idiotic tripe where it belongs."

"Very good, sir." The footman bowed, but as he moved to depart with the now neatly folded newspaper, Sebastian's curiosity once again got the better of him. He reached out and snatched back the paper, then he waved the footman out of the dressing room and sat down in his shaving chair. While Abercrombie soaped a shaving brush, Sebastian continued to read the review. It was an infuriating exercise.

The play, this Mr. Lindsay declared, was based upon a flimsy misunderstanding, and its hero, Wesley, was too dim for words. A simple explanation by him to his lady love, Cecilia, in Act Two would have resolved everything. Wesley's attempts to court Cecilia were no doubt meant to amuse the audience, but were in truth, painful to watch and made one embarrassed for the poor fellow. The ending of the play, however, was immensely satisfying in that it *was* the ending.

"Ha-ha," Sebastian muttered, his lip curling. "So clever, this Mr. Lindsay. Full of wit."

He told himself to stop reading such idiocy, but he was nearly done, and he decided he might as well finish.

Those who had hoped Sebastian Grant's emergence from such a long hiatus would hail a return to the powerful, deeply moving work of his early career will be disappointed. Once a lion of English literature, he has chosen to present us with more of the slick, trivial pabulum that has marked his writing for eight years now. This reviewer cannot help but feel saddened that Sebastian Grant's most brilliant work is nearly a decade behind him.

Sebastian snarled, uttering a curse worthy of a Lascar seaman, and once again hurled the newspaper. It sailed over Abercrombie, who'd had the sense to duck, and fluttered to the floor.

As his valet straightened, Sebastian stared at the untidy heap of newspaper on the floor and felt an overwhelming desire to read the review again. Instead, he leaned back in the chair and closed his eyes, but as his valet began their daily shaving ritual, Sebastian could not stop George Lindsay's words from echoing through his mind.

. . . like a visit to the dentist . . . a second-rate Oscar Wilde . . . most brilliant work is nearly a decade behind him . . .

He had long ago accepted the rantings of critics as an inevitable part of his profession, but this scathing condemnation passed all bounds. And coming from the *Gazette*, a newspaper owned by his own publisher, was insult added to injury.

Who was this George Lindsay anyway? What qualifications did he possess that entitled him to slaughter a writer's work and call it rubbish?

"My lord?"

Sebastian opened his eyes, watching as Abercrombie stepped back to reveal his butler, Wilton, standing nearby with a salver in hand. "A letter has come from Mr. Rotherstein, sir," the butler informed him. "Hand delivered by his secretary. I thought it might be important, so I brought it up to you straightaway."

Sebastian sat up, taking the letter from the tray with a feeling of foreboding. He broke the seal, unfolded the note, and read it, not surprised by the lines penned in Jacob Rotherstein's bold black script.

Ticket sales for tonight already down thirty percent from last night. If trend continues, the play could be forced to close by week's end. Word is the Gazette *had it right—that the play is a failure. What the devil? Can't we at least expect a decent review from a paper owned by your publisher? Suggest you discuss the situation with Marlowe at once.*

J.R.

Sebastian tossed the letter back onto the tray with an oath. Rotherstein was right, of course. Something had to be done. He'd pay Marlowe a visit this afternoon, he decided, and make the situation clear. George Lindsay might not know it yet, but his career as a dramatic critic was over.

Chapter 2

*I have your review in front of me. Soon it will
be behind me.*

George Bernard Shaw

"Why George Lindsay?" Lucy glanced up from
the newspaper in her hand to meet her sister's gaze
across the breakfast table. "What made you choose
that pseudonym?"

"Many great women of literature have chosen to
write under the name of George," Daisy explained
and took a sip of her morning tea. "George Sand.
George Eliot."

The other ladies gathered in the dining room of the
lodging house at Little Russell Street were too polite to
point out that Daisy was not yet a great woman of literature, but was at present merely a literary critic, and
a temporary one at that.

"As for Lindsay," Daisy went on, "I think it sounds quite intellectual and literary."

Her friend Miranda Dickinson spoke from beside her. "Yes, but why have a pseudonym at all? Aren't you disappointed not to have your true name on your first published piece?"

Daisy was too excited to feel any disappointment. "A critic can't use her true name. Imagine the repercussions! Resentful writers would be coming to vent their spleens at the poor critic whenever they received an unfavorable review."

There were concurring murmurs from the other ladies, and then their landlady spoke. "Regardless of what name you use," said Mrs. Morris, "you are now a published writer, Daisy. We are all very happy for you."

"And envious, too!" Miranda added, laughing. "Tickets to the opening of a Sebastian Grant play and ten shillings in pay to write a review of it for the newspaper? I wish I'd thought to approach Marlowe and offer to write reviews for him!"

She hadn't exactly offered to do it; when she'd called on Lord Marlowe the previous afternoon to inquire about the possibility of earning her living as a writer, he had just learned that his usual theater critic was ill and would be unable to attend the opening that night of Sebastian Grant's new play. Daisy's first piece of published writing had been the result of fortuitous timing.

"One review isn't much, but it's a start." Daisy cast an uneasy glance at her sister. "Lord Marlowe has agreed to read one of my novels and give his opinion of its suitability for publication. I am to deliver the manuscript to his offices this afternoon."

Several of the other ladies expressed congratulations at this news, but Lucy was not among them. "You asked Lord Marlowe to read your work?" she asked, a frown drawing her blonde brows together. "You imposed upon Emma's husband?"

"I didn't impose upon him," Daisy assured her at once. "He told me he welcomed the chance to read a new writer, and said our friendship with his wife had nothing to do with it."

Lucy gave a sniff. "Of course he would say that. He is a gentleman. Why didn't you tell me about this last night?"

"There wasn't time. You arrived home just as Mrs. Morris and I were leaving, and I couldn't stop to explain, for we were already late. I was fortunate Mrs. Morris could chaperone me."

"I was delighted to do it." Their landlady glanced at the other young women gathered around the table. "Being a widow, I am well able to act as chaperone to any of you ladies should you require it. I'm quite happy to do so, in fact."

"What on earth spurred you to take your writing to Lord Marlowe?" Lucy asked, returning to the subject at hand. "I had no idea you were contemplating such a course."

"Neither did I," she admitted. "But I was on my way home, and the omnibus stopped right by Marlowe Publishing to take on passengers, and the idea to talk with his lordship just came to me." She paused, knowing she had to tell Lucy she'd lost another job, but she didn't want to discuss the embarrassing incident with Mr. Pettigrew in front of the others, and she attempted to skirt the issue. "I never expected him to give me a writing assignment that very day. And when he offered to pay me to write a review of Sebastian Grant's new play, I couldn't believe it. *Sebastian Grant*? One of the most famous writers in the world?"

"Infamous, you mean," Miranda put in. "Prudence knows about him, I'm sure. I read in some scandal sheet that he and the Duke of St. Cyres were quite the wild men about town while they were both living in Florence—women, drinking, scandalous parties. Before the duke came home and married our Pru, of course," she added, referring to their friend and former fellow lodger, Prudence Bosworth, who'd been a seamstress before unexpectedly inheriting millions of pounds and marrying the once-notorious Duke of St. Cyres.

"Maria knows him, too," Daisy added, mentioning another former tenant of Little Russell Street as she reached for the jam pot. "Knows Sebastian Grant, I mean. Mrs. Morris and I saw her in the foyer of the

Old Vic last night before the play. We didn't have much chance for conversation, but she mentioned that her husband was backstage with him to wish him luck. She said her husband thinks the man has brilliant talent."

"Well, our Daisy doesn't seem to agree," Lucy commented with a hint of amusement as she passed the paper to Eloisa Montgomery, seated beside her.

"But I do think he's brilliant," Daisy protested, pausing in the act of spreading jam on her toast.

"One wouldn't know that from your review," Lucy pointed out. "It hardly does the man or his writing any credit."

Daisy felt a pang of dismay. "I was too blunt, wasn't I?"

"Blunt?" Lucy lifted a brow. "Dearest, you likened viewing his play to visiting the dentist."

"Daisy, you didn't!" Miranda gave a half laugh as if she didn't know whether to be shocked or amused. "Hurry up, Eloisa, and pass the *Gazette* this way. I must read this review."

"Writing it was much more difficult than I thought it would be," Daisy admitted. "When the viscount told me he wanted me to review the play, I had so hoped I would enjoy it. What a letdown," she added with a vexed sigh and plunked the spoon back into the jam pot. "Why does the man insist upon writing these light, fluffy pieces nowadays? There's no substance to them! His earlier work is so much better, much more powerful and exciting. I didn't mean my review to be unkind, truly, Lucy, but I was being paid to be a critic. I had to give my opinion honestly."

"I cannot imagine you ever being anything but honest, dear Daisy," Mrs. Morris put in with a smile. "But in future, dear, it might behoove you to cultivate a talent for delicacy. Particularly if you are reviewing the work of a man."

"I shall keep that in mind, ma'am, though I doubt I shall be writing any further reviews. I did this one only because the critic of the *Gazette* was ill. I arrived at the viscount's office at just the right moment. Fate, you might say."

"However it came about, I cannot help but applaud your initiative," Lucy said. "You received an evening's entertainment and earned some pin money as well. Pettigrew and Finch pays you a generous wage, but ten additional shillings never goes amiss."

At the mention of her former employers, Daisy wriggled in her chair. "Yes . . . well . . ." she mumbled, her secret suddenly feeling like a ten-ton weight on her shoulders. "Er . . . yes."

Lucy perceived her discomfiture. "What's wrong?" she asked. "What are you not telling me?"

Caught, Daisy braced herself for the inevitable confrontation. "I'm no longer working for Pettigrew and Finch. I intend to make my living as a writer."

"You resigned your post at Pettigrew and Finch to be

a writer?" Lucy cried. "Are you mad?" The latter question displayed a lapse in tact most uncharacteristic of Lucy, and she seemed to sense it, for she paused, and it was several moments before she spoke again. "Writing is not a practical means of earning a living," she finally said. "We decided that long ago."

No, you decided, Daisy thought, with a flash of resentment. She forced it down. "I've always enjoyed writing, and I thought it might be an excellent thing if I were paid to do something I enjoy for a change."

"I daresay it would," Lucy countered at once. "And while you enjoy yourself, the burden of supporting us both once again falls wholly upon me."

That stung, for it was nothing less than the truth. Their father's death fifteen years before had left them with nothing. Lucy, four years older, had been burdened with the majority of responsibility for their financial security. Daisy was painfully aware she hadn't been of much help in that regard, but this was her chance to change all that. "I'm sorry," she said with dignity. "I've let you down again, I know, but I did not do so on purpose."

"Perhaps you could go back to Pettigrew and Finch and ask to be reinstated," Lucy suggested, a hint of desperation in her voice. "Tell them you regret your resignation, that you realize now it was a rash mistake."

If one was confessing the truth, one might as well confess it all. "I didn't resign. They sacked me."

Lucy groaned. "I should have known. What did you do? Let your tongue run away with you again, no doubt."

"This was not my fault!" she shot back. "Mr. Pettigrew cornered me in the closet, the old lecher—" She stopped, remembering too late that she and her sister were not alone in the room. A hot blush flooded her cheeks, and she took a quick glance around, but the other women at the table seemed to have developed a sudden interest in their breakfast plates. Grateful, she returned her gaze to her sister, and saw that Lucy fully comprehended what had occurred.

"Oh, God," Lucy whispered, looking horrified. "What happened? Are you all right?"

"I am perfectly well, but I was insulted beyond bearing. Believe me, dear sister, I had sufficient cause to resign, but Matron terminated my employment before I could do so. And she refused to give me a letter of character."

"Oh, heavens." Lucy looked stricken. "And to think I found you that post."

"It's all right," she hastened to say, wanting to forget the entire sordid episode. "It doesn't matter. I called upon Lord Marlowe, as I said, about the possibility of writing as a profession, and he was generosity itself. He agreed at once to read my work, and he didn't seem to feel the least bit put upon. Oh, wouldn't it be wonderful if he published one of my novels?"

Lucy did not reply, and as Daisy waited for her sister to say something, she became more and more certain that a lecture on the uncertain nature of writing as a profession was forthcoming, along with several unappealing suggestions for other, more suitable, occupations.

But Lucy surprised her. "It's a good thing, I suppose," she said with a sigh, "that we don't need your income to survive."

Daisy blinked. "You don't intend to tell me to stop dreaming about being a writer and find a reliable post?"

"No."

"You don't intend to point out how much more sensible it is to be a typist? Or remind me how low our savings are?"

"No. The agency is doing well enough to support us long enough to see if you are serious about this and if you can make a go of it. I cannot pretend I don't have doubts about this venture, but I'm running out of posts for you to try."

With a shout of exultation, Daisy jumped to her feet and moved to come around the table and hug her sister, but Lucy's next words made her pause.

"On the other hand," her sister added with a sternness that impelled Daisy to sink back into her chair, "you may soon have greater responsibilities than you realize. It's all very well to attend one play and write a review. But if Lord Marlowe agrees to publish your novel, he'll surely want another, and then another. You'll have to meet deadlines, fulfill contracts."

"Of course I shall live up to any commitments I might make to Lord Marlowe."

Her sister did not seem very reassured. "Marlowe is a friend of our family," she reminded. "Don't disappoint him." With that, she stood up. "Now, I must be off for the agency. If you are to be a writer, Daisy," she added as she started for the door, "I should advise you to deliver your best novel to Lord Marlowe as soon as possible. Let us hope it impresses him favorably, for he is no doubt having apoplexy about your review."

Daisy frowned, puzzled. "Why should he be?"

Halfway out of the dining room, Lucy stopped and looked at her over one shoulder. "Sebastian Grant's novels are printed by Marlowe Publishing. He is their most successful author."

"And I said he was a second-rate Oscar Wilde whose best writing was behind him!" Daisy gave a groan of dismay. "How do I always manage to put myself in hot water like this?"

"It's your special gift, dearest," Lucy said with a rueful smile and vanished out the door.

"Did you really call him a second-rate Oscar Wilde?" Miranda asked.

"I did," she admitted with another groan. "I didn't even think about the fact that Lord Marlowe publishes his novels. Oh, what must the viscount think of me?"

"Surely, he won't be angry," Eloisa said in an attempt to console her as she handed the paper across the table to Miranda. "He is a very nice gentleman. Besides, he wouldn't want you to lie, would he, and say you liked the play if you didn't?"

"Perhaps not," Mrs. Morris interjected, "but Lord Avermore might not be so appreciative of our Daisy's candidness. As I said before, gentlemen are very sensitive. Even the slightest criticism can quite upset them."

Daisy stared at her landlady in surprise. "You think my review might have hurt Sebastian Grant's feelings?"

"I think it's possible, my dear. Don't you?"

Daisy couldn't credit it. "But he's a titled gentleman, an earl, far more significant in the world than any literary critic. And given the notorious reputation he developed in Italy, it's difficult to imagine he cares what people say about him. And besides, he's written some truly breathtaking books. He's famous," she added with a laugh. "The most famous English literary figure since Sir Walter Scott! A review by a little nobody like me couldn't possibly have any effect on him."

It was wrong to contemplate murder, Sebastian supposed. Even if the intended victim was a critic.

On the other hand, he was a writer, he reflected, as he leaned back against the seat of his carriage and closed his eyes. He made his living with his imagination, so plotting ways George Lindsay might meet an unfortunate end could not really be wrong, could it?

These somewhat hostile thoughts dominated Sebastian's mind as his landau made the long, slow journey from Mayfair into the City. Rolled in his fist was a copy of that morning's *Social Gazette*, but there was no need to refer to the theater page to recall the words printed there. They were burned upon his brain.

Implausible . . . trite . . . as amusing as a visit to the dentist. . .

There was a pistol in his desk, he remembered. A .22-caliber affair with a pearl handle. It might even be loaded.

The carriage stopped, and Sebastian forced aside the pleasurable notion of shooting critics. He opened his eyes, but one glance around told him he had not yet arrived at Marlowe Publishing. His driver was waiting for a break in the traffic that clogged Trafalgar before turning onto the Strand, and Sebastian closed his eyes again.

. . . his most brilliant work is nearly a decade behind him . . .

Fear rose up within Sebastian—dark, smothering fear. A surprising thing that those words should evoke such emotion, for he'd accepted that truth quite some time ago. What was there to be afraid of now?

He moved restlessly in his seat. Perhaps he should leave London, go away again. He'd only just arrived home, but it wasn't as if he had to remain. He'd attended the opening of his new play. There was nothing, really, holding him here.

Africa, he considered, and felt a slight stirring of interest. He'd already been to Morocco and Tunis. But he could venture farther south . . . He began to imagine a trek through Kenya on safari, roaming the bush amid lions and elephants, inhaling the scent of danger; surely, that sort of experience would spark some sort of creative impulse, wouldn't it? Of course, how he would pay for a journey to Africa was questionable. He was stone-broke, and, thanks to Mr. Lindsay's review, he was likely to remain so for the foreseeable future.

A second-rate Oscar Wilde . . . second-rate . . . best writing nearly a decade behind him . . .

Damn all critics to hell. Parasites, they were; unable to write anything themselves, they fed off of the people who had the talent, did the work, took the risks, and paid the price.

The carriage stopped, jolting Sebastian once again out of his resentful contemplation of critics, and this time when he opened his eyes, he found himself at his destination. He didn't wait for Saunders to open the door for him. He did it himself, jumping down from the carriage as he issued a command to his driver. "Call for me in an hour, Merriman."

"Very good, sir." The driver clicked the reins, Saunders jumped back on the dummy board at the boot, and the landau rumbled down the street in search of a mews as Sebastian entered the offices of Marlowe Publishing.

He didn't bother with the lift. Instead, he took the stairs to the fourth floor, and with each step closer to Marlowe's office, his frustration rose another notch. *Girl with a Red Handbag* might not be the best thing he'd ever written, but did his own publisher's newspaper have to be the means of pointing that out to all of London? It was one thing for him to disparage his own work—he always did, for his writing never lived up to his own expectations and he was never satisfied. But it was quite another matter to be ripped apart by a newspaper of his own publisher, to watch the scribbling of an insignificant little nobody ruin his chance to wipe out his debts and derive a bit of income.

As he entered Marlowe's office suite, the viscount's secretary stood up with an inquiring look, but when Sebastian introduced himself, the secretary's polite curiosity changed to an expression of dismay. "L—Lord Avermore, we . . . umm . . . we were not expecting you." He reached for a leather-bound appointment book. "Did you have an appointment with Lord Marlowe?"

"No." Sebastian stepped around the secretary's desk, making for the closed door into Marlowe's private office. "Is he in?"

"Yes, my lord, but—"

"Excellent," Sebastian cut him off and opened the door.

As he shoved the door wide and entered the room, he spied Marlowe at once. His publisher was standing on the other side of his big mahogany desk, a twine-tied manuscript in his hand. "Sebastian?" he said in astonishment and set aside the bundle of papers. "Sebastian Grant, upon my soul, you're home from abroad at last."

From the doorway, the secretary spoke. "I'm sorry, sir. Lord Avermore insisted upon seeing you."

Marlowe waved the other man out of the room. "It's all right, Quinn. You may go." He returned his attention to Sebastian. "God, man, how long has it been? Eight years?"

At the moment, Sebastian wasn't interested in catching up on old times. He tossed his crumpled copy of the *Social Gazette* onto his publisher's desk. "What happened to Basil Stephens, Harry? Did you sack him when you bought the *Gazette*?"

Much to his chagrin, his publisher began to smile. "Mr. Stephens had a cold. I found someone else to review your play."

"And where did you find this cretin? Your favorite pub?"

"Cretin?" Harry laughed. "If you ever met George Lindsay, I doubt you would describe him so."

"No doubt a moment's conversation with him would enable me to add the words 'idiotic' and 'inarticulate' to my description."

"How cross you are! And I can't agree with your assessment. I thought George Lindsay displayed remarkable eloquence in his thrashing of your play."

"Thank you, Harry. Your concern for my feelings warms my heart. Since Mr. Stephens has a cold, I take it Mr. Lindsay's career as a dramatic critic is only temporary?"

"I wouldn't say that. I might have him write more reviews in future." His publisher ignored his snort of disgust and gestured to the manuscript he'd just placed on his desk. "I've agreed to read his novel as well."

"My condolences."

"If it's good, I'll publish it, of course."

"Good?" Sebastian couldn't believe what he was hearing. "How could it possibly be any good? No writer worth his salt ever becomes a critic."

"You're only saying that because you're in a snit over the review he gave *you*."

"That's absurd," Sebastian snapped. "One undiscerning opinion has no effect on me."

"Glad to know you're not upset."

He ignored that breezy reply. "But it will have an effect on other people. Everyone reads the reviews in the *Social Gazette*. Everyone is influenced by them. This review could hurt the play." He leaned forward, resting his fists on the desk. "I want a retraction."

Harry also leaned forward, mirroring his aggressive stance. "No."

"An alternate opinion, then."

"No."

Sebastian let out his breath in an exasperated sigh and straightened away from the desk. "Ticket sales have dropped by thirty percent since yesterday."

Harry shrugged. "What do I care? I only publish your novels. I have no stake in your plays."

"I need the money, damn you!"

Harry met Sebastian's aggravated gaze with a hard one of his own. "If you had written the novel you were due to give me three years ago, you wouldn't be short of funds, would you?"

Sebastian glared back at his publisher, and it occurred to him that perhaps his contemplations of murder this morning had been centered on the wrong victim.

Something of what he felt must have shown in his face, for Marlowe shook his head, looking at him in mock sadness. "You're so disagreeable. Living in Switzerland doesn't seem to have suited you. What, was the climate there too cold after living in Italy for so many years?"

"It's clear I've been away from England too long," Sebastian shot back. "In my absence, you've transformed the *Social Gazette* from the definitive arbiter of London theater to a comedic paper worthy to rival *Punch*! That review was laughable."

"Pity the same couldn't be said of your play," muttered a vexed feminine voice behind him before Harry could reply.

Sebastian frowned in puzzlement, for that impertinent remark had definitely not been uttered by Harry's secretary. He turned toward the open doorway, but he saw no one standing there, a fact which only deepened his puzzlement. But then the door moved, swinging shut to reveal a feminine figure which had until this moment been concealed behind it. Her position beside the coat tree, a dark green cloak in her hand, made it clear his abrupt entrance to the room had trapped her behind the door and prevented her departure.

His brows rose as he glanced over the unexpected eavesdropper. She made quite an incongruous picture standing in his publisher's office. She wore a straw boater hat, a starched white shirtwaist buttoned up to her chin, a serviceable navy blue skirt, and knitted white gloves. It was the uniform of both schoolgirls and spinsters, but in his first cursory glance, Sebastian, usually adept at assessments of the fair sex, could not quite decide which category she belonged in.

She had the slim, coltish figure, rose pink lips, and luminous skin of a girl, but when he took a step toward her for a closer inspection, he saw the faint, unmistakable lines across her forehead that made it clear she had put aside French lessons and sewing samplers at least a decade earlier. Not a schoolgirl, no, but a fully mature woman, and yet, there was something about her that spoke of youth, something in the dusting of freckles across her nose and cheeks and in the heart shape of her face, something artless and open that would enable anyone with an ounce of discernment to read her like a book.

He noted the slight crinkle of a frown between her brows, and he lowered his gaze a notch to look into her eyes. When he did, he caught his breath, for their color was remarkable—a deep, vivid blue-green that his writer's mind struggled at once to describe. Like a teal's wing or a eucalyptus forest or the light-tricked waters of Monet's pond at Giverny. Surrounded by a heavy fringe of auburn lashes, they were gorgeous.

Tendrils of her bright red hair peeked from beneath her boater hat, and despite the hellish morning he'd had, the sight of them almost made him smile. She probably hated the color of her hair—most people did who possessed that fiery shade—but an image flashed through his mind of how that hair would look if it were undone and falling down around her bare, white shoulders. It was a very fetching picture.

His gaze slid downward. She was tall for a woman, only a few inches beneath his own height, and very slender, but he could see that there were distinct curves beneath those dreadful clothes.

He turned toward Marlowe, lifting an eyebrow. What was this vibrant, pretty creature doing behind closed doors in his publisher's office? A vague memory passed through his mind about the viscount having married a few years back. If this was Harry's wife, all well and good. If not . . . naughty, naughty Harry.

"Your play *was* meant to be a comedy, wasn't it?" she asked, interrupting his speculations and returning his attention to her. "If you ever write another," she added with a sniff, "I should advise you to make people actually laugh."

With that remark, her flaming hair and gorgeous eyes began to lose their charm for him. She had to be a spinster, he concluded, for no man would marry a woman with such a vinegary tongue. "Who the devil are you?"

Harry's laughter interrupted any answer she might have made. He came around from behind his desk to stand beside Sebastian. "Permit me to introduce you," he said and gestured to the woman with a flourish. "Sebastian, meet George Lindsay."

Chapter 3

Writing is like prostitution.
First you do it for love,
and then for a few close friends,
and then for money.
Moliere

$\mathcal{D}$aisy supposed most people would find Sebastian Grant a bit intimidating. There weren't many things that intimidated her, but in her first glimpse of the famous writer, even she had to admit he was rather a daunting figure.

He was a big man, for one thing, taller than most men—with exceptionally wide shoulders, a broad chest, and powerful arms. His physique did not seem at all in keeping with what she would have imagined. Britain's most successful author ought to be a slender, bookish sort of fellow, with spectacles, perhaps, and an intellectual brow. This man, big and virile and irascible, seemed larger than life. With his unruly black hair and his eyes the color of gunmetal, she could well believe he had earned his wild reputation. He ought to be navigating rivers in the Argentine, she thought, or brawling in a Bangkok tavern, for the idea of him seated at a desk with quill and ink, or pecking away at a typewriting machine, seemed ludicrous in the extreme.

With Lord Marlowe's blithe introduction still hanging in the air, she watched the famous author's black brows draw together in a frown. His eyes narrowed on her with riveting intensity, and a muscle worked at the corner of his strong, square jaw. All in all, he gave the impression of a recalcitrant bull. If his splendid, straight, Roman nose had begun flaring at the nostrils, she wouldn't have been surprised.

"You are George Lindsay?" he asked and cast another peremptory glance up and down her person. "You?"

It was a disconcerting thing for a critic to meet the displeased author she had just panned, but he'd already gotten a bit of his own back with his disparaging conclusions about her. Daisy met his smoldering gaze with a defiant one of her own. "George Lindsay is my pen name, yes," she answered. "And by all the bellicose ranting you've been doing since you so rudely walked in, I take it you are Sebastian Grant."

A laugh from Lord Marlowe interrupted any reply the author might have made. "You presume rightly," the viscount told her, gesturing to the man beside him. "Allow me to present Sebastian Grant, Earl of Avermore. Sebastian, Miss Daisy Merrick."

She could tell Avermore was fighting to regain a semblance of civility. He bowed to her and when he straightened, the frown was gone from his face, though she suspected it had not vanished without effort. "How do you do?"

She dipped a perfunctory curtsy in response. "Lord Avermore."

He turned a bit to address the man beside him, but he kept his gaze on her face. "This is quite a surprise, Marlowe. You should have given me a bit of warning when I walked in."

"Sorry, old chap," the viscount answered, not seeming the least bit contrite, "but you didn't give me much of a chance."

Lord Avermore looked her over once more, and his piercing stare made her feel like a butterfly on a pin. "So you are the poisonous critic who shredded me into spills this morning."

"I regret my review was not to your liking, my lord, but I had an ethical obligation to give my honest opinion of your play."

His brows rose. "An ethical critic. How . . . unusual."

There was unmistakable mockery beneath the well-bred accents of his voice. It flicked her on the raw, and though she knew engaging in arguments with Sebastian Grant in front of his publisher, the man she hoped would buy her own writing, was probably not a wise thing to do, Daisy felt impelled to respond. "If you can't take the heat, my lord," she said sweetly, "perhaps you ought to leave the kitchen."

He made a sound of derision. "Yes, critics always say that. The reason is that their own work is never at risk for public ridicule. It's much easier to offer criticism than endure it."

"For some, perhaps, but if I am fortunate enough to see my novels published, I shall be perfectly willing to endure the criticism of others regarding them," she assured. "And I hope to take their opinions in the proper spirit."

"Trust me, petal, you won't."

Daisy wanted to dispute that cynical contention about her, but he spoke again before she could do so. "What is the proper spirit, by the way?" he asked. "How should an author respond to a scathing review?"

Lord Marlowe gave a cough. "By ignoring it?" he suggested, sounding hopeful.

"Ignore it?" Avermore echoed. "But if we ignored critics, Marlowe, there would be no purpose to their existence." He paused, giving Daisy a wide smile. "How tragic that would be."

He was trying to goad her, but Daisy had no intention of allowing that to happen. "I think the author would be well served to examine the critique, consider the points made in a balanced light, and perhaps learn from the experience."

"Learn from the experience?" That made him laugh. "Good God."

She lifted her chin a notch. "I don't see what is so amusing."

"My apologies," he said at once, but he didn't look the least bit sorry. "In all honesty, Miss Merrick, do you believe a critique can teach a writer anything?"

Despite his mockery, Daisy considered the question in a serious fashion. "Yes," she answered after a moment. "I do."

"Then you know nothing about it. The only way a writer learns anything is by writing."

"I don't agree. There is always the potential to learn from others, if one is open-minded." She met his amused gaze with a pointed one of her own. "And humble."

"Indeed?" His lashes, thick and straight and black as soot, lowered a fraction, and the mockery vanished from his countenance, though he still seemed amused, for one corner of his mouth remained curved in a slight smile as he tilted his head to one side, studying her. "And if I give you the chance, petal," he murmured, "what will you teach me, hmm?"

That question, so softly uttered, made her blush, and she felt in desperate need to say something. "Perhaps it is impertinent for a novice such as myself to offer advice to someone of your vast experience, but since you asked, I will answer. In my opinion, your play has the potential to be good."

"Why, thank you," he said with a bow, sounding so much like an indulgent adult patting a child on the head that Daisy's temper flared. But she tamped it down, counted to three, and went on. "In order to make it truly worthwhile—in fact to make it work at all—you would have to rewrite it."

"Rewrite it? The play's in production, my dear girl. Only a novice would suggest rewrites at this stage."

Despite his patronizing attitude, Daisy persevered. "I agree that for this run of the play, it's too late. But if you ever put it on again, you could rewrite it, and if you did, the problems could be resolved without much difficulty."

"It's never difficult to resolve the problems when it isn't your play. But you've piqued my curiosity, I admit." His amusement vanished, and suddenly something flashed in those eyes, something dangerous. "How does one fix a play that is as painful as a visit to the dentist?"

"Sebastian," Lord Marlowe put in, "you really shouldn't put the girl on the spot this way."

"But Marlowe, Miss Merrick pointed out the problems with my play, and she sees a way to resolve them. I can't resist inquiring further. Advise me, Miss Merrick. How can my utterly implausible story line be fixed?"

His voice was pleasant, his manner genial, but it was a thin veneer. Beneath it, his resentment was palpable, and she realized in some surprise that Mrs. Morris had been right to caution her. She had wounded him with her review. Sensing the bull might be about to charge, she decided it would be wise to employ tact for a change, disengage from this argument, and depart. "Lord Avermore, I don't believe you truly desire my opinions. Besides, I seem to have said quite enough already."

She started to turn to Lord Marlowe and bid him good day, but Avermore spoke again before she had the chance. "Come, come, Miss Merrick. Prove to me that you have more to offer than criticism. How would you resolve the problems in the play?"

There was challenge in that question. He thought she had nothing useful to say, and he was daring her to prove him wrong. She could not bear to let the challenge pass unanswered. "You only needed to do one thing in the first act, and you would have had a workable plot. You should have made Wesley's letter a condemnation of Cecilia."

"What?" He stared at her in disbelief, as if he couldn't believe anyone would suggest something so ridiculous.

Daisy stuck to her guns. "Wesley's condemnation would have established a true conflict between the lovers, not one based on a misunderstanding. By having Wesley tear Cecilia to shreds in that letter, she would have been publicly humiliated when Victor read the letter aloud at the house party. You would then have had a conflict—"

"Yes, yes," he cut in dismissively, "I would have had a conflict worthy of a silly lady novelist."

Any momentary guilt she might have felt over wounding his feelings went to the wall. She stepped forward and rose onto her toes, bringing herself to his eye level. "Better the conflict of a lady novelist," she countered, "than a stupid misunderstanding and no conflict at all!"

"All right, you two," Lord Marlowe interjected, "that's enough literary debate for one day, I think. Stop teasing the girl, Avermore."

"I'm not teasing her," Lord Avermore countered with a hint of reproof, pressing a hand to his chest with a galling pretense of humility. "I am hoping to learn."

He ignored the other man's sound of skepticism. "You must keep me informed about your own writing, Miss Merrick." His smile returned. "I shall dearly love to know what you learn from the critics if you ever manage to publish a novel."

"An occurrence likely to happen long before we see a new novel from you," she shot back, tired of his insufferable air of superiority. "Hasn't it been about three years since your last book was published?"

His smile did not falter. "Nearly four, petal," he corrected, his voice light. "Lord, I didn't realize anyone was still keeping count."

"I am," Marlowe put in with emphasis. "Speaking of which, I'm glad you came by, Sebastian. This is the perfect opportunity for us to discuss that next novel of yours, since my letters and cables to you on the subject seem to keep going astray." He glanced at Daisy. "If you will forgive us, Miss Merrick?"

"Of course." She was happy to escape. If she stayed here much longer, letting this man toy with her like a cat with a mouse, she would surely say something she'd regret.

Daisy forced herself to give the earl a polite curtsy before she turned to Lord Marlowe. "Shall we meet again next week, my lord? Before we were interrupted," she couldn't help adding, "I believe you had made that suggestion?"

"So I did," Lord Marlowe said, moving to her side to offer his arm. "See my secretary about an appointment for Thursday or Friday," he said as he escorted her to the door. "That should give me enough time to read your manuscript."

"Thank you." As Daisy walked out of Lord Marlowe's office she breathed a sigh of relief. Her unexpected encounter with Sebastian Grant had been most disagreeable. She had finally met the legendary author, and it would be perfectly acceptable to her if she never met him again.

Silly lady novelists, indeed! Horrid man, so arrogant and condescending. Daisy had no doubt his assessment of her was equally unflattering, but she didn't intend to lose any sleep over the fact.

* * *

It was a travesty, Sebastian thought with chagrin, eying the curve of Miss Merrick's hips as she walked out of Marlowe's office. A travesty that a woman with such a shapely backside should be a critic.

As Marlowe closed the door behind her, an image of her face came into Sebastian's mind, and he felt even more aggrieved. Nature had a twisted sense of humor indeed to put such a lovely pair of eyes into the same head with such a vinegary tongue and such a clever brain.

She was a cheeky baggage, too. Offering her opinions with such blithe confidence and without any bona fides to back them up. Deuce take it, he had twenty years of hard writing behind him, including ten novels, seven plays, and half a dozen short story collections. One review aside, she was an unpublished nobody. Who was she to be giving him literary advice?

Make Wesley's letter a condemnation of Cecilia. Of all the idiotic ideas.

"Was she right?"

Harry's voice broke into Sebastian's thoughts. "Hmm? What?" He turned, watching as his publisher circled back around the desk. "Sorry. What did you ask me?"

Harry resumed his seat. "Was she right?"

Sebastian pulled out the chair on his side of the desk and also sat down. "About what?"

"Don't be coy. What she said about the play. Was she right?"

He shifted in his chair, impatient. "Of course not. She was talking nonsense."

"Indeed? What she said sounded sensible to me."

"The only sensible thing Miss Merrick said was how impertinent it was for a novice such as she to offer me writing advice!"

"My, my," Harry drawled, "she *has* gotten under your skin. I don't think I've ever seen you this outraged about a review. You came storming in here, sneering at the poor girl—"

"I was not sneering!"

"—disparaging her and her review, demanding I print retractions and alternate opinions, and when you find she's overheard every word you've said, what do you do? Do you behave like a gentleman? Oh, no. God forbid you should apologize, I know, but you don't even politely withdraw. Instead, you goad her and laugh at her. You demand her opinions, and then dismiss them when she offers them. In short, you've been acting like an ass ever since you walked through the door. I'd love to know why."

Sebastian looked away. "I told you," he said after a moment. "That review was important. I need the money from ticket sales—"

"Sod the ticket sales. You want to know what I think?"

He set his jaw. "Not particularly."

"You're outraged about this review because it was the truth, and your artistic conscience is smiting you. At long last, you are feeling guilty because your writing has become so unworthy of your talent."

"That's absurd!" he said at once, but the sick twist in his guts belied his denial.

"I saw the play last night. I wasn't intending to go, but at the last minute I changed my mind. After viewing it, I can safely say that Miss Merrick's review was spot on in every respect, including the assertion that you wrote it for the money."

"Of course I did!" Sebastian shouted before he could stop himself. He twisted in his chair, jabbing a finger over his shoulder toward the door behind him. "I didn't need that fire-haired, serpent-tongued spinster to tell me *Girl with a Red Handbag* is trivial, and trite, and just plain silly! I knew that already, but I had to agree to put the thing into production. I didn't have a choice."

Sebastian let out his breath in a sigh. "Rotherstein wrote to me three years ago. He asked me to write a play for him. He offered me two thousand pounds up front and twenty percent of the gross. I hadn't written anything for over a year, Harry. I was absolutely flat and going into debt, and I couldn't afford to refuse." He gave a short, humorless laugh. "What was it Moliere said? Writing is like prostitution? It's so true."

"Well, if that's so, do you think you could whore yourself long enough to write a novel for me?"

Sebastian stared at his publisher in disbelief. "You're enjoying this," he accused. "That woman slaughtered me and quite possibly ruined any chance my play had for success, and you are enjoying it."

Harry didn't deny it. "Do you blame me? I'm thinking you got just what you deserve. The quality of your work has been deteriorating ever since you went to Italy. You were writing with such speed, but the substance was lacking. Each novel, each short story, became a little more slick, a little more shallow, until I could no longer recognize the brilliant talent I first published eighteen years ago. I tried to warn you. I tried to tell you that you needed to slow down. I wrote letter after letter, but you wouldn't listen. You ignored my requests for revisions and left me no choice but to publish your work as it was and let the critics slaughter you. Which they began to do with tiresome regularity."

"Harry—"

"The sales of your past few books have declined steadily," Harry interrupted, cutting him off. "Your last novel was due to me over three years ago, a novel for which you had already been partly compensated, but I have not seen a single page of manuscript. Despite your sinking career, you seemed to be having quite an enjoyable time in Florence. I heard all about the parties, the women, your escapades about town with St. Cyres—"

Sebastian stiffened, fearing the worst. "What did he tell you?"

"Give the man a little credit. He told me nothing. But he didn't have to, Sebastian. It was in all the scandal sheets, including mine. I got to read about your exploits in my own damn newspapers. As I said, I wrote to you repeatedly with my concerns, but received no replies. You couldn't even be bothered to respond when I cabled you saying I had married and that my wife and I were coming to Florence during our honeymoon because I wanted her to meet you."

"You wanted an excuse to see me because you wanted the damned book," Sebastian shot back.

"Well, it wasn't because you'd been any sort of a friend."

Sebastian sucked in his breath, feeling those words like the lash of a whip.

"Imagine my surprise," Harry went on, "when I called at your *pensione* in Florence and found you were no longer living there. Upon inquiring at Cook's Tours, I learned you'd gone gallivanting off to Switzerland months earlier."

"Gallivanting? For God's sake, I wasn't touring the European capitals like some awestruck American with a Baedeker! I was—" He broke off, for he had no intention of telling his publisher what had taken him to Switzerland. But before he could think of any alternate explanation to offer, Harry spoke again.

"I know what you were doing."

"You do?" he asked even as his mind tried to deny

it. *You can't know*, he thought. *You can't. No one knows*.

"Your aunt was kind enough to explain that you were perfectly well, holed up in some Alpine cottage, writing away."

Relief flooded him. Aunt Mathilda, of course. She knew only what he had told her, and she would have passed that information on to his acquaintances and friends in all good faith.

"But then another year passed," Harry continued, "and another, and another, and yet, I still had no book and no word from you. The only reason I knew you weren't dead was Mathilda, who kept assuring me that you were indeed writing. And then, last autumn, I happened to encounter Rotherstein at a party. Imagine my surprise when I learned from him that you had a new play opening at the Old Vic in April. You hadn't been in Switzerland writing the novel you owed me. You were writing a play for him."

"I wasn't—"

"And now, after all this time, you come barreling in here, full of righteous indignation, interrupting me in the midst of a meeting, making demands and grumbling about your damned lack of income? Forgive me if I lack the proper sympathy."

He couldn't deny it. It was true, all of it, and his publisher's condemnation was no less than he deserved. His resentment crumbled, leaving only a terrible helplessness. He leaned forward, plunked his elbows on the edge of the desk, and rubbed his palms over his face. "I wrote the play before I left Italy," he mumbled, resting his forehead against the heels of his hands. "I didn't write it in Switzerland."

"So what the hell were you doing in Switzerland?"

He lifted his head, staring at his publisher. He couldn't explain about Switzerland, about the long, painful withdrawal from cocaine and the dearth of creativity that had followed in its wake. About the endless hours of staring at a blank sheet of paper, feeling no spark of inspiration but only the hungry need for a drug he could no longer have. About how desperation had turned him to new distractions—he'd climbed mountains and crossed ravines, he'd learned to use skis and snowshoes. Hell, he'd even learned to milk a goat. Anything to help him forget cocaine, the only thing that had ever made writing easy.

It was time to face things, wasn't it? He straightened in his chair. "I finished that play three years ago, and it was the last thing I wrote. I tried after that, but it was no use. Harry, I can't write anymore."

Harry's gaze was thoughtful and not without compassion. "Periods of drought happen to all writers. In your case, it's understandable. You produced a massive body of work in a short period of time. It's temporary, Sebastian. It'll pass."

"No, Harry." Without cocaine, writing made him feel

as if he were a fly drowning in treacle. "That play, that stupid, silly play, was the last thing I'll ever write. I'm tired." He slumped back in his chair. "So damned tired."

Harry clasped his hands together on the desk top. "I never give advice to my writers because it's usually a waste of breath. But in this case, I shall offer it anyway. Humor me for a change and take it." He paused, and when he spoke again, there was a gravity in his voice Sebastian couldn't ignore. "Stop flogging yourself for a few less-than-perfect stories. Stop taking the counsel of your doubts." He leaned forward in his chair. "Stop avoiding your typewriter. Sit down and start work. The story will come."

"There is no story. And I don't give a damn about inventing one. That's the trouble, you see. I just don't care."

"Sebastian, the only way to overcome something like this is by doing it. You have to sit down every day and write. Even if you think it's god-awful, which—let's be honest—is what you always think, write anyway. One word, then another, then another, until you have a book."

"Damn it, are you deaf, man? There is no book. There isn't ever going to be another book. I have nothing to say."

"A writer always has something to say. You're just not sitting down at your typewriter long enough to know what it is." He frowned, looking thoughtful. "Have you ever thought about taking on a partner? About working with another writer?"

"Oh, no." He shook his head. "No, no, no. I don't collaborate. Writing is something one does alone."

"You wouldn't have to collaborate on the actual writing. Listen to me for a moment," he added as Sebastian once again started to protest. "I know you writers. I know how this sort of thing goes. You sit down, it's hard, you struggle, you give up. You try again, it's even harder, you struggle, you give up. Each time it becomes more difficult to sit down in that chair. Discouragement sets in like dry rot, and before you know it, years have gone by and you haven't written a thing."

"Thank you for reiterating the past few years of my life."

Harry ignored that. "A partner would encourage you to keep trying, would see that you don't walk away every time things get difficult, and help you see the good in your work when you believe there is none. You could do the same for him. The pair of you could offer each other criticism and advice, toss ideas around when you're stuck, that sort of thing."

Sebastian knew some writers sought the help of their peers, but he wasn't made that way. For him, writing was a long, hard strenuous climb alone, a climb he no longer had the strength to make. Harry would eventually have to accept that.

"I don't need a partner." He pulled out his watch.

"What I need," he went on, forcing a lightness into his voice he was far from feeling, "is lunch."

Harry didn't seem to hear. "It would have to be someone you can't bully," he said, obviously still enamored with his idea. "Someone who won't go scurrying off like a frightened mouse every time you lose your temper."

This was becoming irritating. "I do not have a temper!" He shoved his watch back into his waistcoat pocket, scowling. "Do you wish to dine with me, or not?"

"Dine?" Harry stared at him for a moment, then shook his head as if coming out of a daze. "Yes, of course," he said and stood up. "By all means."

They dined at the Savoy, and much to Sebastian's relief, Harry left off any conversation about writing during their meal. Instead, they discussed politics, possible winners for the upcoming Ascot, and the exciting potential of that recent scientific invention called X-rays as they consumed an excellent meal of lamb cutlets and apple tart.

When Sebastian departed, he left Harry to pay the entire bill. Even though he hadn't produced a book in four years, and he had no intention of producing one in the future, he felt no pang of conscience about it. Publishers, in his opinion, never paid enough for the books. Providing lunch to their poverty-stricken authors was the least they could do.

Chapter 4

If you wish to be a writer, write!
Epictetus

Daisy felt her meeting with Lord Marlowe had gone well. The viscount had made no mention of her blistering review of his most famous author, and he had accepted her novel, *The Withering Moon*, with an enthusiasm she found most encouraging. Though the encounter with Sebastian Grant had been most disagreeable, Daisy had departed Marlowe Publishing filled with high hopes.

During the week that followed, she worked on her writing with the utmost zeal and dedication. In the hope that Marlowe might like her latest novel enough to ask for more of her work, she pulled out her older manuscripts, chose one, and tucked it into a leather dispatch case she'd borrowed from her sister. She then returned her remaining manuscripts to the recesses of the drawer where she'd kept them, tried to stop any further speculations as to what Lord Marlowe's opinion would be, and resumed the writing of her current novel. As she sat at the cramped writing desk in her bedroom and scribbled pages, she felt a sense of happiness and conviction she'd never felt before, and more strongly than ever, she felt being a writer was her destiny.

Despite this conviction, by the day of her second meeting with the viscount, she was a bundle of nerves. As an omnibus took her into the City, apprehension began to overtake her happiness and excitement, and she attempted to quell her doubts and fears with dreams of success. She dreamed of publication, notoriety, and critical acclaim. She dreamed of the day when she could hold out a copy of her first published book to Lucy, thereby presenting to her sister with tangible proof that she could succeed at something. She wanted that more than anything else.

By the time she reached Marlowe Publishing, Daisy's nervous excitement was like a huge, glistening bubble inside her that pressed painfully against her chest. The viscount received her with even more charm and friendliness than he had displayed before, and as she sat down opposite him, watching him over the stacks of manuscripts that littered his desk, Daisy suddenly felt as if she couldn't breathe.

"I have read the novel you gave me," he said, gesturing to a particular stack of pages on the desk.

With those words, Daisy's usual sunny optimism deserted her. She clasped her gloved hands together in her lap so tightly her fingers ached. "And?" she whispered, her heart in her throat.

"I'm pleased to tell you that you have a natural talent, Miss Merrick."

That eased her apprehension a little.

"Your story is unique and interesting, and I liked its premise very much." he went on. "Your work shows great promise."

Her spirits began to soar.

"You have a great deal to learn, however," he added before she could savor the happiness of the moment. "I'm afraid your story is too raw for immediate publication. I'm sorry."

Her bubble burst. She watched in a haze of sinking hopes as Lord Marlowe picked up her manuscript and held it out to her over the top of the desk. She stared at it for a moment, stunned, wanting to deny that this had happened, and at the same time, berating herself for having been so unrealistic in her expectations. She forced herself to take the stack of pages from him, then she ducked her head, trying to shove down her disappointment and think of something to say. "Are there . . ."

Her throat closed up. She paused and swallowed hard

before trying again to speak. "Are there any constructive suggestions you can offer me?" she asked, the pages in her lap blurring before her eyes. "Have you any advice as to how I can do better?"

"I've included a summary of my thoughts for you," he said in a gentle voice.

She blinked several times to clear the blurriness of tears from her vision, and saw that there was a typewritten letter signed by the viscount on top of her manuscript. Part of her wanted to read the letter right then, for she burned to know what she had done wrong, but another part of her wanted to shove it all into the closest fire she could find and never try again. "I look forward to reading your comments." She opened the case and tucked the manuscript in beside the older one, the one he would probably never read now.

"I hope you find my evaluation useful," he said as she closed the case. "If you are willing to learn, if you keep writing and strive to improve, I have no doubt you will become an accomplished author one day."

Daisy's hands stilled, and she couldn't help remembering her assurances to Sebastian Grant in this very room that she would take any criticism in the proper spirit and learn from the experience. How he would laugh if he knew of this.

Still, she was no humbug. She intended to live up to her own words. Daisy took a deep breath and lifted her head, doing her best to conceal her disappointment.

"Thank you, my lord. I am most grateful for your time and your consideration."

"Not at all. And I would be glad to read your future work."

That was a bit of a comfort, but not much. "I appreciate that," she mumbled and started to rise, but his next words stopped her.

"My wife tells me you are without a suitable employment situation at present."

Daisy sank back down in her seat and felt her cheeks begin to burn at the reminder of her present circumstances. "Yes."

"She also tells me that you have been in this sort of difficulty before, mainly due to your talent for speaking your mind. Do you believe that to be an accurate assessment? Forgive me," he added at once, "but though these questions may seem intrusive, I have my reasons for asking them."

Daisy forced herself to answer. "Yes, I fear I am far too frank in my opinions for my own good." She tried to smile. "No doubt you have already observed that particular weakness in my character for yourself, my lord. So has Lord Avermore, I fear."

Marlowe smiled back at her, appreciating this reference to the incident in his office the week before. "I assure you, I do not consider outspokenness a weakness. As for Avermore, it's good for him to be knocked back on his heels once in a while. He's too arrogant by half. The worst things anyone can do are pander to him or pamper him." The viscount fell silent and leaned back in his chair, tapping a pencil against the desk and studying her for several moments before he spoke again. "Your review makes it clear you've read his other works."

Daisy stared. "Of course I have. All of them. He's written some wonderful books. *Teeth of the Storm. The Bishop's Reckoning.* And his play *The Third Wife*—oh, I was on the edge of my seat for the entire performance."

"But you do not care for his more recent efforts."

She bit her lip and said nothing. She was trying—she really was—to learn when to keep her mouth closed.

Marlowe picked up a newspaper and read, " 'Once a lion of English literature, he has chosen to present us with more of the same slick, trivial pabulum that has marked his work for eight years now. This reviewer cannot help but feel saddened that Mr. Grant's most brilliant work is nearly a decade behind him.' "

Daisy plunged into speech. "When I wrote that, I didn't know . . . that is, I didn't think about how Marlowe Publishing prints his books. Of course you're angry. You must be, and when we met before, I was sure you would bring it up, but when you didn't—"

"Miss Merrick, pray do not distress yourself. I knew about the review before it went to press that night. Mr. Tremayne, the editor of the *Gazette*, placed a telephone call to my home late that evening and read the review to me, asking if I wished him to edit it. I told him not to change a word."

"You did?"

"I saw the play, Miss Merrick. Your assessment was wholly accurate. Furthermore, Avermore knows it."

"He does?" Daisy gave an incredulous laugh. "Forgive me if I find that a bit hard to accept."

"Nonetheless, it's true." He paused, then went on, "Though your fictional work is, in my opinion, too raw for you to be immediately published, I have observed certain other qualities in you that interest me greatly."

Daisy was astonished. "Other qualities?"

"Yes. As we've already discussed, you have the extraordinary ability to be frank. I find that refreshing."

She couldn't help a rueful smile. "I believe you are the first person who has ever given me that particular compliment."

He grinned back at her. "I am not surprised. You also have the ability to enunciate your opinions with clarity, a talent you demonstrated when you wrote your review of Avermore's play. I can appreciate that some people, Lord Avermore among them, might not see that trait of your character as valuable, but I do." He leaned forward in his chair and tossed aside the pencil. "I have an unusual proposition to offer you. If you accept, you could be of great help to an old friend of mine, and improve your own writing skills at the same time."

"I'm not sure I understand you, my lord. What exactly are you offering?"

"A job, Miss Merrick. I am offering you a job."

Sebastian's dire prediction to his friend Lord Kayne on opening night proved more accurate than either man would have thought possible. The financial backers of *Girl with a Red Handbag* closed the play after a one-week run. Never had a Sebastian Grant play closed after a mere seven days, but a slate of reviews almost as brutal as that of the *Gazette*, combined with dwindling ticket sales, had prompted the decision. Rotherstein was furious and blamed Sebastian. Sebastian found it hard to care. Gin, he found, took the sting out of even the most crushing defeat. At least, until the next day.

He was roused from sleep by Abercrombie, who, for some idiotic reason, insisted upon messing about in his rooms with a fireplace poker.

"For heaven's sake, man, cease banging that thing!" Sebastian muttered, slamming a pillow over his ear. "It's May. We don't need a damned fire."

"Of course not, sir. Sorry, sir."

To his relief, his valet left off toying with fireplace implements, but Abercrombie had barely departed before Saunders appeared, coming into Sebastian's bedroom with the ringing announcement, "Morning post's come, sir."

Why did people have to shout so? he wondered with

a grimace. Unable to work up the slightest interest in his morning's letters, he grunted, rolled over, and went back to sleep.

But spending his entire day in bed was not to be. He didn't know how long he slept following Saunders' departure before his rest was again interrupted, this time by his housekeeper.

"Good morning, sir," Mrs. Partridge said in her deep, ponderous voice, banging the door wide.

Sebastian jerked, startled by these sounds that had so rudely disrupted his slumber, and opened his eyes. "Yes, Partridge, what is it?"

"Eleven o'clock, sir," she answered, as if he'd asked the time. "Breakfast has been waiting for you in the dining room, sir, in warming dishes on the sideboard. Cook wants to clear it away, being that it is so late in the day, but I've come to inquire as to your wishes."

His stomach lurched in protest at the mere mention of food. "No breakfast," he said hoarsely, baffled as to how anyone could think eleven o'clock late in the day. "I just want to be left alone." He started to roll over, intending to go back to sleep, when his housekeeper spoke again.

"I suspected so, sir. I will have Cook clear the table."

Sebastian waited for the closing of the door, indicating the housekeeper's departure, but when that did not happen, he dared to glance at his housekeeper over his shoulder.

This nonverbal cue was sufficient encouragement for Partridge. "Temple and I are waiting to do the rooms, sir."

He had no idea what "doing the rooms" entailed, but the firmness of the housekeeper's voice seemed to anticipate no opposition from the mere master of the house, who by lying abed all day was clearly impeding the precise timetable of British household routine. Sebastian, however, didn't care. "Partridge," he said, licking his dry lips, "you are an excellent housekeeper, and I appreciate your efficiency. Now, get out."

He watched the formidable housekeeper's impressive bust heave with disapproval; but she departed without a word, much to his relief. He closed his eyes again and drifted off.

The thunderous gush of water through the drainpipes of the adjoining bath was the last straw. "For the love of God!" he roared, and regretted it at once. The act of shouting sent agonizing pain through his head, and he clamped his hands over the sides of his skull with a groan. Once the pain had subsided, he eased himself to a sitting position.

As if on cue, Abercrombie came in. "Ah, I see you are awake, sir. I am drawing a bath for you."

"Yes, I comprehended that," he muttered, pressing his palms to his skull. "Though a pistol might be more to the point."

"A pistol, sir?"

"So I could rid myself of this beastly headache by blowing my brains out," he explained as he pushed aside the sheets and stood up, moving with great care.

Despite the slowness of his movements, his valet was as efficient as the rest of his household, and an hour later, Sebastian had bathed, shaved, and dressed. After downing Abercrombie's special secret remedy for the aftereffects of too much alcohol—a vile concoction of willowbark, peppermint, and various other more mysterious ingredients—Sebastian began to think life might be worth living. Though what he would do to occupy his time for the rest of that life was open to question.

He wandered down to his study, where he encountered Saunders just entering the room with a packing crate. Curious, he followed, and found that crate was not the only one his footman had brought into the room. A dozen or so similar crates littered the floor, along with two steamer trunks. "What's all this?"

The footman bent to set the wooden crate on the floor. "The last of your things have arrived from Switzerland, sir," he explained as he straightened. "Mr. Wilton thought you might wish to go through them before we take them to the attic."

Sebastian had no idea what was in these boxes, for Abercrombie had packed them. But having been home a month, he couldn't imagine these crates and trunks contained anything he might need now. Still, why not go through them? It wasn't as if he had anything else to do.

He gave a nod, and the footman departed. Sebastian removed his jacket, unfastened his cuff links, rolled up his shirtsleeves, and set to work.

The trunks were filled with old clothes. The first two crates held books, and the third various stationery supplies. In the fourth crate, he found his typewriting machine.

Sebastian sat back on his heels, staring at his battered, once-beloved Crandall. Its black enamel was scratched and dented here and there, and the mother of pearl inlay was chipped, but all in all, it was in surprisingly good shape for a machine that had been pounded on a daily basis—sometimes with savage ferocity—for over a decade.

He stared at it, feeling nothing. Strange. This typewriting machine had once been the most important item he owned, and yet, staring at it now, he felt curiously detached from any emotion, as if he'd run into someone who hailed him as an old friend, but whom he did not even recognize.

He reached into the crate with both hands and pulled out the machine. Below it was a yellowed stack of paper tied with twine—an old manuscript. Sebastian froze, the typewriter in his hands, staring at the stack of pages nestled amid the bits of straw and shredded burlap used to pack the crate. A very old manuscript, he realized, noting the lines penned in his handwriting.

"He Went To Paris," Sebastian murmured, reading the title aloud. A vague memory stirred and he began to laugh. "My God."

This was the first complete novel he'd ever written. He set aside the typewriter and pulled the bundle out of the crate, and as he did, Sebastian's mind went tripping backward to when he'd written it, back to the very beginning.

It was his first summer abroad, after Eton and before Oxford, and he'd spent it in Paris. There, he'd been able to write without any risk of his father's censure or contempt. He'd sat in cafés, his quill racing madly across these pages, word after word pouring out of him, his seventeen-year-old heart so hungry, his writing so raw. He hadn't been concerned with plot or dialogue, only with putting on paper the story in his head. But when he'd reached the end, he'd realized it wasn't good enough to publish. He'd packed it away, gone on to Oxford, and forgotten it.

It was in his final year at university that he'd started his second manuscript, a far more difficult endeavor than his first, for he'd been determined that this time every word should be right, determined to succeed at writing and prove his father wrong. That manuscript had taken him three years to complete, and to his mind, it still hadn't been worthy of publication, but Phillip had convinced him to send it off to their friend Marlowe, who had just started a publishing company. Harry bought the book and published it, launching Sebastian's career as an author.

More novels followed, all of them immensely popular, along with a dozen short stories and three successful plays. He was showered with both literary acclaim and monetary success, and though his father scorned his profession and disowned him for it, Sebastian ceased to care what his father thought. He bought the Crandall and carted it across the globe, traveling and writing, and living out the dream he'd had as far back as he could remember.

But the dream had a price. Each story proved harder to write than the one before. Each year the writing felt more stale, the process more painful, until he couldn't shut out the endless parade of self-criticism, until each word felt ripped out of him. But then, he'd discovered cocaine, and cocaine had changed everything.

So harmless it had seemed at first, an amusing experiment in a Parisian salon. But later, while living in Italy, he had discovered what it was like to write under the drug's influence, and cocaine had become the magic elixir, warding off the crippling uncertainties that had come to plague his writing. With cocaine, writing became a joy again, as free and exciting as it had been that first summer in Paris, and what followed proved to be the most prolific period of his career, generating six more novels and four more plays.

He couldn't pinpoint exactly when everything had started to go wrong, when the exhilarating joy of writing on cocaine became an addictive need for the drug itself. Instead of being the ruling passion of his life, writing became the irksome duty that interfered with his amusements. Italy, instead of being a source of inspiration to his work, became an endless round of parties and women and an elixir that wasn't really magical at all.

Sebastian set aside the manuscript and returned his attention to the Crandall. He ran the tip of his finger across the upper row of typewriting keys, thinking of that fateful afternoon in Florence three years ago when he'd written *Girl with a Red Handbag*. He'd fired off the three-act comedy in just twenty-four hours, pounding away at the typewriting machine with all the speed and cocksureness that only cocaine could give him. Afterward, he hadn't bothered to edit it, or even read it. He'd posted it to Rotherstein in London, demanded his first payment on the contract, and rewarded himself with a three-day binge of drinking, debauchery, and more cocaine.

He didn't remember inhaling the final dose. He didn't remember losing consciousness. But he did remember waking up in a Florentine alley with the revolting smell of his own vomit in his nostrils. He remembered his friend St. Cyres kneeling beside him, shouting for a doctor in Italian that sounded strangely slow and slurred to his ears. And then had come a bright light that hurt his eyes, and a queer pulling sensation, as if someone had grabbed him by the pectoral muscles within his chest and lifted him off the ground; and yet, he felt no pain from the experience. That was when he'd realized he was dying.

He'd fought, he remembered, kicking and cursing and telling God and the devil to both sod off, that he wasn't going anywhere with either of them because he didn't want to die. He wanted to live.

He'd gotten his wish in the end, coming to his senses in an Italian hospital, racked with the pain of withdrawal from cocaine. It was there that a long-faced British doctor had refused to administer the drug required to ease his suffering, informed him cocaine would kill him if he continued to take it, and recommended a quiet, discreet place in the Swiss Alps.

Having fought so hard for his life, Sebastian intended to fight just as hard to keep it. He'd gone to Switzerland, he'd freed himself of his physical need for cocaine. But freeing himself from the emotional need for the drug had proved much harder. Even now, three years later, there were times when he longed to go back to his frenetic, quixotic days in Italy, to relive a time when all his doubts were silent and he felt invincible. No matter that the writing itself had been some of his worst—

he hadn't known that then, and he hadn't cared; he'd loved the bliss of self-deception. His physical addiction was past, but the feeling that came with it, the euphoric feeling of being invincible—the craving for that never went away. It never would.

He tapped the tip of one finger against a typewriter key, and Harry's words of a week ago echoed through his mind.

You have to sit down and type . . . one word, then another, then another, until you have a book.

If only it were that easy.

Sebastian grabbed the typewriting machine and stood up. Weaving amid the trunks and boxes, he made his way to his desk. He plunked the typewriter down on top of his blotter and pulled a stack of notepaper from the center drawer of his desk. He sat down, rolled one sheet into the machine, took a deep breath, and put his fingertips on the keys.

It came at once—that yawning emptiness, that stark, blank, irrational fear. He set his jaw.

Write something, he told himself. *For God's sake, write something.*

The door opened. Relief flooded through him and he looked up, hopeful of possible distraction, but at the sight of his butler in the doorway, he knew his hope was a futile one. When it came to providing distractions, Wilton was hopeless. "Yes, what is it?"

"You have a visitor, my lord," the servant informed

him in that bored, superior fashion butlers were so fond of using. "A young woman."

That was all having a title and estates did for a fellow. "Devil take it, man, haven't I told you not to bother me with visits from silly marriage-minded debutantes and their matchmaking mamas?" He tapped the keys of the Crandall and donned a virtuous air. "I am working."

"My apologies, sir, but I thought you might wish to see this particular young woman."

Wilton's insistence stirred Sebastian's interest. His butler was not usually so presumptuous. "Why? Is she pretty?"

It was impossible to fluster Wilton, who had previously been the head footman in Aunt Mathilda's household. Mathilda, his staunchly proper maiden aunt, expected her servants to display an unruffled demeanor at all times, regardless of any circumstances they might face. Trained by her, Wilton had become unflappable long before he'd been promoted to his current position as butler to Mathilda's notorious nephew. "I believe any gentleman would consider her to be very pretty, sir," he said with no change in expression.

There was a pause, and Sebastian sensed there was more information the butler wished to impart. "And?" he prompted.

"She is unaccompanied, sir."

Sebastian's brows rose at this significant piece of information. A respectable young woman who was unaccompanied coming to call upon an unmarried man was one of those things that Did Not Happen. Therefore, she must not be respectable. His mind began imagining an interlude of amorous intrigue, he felt an immediate rise in his spirits, and any notions of trying to write went to the wall.

He smiled and stood up. "You always find a way to brighten my day, Wilton."

"Thank you, sir."

"Does this young woman have a name?" Sebastian asked, brushing dust and bits of straw from his shirt-sleeves as he glanced at the butler.

Wilton lifted the calling card in his hand. "Miss Daisy Merrick," he read. "Thirty-Two Little Russell Street, Holborn."

Sebastian groaned, his hopes dashed at once. "Not that saucy little baggage! What on earth is she doing here?"

"She is here at the request of Viscount Marlowe."

Worse and worse. "I don't care if she's here at the request of the Queen! Miss Merrick is one of those modern, emancipated spinsters who speak their minds with impunity and absolutely no sense of delicacy. You see her sort forcing their way in everywhere, marching through the streets with placards, chaining themselves to railings, demanding the right to earn their own living." He cast a resentful glance at the typewriter on his desk. "As if anyone with sense would want to earn a living."

"Not spinsters, sir," Wilton corrected him with complacence. "Girl-bachelors, I believe they are called nowadays."

"Girl-bachelors? Ye gods, what a term. Call her what you will, but Miss Daisy Merrick is the worst thing any human being can possibly be: a critic. She imparts her pert opinions to all and sundry even when she doesn't know what on earth she's talking about. Marlowe obviously thinks it amusing to send her here to plague me." He made a dismissive gesture with one hand. "Send her away."

Wilton gave an apologetic little cough. "Begging your pardon, sir, but given the . . . umm . . . uncertain nature of things at present, and considering the fact that Lord Marlowe did send her himself, perhaps you might deem it wise to . . . ahem . . . give her a few moments of your time?"

He met his butler's limpid gaze and remembered that he owed the fellow three months' wages. Wilton, along with his cook, housekeeper, footman, housemaid, and driver had been sent down from Devonshire by his aunt to do for him upon his arrival home in February, but unfortunately, Mathilda hadn't sent the blunt with which to pay any of them. If he couldn't come up to scratch soon, all of them would leave his employ, a fact of which Wilton was delicately reminding him. Even Abercrombie, a loyal old bird who'd stuck by him through those dark days in Switzerland, might leave if he couldn't pay proper wages.

Sebastian rubbed a hand across his jaw, considering. His play had closed, leaving him without a shred of income. Due to his father's demise, he owed Her Majesty's government an exorbitant amount of money in death duties, and given his current lack of writing success and his formerly lavish lifestyle, he had other debts as well. His estate in Devonshire was already heavily mortgaged, and what with the agricultural woes that had been plaguing the British economy, Avermore Park wasn't likely to produce much in the way of income anyway. His financial situation was grim indeed.

Unlike him, however, Lord Marlowe was a very rich man, and Sebastian might soon be forced to request another advance from him on the nonexistent next book. Whatever joke Marlowe was having at his expense by sending Miss Merrick here, it was best to be civil. And though she might be an opinionated spinster with a devilish supply of impudence, she was far prettier to look at than a blank sheet of paper.

"You're a wise man, Wilton," he said. "Where have you put the girl? In the drawing room, I suppose?" When the butler nodded, he went on, "Very well. Tell her I shall be down directly."

Wilton was not so ill-bred as to display any sign of

relief, but Sebastian sensed it just the same. "Yes, sir," the butler answered and withdrew.

Sebastian did not follow at once. Instead, he lingered behind, trying to fathom what Harry was up to, but after a few moments, he was forced to give it up. His publisher was an unaccountable fellow at times, and there was no point in guessing what crazy notion he'd gotten into his head. Sebastian rolled down his cuffs and fastened them with his cuff links, then gave a tug to the hem of his slate-blue waistcoat, raked his fingers through his hair to put the unruly strands in some sort of order, and smoothed his dark blue necktie. He went down to the drawing room and paused beside the open doorway.

Miss Merrick's appearance, he noted as he took a peek around the doorjamb, was much the same as before. The same sort of plain, starched white shirt-waist, paired with a green skirt this time. Ribbons of darker green accented her collar and straw boater. She was seated at one end of the long yellow sofa, her hands resting on her thighs. Her fingers drummed against her knees and her toes tapped the floor in an agitated fashion, as if she was nervous. At her feet was a leather dispatch case.

He eyed the dispatch case, appalled. What if Harry wanted him to read her novel and give an endorsement? His publisher did have a perverse sense of humor. It would be just like Harry to pretend he was publishing the girl and blackmail Sebastian into reading eight hundred pages of bad prose before telling him it was all a joke. Or—and this was an even more nauseating possibility—she might actually be good, Harry did intend to publish her book, and they truly did want his endorsement.

Either way, he wasn't interested. Striving not to appear as grim as he felt, Sebastian pasted on a smile and entered the drawing room. "Miss Merrick, this is an unexpected pleasure."

She rose from the sofa as he crossed the room to greet her, and in response to his bow, she gave a curtsy. "Lord Avermore."

He glanced at the clock on the mantel, noting it was a quarter to five. Regardless of the fact that it was inappropriate for her to call upon a bachelor unchaperoned, the proper thing for any gentleman to do in these circumstances was to offer her tea. Sebastian's sense of civility, however, did not extend that far. "My butler tells me you have come at Lord Marlowe's request?"

"Yes. The viscount left London today for Torquay. He intends to spend the summer there with his family. Before he departed, however, he asked me to call upon you on his behalf regarding a matter of business."

So it was a request for an endorsement. "An author and his sternest critic meeting at the request of their mutual publisher to discuss business?" he murmured, keeping his smile in place even as he wondered how best to make the words 'not a chance in hell' sound civil. "What an extraordinary notion."

"It is a bit unorthodox," she agreed.

He leaned closer to her, adopting a confidential, author-to-author sort of manner. "That's Marlowe all over. He's always been a bit eccentric. Perhaps he's gone off his onion at last."

"Lord Avermore, I know my review injured your feelings—"

"Your review and the seven others that came after it," he interrupted pleasantly. "They closed the play, you know."

"I heard that, yes." She bit her lip. "I'm sorry."

He shrugged as if the loss of several thousand pounds was a thing of no consequence whatsoever. "It's quite all right, petal. I only contemplated hurling myself in front of a train once, before I came to my senses." He paused, but he couldn't resist adding, "Hauling you to Victoria Station, on the other hand, still holds a certain appeal, I must confess."

She gave a sigh, looking unhappy. As well she should. "I can appreciate that you are upset, but—"

"My dear girl, I am not in the least upset," he felt compelled to assure her. "I was being flippant. In all truth, I feel quite all right. You see, I have followed your advice."

"My advice?"

"Yes. I have chosen to be open-minded, to take your

review in the proper spirit, and learn from your critique." He spread his hands, palms up in a gesture of goodwill. "After all," he added genially, "of what use to a writer is mere praise?"

She didn't seem to perceive the sarcasm. "Oh," she breathed and pressed one palm to her chest with a little laugh, "I am so relieved to hear you say that. When the viscount told me why he wanted me to come see you, I was concerned you would resent the situation, but your words give me hope that we will be able to work together in an amicable fashion."

Uneasiness flickered inside him. "Work together?" he echoed, his brows drawing together in bewilderment, though he forced himself to keep smiling.

"Yes. You see . . ." She paused, and her smile faded to a serious expression. She took a deep breath, as if readying herself to impart a difficult piece of news. "Lord Marlowe has employed me to assist you."

Sebastian's uneasiness deepened into dread as he stared into her upturned face, a face that shone with sincerity. He realized this was not one of Harry's jokes. He wanted to look away, but it was rather like watching a railway accident happen. One couldn't look away. "Assist me with what, in heaven's name?"

"With your work." She met his astonishment with a rueful look. "I am here to help you write your next book."

Chapter 5

The road to ignorance is paved with good editors.
George Bernard Shaw

To say that Sebastian Grant looked displeased was something of an understatement. As those steel-gray eyes of his narrowed, resentment emanating from him like a blazing bonfire, even the ever-optimistic Daisy began to lose hope for the mission that had brought her here.

Since leaving Lord Marlowe's office yesterday afternoon, she had rehearsed this moment at least a dozen times. But the reality of telling one of England's greatest writers his publisher had sent a novice to help him with his work was proving to be a far more daunting prospect than it had been in her imagination. He looked ready to slice her into pieces and feed her to a pack of hungry dogs.

She couldn't blame him. He had every right to resent her. She'd thrashed his play, and now, when he was in the midst of a writing drought, she was here to come to his aid. It had to be a galling situation for him.

Still, she had accepted Lord Marlowe's offer, and there was no going back. Wishing she possessed even a fraction of her sister's tact and *sang-froid*, Daisy took a deep breath, gathered her nerve, and attempted to explain what the viscount had in mind without offending the man before her any further.

"Lord Avermore, I know this situation is a bit unusual—"

"You are to assist me with writing? You? The critic who loathes my work?" He laughed, a harsh sound that made her wince. "This has to be a joke. It's too absurd to be anything else."

"If it were a joke, Lord Marlowe would never choose me to implement it," she told him, trying to smile. "I've no talent for jokes. I always make a terrible muddle of them."

"Then it's an insult. Who are you to think your opinion is worth a damn? When you've two decades of writing behind you, and some published works to your credit, I might set some store by your opinion. Until then, you can go hang, and Marlowe with you."

She pressed her lips together, eying him with a hint of compassion. "I am sure it seems somewhat insulting to you," she agreed. "But the viscount is genuinely concerned about you. He believes I possess a certain insight that might assist you in overcoming your creative difficulties."

Daisy watched him stiffen as she spoke those last two words, and she feared that her carefully worded speech had been for naught. Those broad shoulders of his squared, harkening back to her first impression of him as an angry bull, and she spoke again before the bull could charge. "Despite what you may think, I do not loathe your work, my lord."

"You gave a damned fine imitation of it a week ago."

"I did not like your latest play, that is true, but—"

"Nor do you seem to have much fondness for any of my recent literary efforts."

She refused to allow this conversation to degenerate into a pointless and petty argument over that review. "Nonetheless, I think you one of the finest writers of English literature ever born, and I would consider it an honor and a privilege to work with you. I've read everything you've ever written, seen all your plays—"

"And just what," he interrupted her again, seeming not at all flattered by her attempts to soothe his pride, "creative difficulties did Harry tell you I am having?"

She decided perhaps it was best to follow his lead and cut to the heart of the matter. "Lord Marlowe said you are unable to write."

"Marlowe is mistaken."

Studying his hard countenance, her hopes for success fell another notch. How?—she wondered for perhaps the twentieth time since yesterday—how was a novice like her going to help a legendary writer like him compose a book, especially when it was plain as day he didn't want any help? Surely, it was impossible.

The moment that conclusion crossed her mind, Daisy shoved it out again. Marlow's rejection had made it clear that being paid for her own writing was a more distant hope than she had thought at first, and he had offered her five hundred pounds to accomplish this one task. But Daisy knew there was more at stake for her than money, and that was the true reason she had agreed to take it on. This was about pride and accomplishment, about self-reliance and self-respect, and about learning to do something well.

She cleared her throat to break the silence that had fallen between them. "If Marlowe is mistaken," she said gently, "then why has it been four years since you last published a book?"

Those gray eyes flashed like glittering steel. "Assuming for the sake of argument that I am having trouble, what in Hades are you supposed to do about it?"

"Lord Marlowe proposes that I become your writing partner."

"I knew it!" He slammed one fist against his opposite palm. "Damn that crazy editor of mine, and his harebrained ideas. Interfering jackanapes. No one writes my books for me. No one." He paused, scowling at her. "Especially not you, for God's sake!"

In the face of such animosity, anyone might have forgiven her for abandoning the whole venture in despair at this point, but Daisy had promised Marlowe that she would try her best, and she was by no means ready to give up. "I am not here to write your book for you," she told him. "I am here to help *you* write it."

He set his jaw and folded his arms across his wide chest. "And how do you intend to do that, hmm?"

Daisy herself wasn't quite sure yet, but she decided Marlowe's explanation to her when he'd hired her would be sufficient to answer that question for now. "I am to be a—a sort of sounding board for you, perhaps provoke thought and discussion that will lead you to ideas for a story. And then—"

"Well, Harry got that right, at least," he interrupted. "You provoke me beyond belief, Miss Merrick. In fact, I have once or twice felt the desire to wring your pretty neck."

"And I sometimes want to slap your insufferable face," she countered at once. "If that would help you write the damned book, I'd do it, too! Now, would you kindly stop interrupting me so that I might finish answering your question?"

Arms still folded across his chest, he gave her a little bow. "My apologies." He made a rolling gesture with one hand, then rested his elbow on his opposite arm, pressed his knuckle to his chin, and looked at her expectantly. "Pray continue. I'm waiting on pins and needles, I assure you."

"As you write, I am to critique your work."

"Oh, now that's a joyful prospect."

"I'd have thought it would be." She looked into his eyes, meeting his mockery head-on. "Since you are also to critique mine."

"Indeed?" A flicker of interest came into his eyes, the only hopeful sign she'd seen yet.

"Yes. You are to sharpen your knives on my work to your heart's content, and I . . ." She paused, forcing herself to smile. "I am to take it in the proper spirit and learn from the experience."

"Clever, petal," he said in an appreciative voice. "Very clever. You've thrown out some bait I'm actually tempted to take."

"Lord Marlowe feels my writing would benefit from your opinions and advice, enabling me to improve."

"Ah." He tapped his knuckle against his chin and gave her a knowing look. "Rejected your book, did he?"

It galled her to admit the truth to this man, but she had no choice. "Lord Marlowe said my writing shows great promise," she informed him with dignity.

"Great promise?" he echoed, sounding amused. "Isn't that a bit like the plain girl being told she has a pleasing personality?"

"Oh! You really are the most insufferable—" Daisy

bit back the insults she so badly wanted to fire off, reminding herself that tact was her new watchword. Still, she knew she could not let such remarks go unchallenged or this man would walk all over her. "Is that your way of saying I am plain, my lord?" she demanded, deliberately misinterpreting his words.

She watched him glance over her, the same assessing perusal that had made her blush so unaccountably in Marlowe's office. She felt it happening again, and she cursed her fair complexion, but she refused to look away. "Is that what you think?"

"What I think is that you're a delicious little morsel with pretty hair, a shapely bum, and a deuced supply of impudence."

Daisy sucked in her breath, shocked by his most improper reference to her backside, and it took her a moment to realize he had also complimented her hair. The idea that he thought there was anything pretty about her was surprising enough, but her *hair*? The carrot-colored mop that had made her such a favorite target for teasing in her childhood?

Daisy frowned. Maybe he was color-blind. Or maybe he was just crazy.

Before she could decide, he went on, "But I don't know if you can write worth a damn."

She strove to recover her poise. "Lord Marlowe said I have natural talent and original ideas."

"That's nice. So why did he reject your manuscript?"

"He also said I have a few things to learn before I am ready to be published."

"And I'm supposed to teach you, eh? Is that his idea?"

"Yes."

He unfolded his arms and took a step toward her, closing the distance between them. "There's a great deal I could teach you, I think," he murmured, leaning close to her, so close she had to tilt her head back to look at him. "But would you be a willing pupil?"

A tingle ran up her spine, an awareness—not of danger, but of something else, something that made her flustered and nervous, but it wasn't fear. He'd asked her a question, but she couldn't seem to remember what it was. He was staring at her, his mouth curved in that slight, one-sided smile. He thought her hair was pretty. She had a shapely bum. She felt the color in her face deepening. She tried to speak. "I . . . umm . . . I . . ." But her voice trailed off as his lashes lowered and he fixed his gaze on her mouth.

He bent his head a fraction, and Daisy realized wildly that he was going to kiss her. Her heart gave a little lurch. Oh, heavens. He was making advances upon her person. Reminding herself that she'd lost her previous employment because of this sort of thing, Daisy jerked back a step and tried to return to the matter at hand.

"The most important thing," she said, her voice sounding strangled to her own ears, "is that I am here to assist you with your writing. And I hope that you can also help me. In addition, I can provide you with clerical assistance. I am an excellent typist. I can act as your secretary, your stenographer, whatever you want to call it."

"I call it idiotic."

Those words wiped out any tingly warmth she might have been feeling a moment before. "I will do whatever I can," she said through clenched teeth, "to see that you provide Marlowe Publishing with a book."

"And Marlowe is paying you for this pointless exercise?"

"Well, I'm certainly not doing it because of your charming demeanor and pleasant temperament."

He gave a shout of laughter. "By God, you've a fair amount of nerve, I'll give you that."

"My primary task," Daisy said doggedly, "is to see that you recover from your creative drought and fulfill the terms of your contract. For that, I shall be paid a fee of five hundred pounds. In addition, it is my fervent wish that your influence and guidance will enable me to become a more accomplished writer. If you are any good at teaching," she added, "Marlowe will publish not only your next book, but mine as well."

An odd expression crossed his face, an inexplicable hint of melancholy. He sighed, raking a hand through his hair. "I can't teach you how to be a writer, petal."

"But you can teach me to improve, to be a better writer than I am now. And perhaps, I can assist you to break free of this dry spell you are in. That is Marlowe's hope. And mine." She paused, studying him. "Yours, too, I think, deep down."

With those words, any trace of softness in his expression vanished. "There is nothing you can do to help me. And as for helping you, it's futile. As I said before, the only way one learns to write is by writing. There's nothing I can teach you. God knows," he added, sounding suddenly tired, "if I could teach anyone to write, I'd teach myself." He bent and picked up her dispatch case, then reached for her hand and wrapped her fingers around the handle. "Good day, Miss Merrick."

"My lord, I know this idea seems unorthodox, but it could benefit us both."

"I doubt it." He let go of her hand, gripped her elbow, and turned her toward the door.

"Surely, it is worth the attempt," Daisy argued as he began ushering her out of the drawing room. "And I truly would like to help you if I could."

He paused just beside the door. "Miss Merrick, there is one way you can help me tremendously."

"Oh?" Daisy's spirits lifted a little. "How?"

"By leaving." His grip on her elbow tightened, and before she knew what was happening, he had propelled her out of the drawing room and into the corridor.

Daisy dug in her heels at the top of the stairs and jerked her elbow free of his grasp. "Lord Marlowe wants us to try to work together."

"Quite a mad fellow, that Marlowe." He wrapped an arm around her waist and lifted her off the ground, ignoring her yelp of protest. "They say insanity runs in his family," he added, starting down the stairs with her body pressed to his side and her feet dangling in the air. "Personally, I think his lunacy stems from years of exposure to writers. That would drive anyone mad."

Daisy knew she couldn't put up a struggle and risk tumbling them both down the stairs. But once they had reached the bottom and he set her on her feet, she dropped her dispatch case and made a grab for the newel post. "But I need your help, too," she said, gripping the carved teakwood pineapple finial and holding on for dear life. "Don't you want to help me?"

"No. I'm such a cad." He began prying her fingers from the finial, and though she tightened her grip, she was no match for his superior strength. It was only a moment or two before he was pulling her away from the newel post.

"Marlowe told me you want to begin a new novel," she said, as he once again lifted her off her feet, retrieved her dispatch case, and started across the foyer toward the front door, marching her past the dour-faced butler who stood by without raising an eyebrow. "He told me your problem is that you can't seem to get started."

"No, the problem is that I don't want to write at all. But even if I did, it would have nothing whatsoever to do with you." He plunked her down beside the front door. "Please tell Marlowe I am touched by his concern on my behalf," he added as he opened the door, "but I do not require a partner or an assistant."

"I can type your manuscripts."

"There is no manuscript, and if there were, I would type it myself, thank you."

She was unable to stop him from shoving her across the threshold, but the moment she was on the front stoop, she turned around to face him. "I can edit your pages—"

"I already have an editor, something Marlowe knows perfectly well, since that editor is he. Good day, Miss Merrick." He bowed and started to shut the door.

"I could help you," she said in desperation. "Really I could, if you'd just—"

The door slammed in her face.

"Give me the chance," she finished, but she was now talking to the bright red panels of the closed door.

She'd bungled it. Daisy's shoulders slumped in discouragement. It was always like this, she thought dismally. Somehow, she always managed to make a mess of these things. Lucy, no doubt, would have handled the entire situation much better.

Thoughts of her sister caught her up sharp, and she put aside any inclinations to feel sorry for herself.

This time, she vowed, was not going to make a mess of things. She wanted the five hundred pounds Marlowe had offered her. It was more than she could earn as a typist in half a dozen years, and surely in that amount of time, her writing would improve enough to make her worthy of publication. Besides, she didn't want to go in search of yet another post. Most important of all, she wanted to prove to Lucy and to herself that she could succeed at something. The man on the other side of this door was the key to accomplishing all of those goals.

Somehow, she had to induce him to write his novel. There had to be a way. Daisy looked through the window and saw him still standing in the foyer, watching her. Their gazes met, and Daisy pressed the electric bell beside the door, but she was not surprised when he folded his arms across his chest and remained right where he was.

Contrary, stubborn fool, she thought in irritation, but with that thought came the memory of Marlowe's words about Avermore.

It's good for him to be knocked back on his heels once in a while. He's too arrogant by half. The worst things anyone can do are pander to him or pamper him.

Daisy considered that for a moment, and as she did, a plan began to form in her mind. It was a bold plan, and it would take nerve to pull it off, but as Avermore himself had pointed out, nerve was something she had plenty of.

Daisy smiled sweetly at the man on the other side of the glass, and she took great pleasure in watching his black brows draw together in a suspicious frown. Still smiling, she waved at him, then turned away and descended the front steps.

Sebastian Grant might not know it yet, but he was going to write that book. She intended to leave him no other choice. Filled with renewed determination, Daisy started down the sidewalk in search of a telegraph office.

Chapter 6

An enemy can partly ruin a man, but it takes a good-natured, injudicious friend to complete the thing and make it perfect.

Mark Twain

*E*very time Sebastian thought of Daisy Merrick's pleased little smile, he became more convinced he had not seen the last of her.

It only took three days to prove him right. He was in his study, going through the last of the crates from Switzerland, when Wilton entered with the announcement that Miss Merrick had once again come to call on him.

He groaned. "I knew it. Good God, does she not comprehend what the word *no* means?"

"Evidently not, sir."

"Well, send her away," he ordered, pulling a book

from the crate at his feet. "I told you before, to that woman I am never home. And send Saunders to me, will you?" he added, shoving the book into the appropriate place on the bookshelf beside him. "Several of these crates need to go to the attic."

Wilton hesitated, glancing at Sebastian's desk. "You have packed away your typewriting machine, sir?"

"I have." He saw no point in torturing himself by having the blasted thing out where he could see it, but he wasn't about to explain his motives to a servant. "Anything more, Wilton?"

"No, sir." The butler departed without another word, but of course, a simple order was not sufficient to dispense with Miss Merrick. Moments later, Wilton reappeared.

"Sorry, sir," he apologized at once, "but the young woman is most insistent upon seeing you. She says she has come regarding a legal matter involving yourself and Marlowe Publishing, something of vital importance."

"Legal matter? Damn it, man, does the girl look like a solicitor?"

"No, sir."

"Well, then, what legal matter could she possibly be here about? Women don't involve themselves in legal matters. They aren't allowed to sit for the bar, thank heavens. If they were, can you imagine the havoc that would ensue? Men would never win any arguments again. Not that we ever do anyway. I told you, send her away."

"Begging your pardon, my lord, but she says this must be handled at once. Marlowe has sent her to ascertain your wishes so the proper actions can be taken by Marlowe Publishing."

"Oh, for the love of—" Sebastian bit back an oath and shoved the book in his hand onto a shelf of the bookcase. This had to be a ruse, designed to give her another go at persuading him to write a book. He started to tell Wilton to send her packing, but then he paused to reconsider.

His publisher had a perverse sense of humor. If this were a genuine legal matter, it was just like Harry to send the pretty and pernicious Miss Merrick to tell him about it. It probably involved nothing more than a request for the translation rights of one of his books into French, or some proposal from an American newspaper to serialize one of his story collections. He hoped it was the Americans. They paid well. The French, on the other hand, were terribly stingy. Either way, it meant income for him, and he could ill afford to be cavalier. If he were in funds, he'd instruct his own solicitors to handle things for him, but he already owed Bassington and Burton quite a bit of money, and incurring more debt was the last thing he needed.

It wasn't as if the girl could persuade him to write anything anyway. Although, he amended as an image of those viridescent blue eyes and that lush pink mouth came into his mind, it might be enjoyable watching her try.

"Very well," he said. "I'll be down in a moment."

Wilton departed, and Sebastian turned to lean back against the bookcase, recalling his last encounter with Miss Merrick. He'd almost kissed her that day. Even now, he didn't know quite why. Granted, she was pretty enough that a man hardly needed a reason, but in this case, that didn't quite explain things. He didn't like her. He found her annoying as hell. She provoked him beyond belief. Yet, strangely enough, those very qualities were what made kissing her such an intriguing notion.

She'd experienced a similar feeling, he knew, and it had rattled her. She'd jumped like a startled deer the moment he'd come too close. Perhaps this time, he could get closer. It occurred to him that getting close to Miss Merrick might be akin to lighting matches near a powder keg, but some risks were just worth taking. Sebastian ventured down to the drawing room.

Sadly, she was once again wearing those spinsterish clothes and carrying that hideous dispatch case, but he took some consolation in the fact that the sunlight through the drawing room windows poured in behind her as she rose from the sofa, outlining her shape beneath the cotton shirtwaist. "My lord," she said, offering a curtsy as she greeted him.

"Miss Merrick. How delightful to see you again." He bowed and gestured for her to resume her seat, but as she did so, he chose not to take the chair across from her. Instead, he sat down. "I hope you are well?"

She scooted sideways until she was at the very other end. "I am quite well, thank you. But this is not a social call," she added, turning a bit so that she could face him on the sofa. "It is a matter of business, so may we begin at once?"

The brisk efficiency of her voice sounded terribly forced and made him want to smile. He was flustering her again. "Of course," he answered. "My butler mentioned you have come to consult me regarding some sort of legal matter?"

"I have." She reached for her dispatch case, opened it on her lap, and extracted a sheaf of documents. "This is a copy of your most recent contract with Marlowe Publishing." She closed the case, set the papers on top, then pulled out the last sheet and held it up for him to see. "Is this your signature, Lord Avermore?"

He felt a glimmer of uneasiness, but he didn't show it. "Yes," he answered, stretching his arm across the back of the sofa, assuming the pose of a man perfectly relaxed. "Why—"

"Excellent," she cut him off and replaced the page in its place. She scanned the top page, using her forefinger as a guide, and paused near the bottom. "Section Two, Subsection A, Paragraph One of your contract states that you agree to deliver a manuscript consisting of a minimum of one hundred thirty-five thousand words to Marlowe Publishing by January 31, 1893." She looked up. "You are late."

Only a fool could not see where this conversation was headed. Damn Harry and his perverse sense of humor. Sebastian moved closer to her, turning and bending his head as if he wanted to read the document on her lap. She stirred, and a wisp of her bright hair fell from beneath the boater perched atop her head. The curl glinted in the sunlight like a burnished strand of fire against the skin of her cheek. Once again, he imagined what she would look like with all that glorious hair undone, but this time he pictured it spread out on green grass all around her, and arousal flickered to life in his body. "Am I truly as late as that?" he asked in a low voice. "Show me."

She didn't look at him, but bent her head over the contract on her lap and tapped the appropriate paragraph with her forefinger. "It is right here."

"Hmm . . ." He pretended to read it, keeping his gaze on her profile. The golden freckles on her cheek were like toffee sprinkles on a dish of cream, and as he imagined kissing them, he was almost able to taste the sweetness of her skin against his mouth. "Yes," he agreed, "I do seem to be a bit behind."

"Three years, three months and twenty days behind, to be precise."

"My, how time does fly." He eased his body closer to hers and caught a fresh, delicate scent he couldn't identify. Somehow it fueled his erotic notions of her beneath him in the grass, and he closed his eyes. Inhaling deeply, he tried to place the elusive fragrance.

Papers rustled as she turned the page. "Furthermore, per Section Two, Subsection B, Paragraph One," she went on, "should you not comply with delivery of said manuscript by the required date, it is your responsibility to request an extension."

He took another deep breath and suddenly realized what that delicate, gardenlike scent was. It was nothing more than soap—Pears' soap to be precise, whose advertisements must be right because she did indeed smell as fresh and sweet as an English garden. Not a scent he'd ever thought particularly erotic, but combined with the images in his mind, it was becoming very erotic indeed.

Beside him, she droned on about his contract. "Any request by you for an extension shall be in writing, and shall be considered solely at the publisher's discretion. Should the publisher agree to an extension, the terms shall be negotiated in good faith. Did you request an extension, Lord Avermore?"

The question forced Sebastian to set aside fantasies of love in the grass for the moment. He opened his eyes to find her staring at him as if expecting an answer. "No. I did not."

"Then none has been granted, despite your seeming assumption to the contrary. Nor has Marlowe Publishing received any other correspondence from you, nor have you replied to any of Lord Marlowe's inquiries on the subject."

At Miss Merrick's reiteration of his publisher's tirade, Sebastian's stirrings of lust toward her began to evaporate. "Harry and I discussed this," he began, but she cut him off.

"Because you failed to request an extension and refused to negotiate extensions proposed by Marlowe Publishing in good faith, you are out of compliance with your contract." She frowned, drawing her brows together in an attempt to look stern. Owing to the abundance of pretty freckles on her face, however, the effort didn't amount to much.

"Yes, it seems I've been very naughty," he agreed languidly. "Am I to be sent to bed without my supper?"

Her frown deepened at his obvious lack of contrition. "It is my understanding that you received an advance payment against this contract of five thousand pounds?"

He gave a sigh of regret as the last vestiges of a most pleasurable erotic fantasy faded away. "I did."

"And can you in good conscience name a date at which you shall be presenting Marlowe Publishing with a manuscript?"

He made a sound of impatience. Harry was still

under the mistaken impression that all he had to do was sit down at his typewriter every day and a book would magically appear in short order. Though why Harry thought sending Miss Merrick to cite petty legalities would spur him to buckle down was rather baffling. "I have already refused to consider Harry's idea of having you as a writing partner, or assistant, or whatever you two want to call it, so now he is using you to remind me of the terms of my contract? Did he think you would be more persuasive in bringing me up to scratch than a long-faced solicitor?"

"Because you are out of compliance with your contract," she went on as if he hadn't spoken, "and because you have categorically refused to negotiate in good faith with Marlowe Publishing for an extension of that contract, you are required to repay your advance to Marlowe Publishing."

He jerked upright. "What?"

She tapped the page on her lap. "It is right here. Section Two, Subsection B, Paragraph Two."

"I don't care what section it's in, damn it all. I thought Harry employed you to persuade me to write a book. This doesn't seem an effective way of achieving that goal."

"Your adamant refusal to discuss writing a new book has led Lord Marlowe to reconsider the situation. You are to repay your advance, thereby voiding your contract."

"Harry knows I can't buy back my contract. He knows I haven't a bean at present." He scowled at her. "A circumstance which is partly due to the fact that a certain critic working for a newspaper owned by my own publisher shredded my play, thereby ruining any chance I had of deriving an income from it!"

She shrugged. "Blame me all you like, but it won't alter a thing. You owe Marlowe Publishing the sum of five thousand, six hundred thirty-four pounds and eleven shillings."

"Marlowe advanced me five thousand. Why is he charging me an additional nine hundred odd?"

"Interest."

"What?" He couldn't help a laugh, for this entire conversation was now venturing into the absurd. "Marlowe intends to charge me interest?"

She tapped the page again with her forefinger. "Pursuant to Section Two, Subsection C, Paragraph One, should you not present the publisher with an acceptable manuscript within a period of three years following the date required for submission of said manuscript, the publisher is at liberty to charge interest on any funds advanced to you, beginning from the original deadline and compounded at a rate of four percent per annum. Hence the amount. Which, by the way, is payable upon demand. That, Lord Avermore, is why I am here."

She held out her hand toward him, palm up, as if expecting him to hand over nearly six thousand pounds then and there.

"Of all the asinine—" He broke off, remembering he was speaking to a woman and too angry to voice what he really wanted to say anyway. "For heaven's sake, Miss Merrick, put your hand down," he said instead. "I don't go about carrying that sort of blunt in my pocket."

She lowered her hand. "If you wish to retrieve your bank book and write a cheque," she said, clasping her hands together and resting them atop the contract, "I would be happy to wait."

"I can't pay over a sum of money like that on such short notice. And Harry damn well knows it."

"If you refuse to comply, then I have been instructed to report your refusal to Mr. Jonathan Ghent, Esquire, of Ledbetter and Ghent. His firm represents the legal interests of Marlowe Publishing, and he will proceed with the appropriate actions against you."

"Sue me in the courts? Harry wouldn't dare."

She nodded as if she had expected such a reply. Once again, she opened her dispatch case and extracted a folded sheet of paper, which she held out to him without a word.

Sebastian snatched the letter, broke the wax seal and opened it. The moment he saw the insignia of Ledbetter and Ghent at the top of the page, and Jonathan Ghent's signature at the bottom, he knew he was in serious trouble. The letter confirmed the legal firm's readiness to begin collection proceedings via the assizes, should Sebastian Grant, Earl of Avermore, refuse to honor his debt to Marlowe Publishing, Limited.

Sebastian looked up from the letter to stare at the woman beside him, appalled. "Good God. A judicial proceeding would turn my private life into a public spectacle."

"Well, yes, the news will be widely reported, no doubt," she agreed with infuriating complacence, "along with the fact that you are no longer contracted with Marlowe Publishing and never will be again. No doubt the scandal sheets will speculate as to the depth of your financial insolvency—"

"Damned right they will! Does Harry realize the damage this will do to me? Given my present circumstances, I wouldn't be able to obtain a loan if my life depended upon it."

"I cannot say what Lord Marlowe realizes or does not realize. I am merely following his instructions."

Sebastian glared at the delicious, infuriating bit of skirt on his sofa, once again chagrined that nature could have fashioned such a paradox. Perhaps he'd died that day in Florence, after all, and he was now in hell. He could well imagine this fire-haired wench had been sent to bedevil and torment him for eternity.

He leaned back against the sofa and rubbed a hand over his face, considering the ramifications of a legal battle with Marlowe. The financial difficulties were bad enough, but there was another far more important consideration. Journalists would begin probing into his private life. The notion that his former cocaine habit could come to light and become fodder for the scandal sheets didn't bear thinking about.

"There is another option."

Her voice intruded and he turned his head to find her watching him. With her big eyes and pretty freckles, she seemed the picture of artless innocence, but Sebastian knew better. "What option would that be?" he asked through clenched teeth.

"You could write the book."

"Damn you!" He jerked to his feet and walked away to the window. "There isn't ever going to be another book. Why can't you people accept that?"

He heard the sound of her footsteps as she came to stand beside him, but he would not look at her. He could not. Anger and frustration burned within him with all the corrosiveness of an acid.

"My lord," she said quietly, "it is Lord Marlowe's wish, as your friend, to see you write again."

He gave a bitter laugh. "Tell my friend to sod off."

"I will convey that message if you wish, but if you choose instead to fulfill your contract, Lord Marlowe would be willing to agree to an extension. A reasonable one, that is."

He took a deep breath. "Define reasonable."

"One hundred twenty days?"

"Four months? You're joking."

"My lord, I told you, I do not joke. It is not one of my talents. Do you wish for the extension?"

There was no way he could write a manuscript in four months. Or four years, for that matter. He would have to endure the scandal, face the financial ruin, and watch the glee with which critics and other writers would comment on the death of his career. Unless—

Sebastian stiffened, feeling a glimmer of hope. "There is no need for an extension, Miss Merrick. Harry wants a book? By God, I'll give him one."

"Where are you going?" she called after him as he started toward the door.

"Wait here." He strode out of the drawing room and went to his study. Among the crates that littered the floor, he sought out one in particular and opened it. How fitting, he thought, staring down at the manuscript he'd found a few days earlier, to end his career with the first book he'd ever written.

Sebastian reached into the crate, then hesitated, his hand curling into a fist as he remembered why he'd never submitted this novel to any publisher. It wasn't good enough.

Still, that hardly mattered now. His literary career had already hit rock bottom, so what did one more piece of bad writing matter? It was this manuscript or nothing. He pulled out the sheaf of paper, slammed the lid back down on the crate, and returned to the drawing room, where he rejoined her at the window. "Here," he said, thrusting the twine-tied bundle at her. "Here is my next book. Tell Harry it's also my last."

He took a grim satisfaction in watching her luscious lips part in surprise as she took the manuscript from his hands "But I thought you said there was no book."

"I was mistaken."

She glanced down. "This is old," she said with a frown, running the tip of her finger over a curled-up corner. "The paper is yellowed. And it's handwritten. You type your manuscripts, you said." She looked up at him again. "When did you write this?"

"What does it matter? It's a complete novel. There's a hundred and thirty-five thousand words there, I daresay."

"But an old manuscript isn't what Lord Marlowe wanted at all! For your own sake, he wants you to write again."

"I don't give a damn what he wants. I have fulfilled my obligation. Take him the book, and tell him I expect to be paid the remaining five thousand pounds due to me under the terms of my contract."

She hesitated, then gave a sigh of acquiescence. "Very well. I will convey your message to Lord Marlowe."

As she took the manuscript from his hands, Sebastian was filled with an immediate, overwhelming relief. It was over. He never had to write another word. It was all over.

She didn't seem to share his view of the matter. Instead of departing, she lingered, staring down at the manuscript in her hands. "Are you—" She broke off and lifted her face to look into his. "What will you do now?"

With that question, Sebastian's momentary relief disintegrated. The deed was done and no going back. He wasn't a writer anymore. With that realization, he felt again that yawning emptiness inside. What was he, if not a writer?

He kept his apprehensions hidden. "Good day, Miss Merrick."

She hesitated a moment longer, then turned away. As he watched her go, he struggled to regain the blissful relief he'd felt moments before, but it was gone.

When she paused at the sofa, he tensed, waiting. *Go*, he thought with a hint of desperation. *For pity's sake, just go.*

Hugging the manuscript to her chest with one arm, she dipped at the knees and picked up her dispatch case with her free hand. She took another step toward the door, but then, she stopped again and turned to look at him over her shoulder.

"What are you waiting for?" he demanded. "You have what you wanted. Now, leave. And don't ever come back."

She pressed her lips together, gave a little nod, and turned away. She walked out of the room without another word, but her departure brought no relief. The image of her unhappy face lingered in his mind, and her question hung unanswered in the air.

What will you do now?

He hadn't answered her because there was only one answer, an answer he could not give.

Write another book.

That was the true reason for this emptiness inside him. The only thing he had ever wanted to do was gone forever, and he knew there was nothing on earth that could replace it.

Chapter 7

When I say writing, O believe me,
it is rewriting that I have in mind.
Robert Lewis Stevenson

Dressed for bed, Daisy was sprawled across the rug in her room at Little Russell Street, lying on her stomach in a pool of lamplight, with Sebastian Grant's manuscript on the wood floor in front of her. Quill, ink, and notepaper were nearby, and she'd made heavy use of them during the past three days, jotting down notes and questions as she waded through his book.

It had been slow going, but she was finished now. She had, in fact, finished quite some time ago. The grandfather clock downstairs chimed its deep, melancholy tones, and she realized to her surprise that she had been staring at the manuscript for over an hour. Rousing herself, she reached for the quill and another sheet of notepaper, intending to jot down her last few thoughts before going to bed. But she hesitated, hand poised over the paper, as the question that had been going through her mind for the past hour echoed yet again.

What if she was wrong?

Daisy gripped the quill tighter in her fingers, trying not to listen to that whisper of doubt, but she couldn't silence it.

Her own work had been rejected. What made her, or the publisher who had rejected her, for that matter, think she could be of any use to another author?

She glanced at the pile of notes she had compiled during the past few days, and Sebastian Grant's angry voice shouted through her mind.

Who the hell are you to think your opinion is worth a damn?

Daisy returned her gaze to the blank sheet of paper before her, but instead of writing comments, she began to doodle, idly drawing flowers and stick figures as she pondered his question.

A knock sounded on her door, and Daisy looked up as her sister, also dressed for bed, entered the room.

"Still at work, I see." Lucy smiled, padding across the bedroom in her stocking feet to place a hand on Daisy's shoulder. "It's terribly late, dearest."

"I know. I'll go to bed soon, I promise." She drew another squiggle on the page before her.

Lucy bent down and gave a little laugh. "Are you editing the man's manuscript by the use of Egyptian hieroglyphs?" she asked as she straightened.

"No, it's just—" She broke off and stopped doodling with a helpless gesture. "I don't know what to do."

"That doesn't sound like the Daisy I know," Lucy commented in surprise. "You aren't usually the least bit indecisive."

"Yes, I know." She set down her quill with a sigh. "I am always plunging full speed ahead like a transatlantic liner."

"What's troubling you?" Lucy settled herself in a nearby chair. "Is the book dreadful? Is that it?"

"It's not dreadful, but I think it needs a lot of work."

"And?" Lucy prompted when she fell silent.

"What if I'm wrong?" Daisy gestured to her notes. "I mean, there are heaps of things in this manuscript I think need to be addressed. Plot threads that lead nowhere. Protagonists doing things out of character . . ." She paused, then added, "But what makes me qualified to tell that to a literary legend?"

"Lord Marlowe believes you to be qualified."

"Yes, and that is part of what baffles me." Daisy sat up, hitching her nightgown up enough to cross her legs beneath her. "I mean, three days ago, when Lord Marlowe rejected my book, I was shocked. I hadn't expected it. Conceited of me, I know—"

"It's not conceit," Lucy interrupted. "It's that confounded optimism of yours. It's something I've often envied, by the way."

"You have?" Daisy was astonished. "But why?"

"You're always so confident, dearest. So sure things will turn out well. You have such faith in people." Lucy pushed her long blonde braid back over her shoulder and hugged her wrapper more closely around her, frowning a little. "I brood and worry, and always assume the worst about everything and everyone."

"At least nothing ever takes you by surprise. When things don't turn out the way I think they should, I'm always shocked."

"True," Lucy agreed. "Shocked, and hurt, too, I think."

Daisy tilted her head, resting her cheek on her bent knees as she looked up at her sister. "You're thinking of Papa, I suppose."

"Not specifically, no, but our father's as good an example as any. I remember the look on your face when he came home from Manchester and you realized he was drunk. Heavens, you couldn't have been more surprised if he'd pulled out a pistol and shot you. Oh, how you hated him for that."

"And you didn't?"

"Not for the same reason. I hated him for hurting you. You hated him because he promised to change and you believed in him and he let you down. Nothing is more crushing than unfulfilled expectations." She gave a sad smile. "I've learned to expect nothing from people. That way, I'm never disappointed."

"I don't think I could ever be as pragmatic as you."

"Probably not," Lucy agreed. "But we've wandered from the subject at hand. What's really troubling you? Was having your book rejected so painful that you've lost faith in yourself?"

"Not precisely. It did hurt to have my novel rejected, and it was a shock, but when Lord Marlowe made the suggestion that I help Avermore, and offered to pay me for it, I agreed at once, but I never thought of what it would entail." She made a wry face. "The transatlantic liner plunging full speed ahead."

"You seem to be talking as if your decision to accept Marlowe's offer was a mistake."

"What if it was? I didn't think about it at the time. I was relieved to have an opportunity to do something worthwhile and redeem myself after being rejected, and the idea of having Sebastian Grant read my work and help me to become better . . . well, I jumped at the chance. And during the past few days, I've been fully immersed in reading it and making notes for revision. But now that I've finished that and I'm ready to present my opinions, I find myself swamped by doubts."

She saw her sister start to reply, but she forestalled her. "Marlowe didn't think my book worthy. In his comments, he said . . ." She stopped, embarrassed, and cleared her throat. "He said my novel was heavy, too bogged down with descriptions. My pace was slow, and I repeat myself too much."

She saw Lucy's compassionate expression, and she tried to smile. "It's not all bad. He did say these are common mistakes among beginning writers, and I take some comfort in that. Oddly enough," she added, struck by a sudden realization, "I'm seeing mistakes very similar to mine in Avermore's novel. Perhaps he wrote it before he ever became published."

"You think it's that old?"

"I don't know," Daisy said slowly, thinking it out. "It would make sense. The style is much more in keeping with his earlier works than with the silly fluff he's been producing of late years." She heaved a sigh. "But what do I know? If I'm not qualified to be a published writer myself, if I am such a beginner that I can't see and correct the mistakes in my own work, how can I assist a writer who is far more experienced? How can I edit his manuscript? What makes me such a proficient?"

"Marlowe hired you to write a review of Avermore's play for the sake of expedience, but he did agree with it. He then employed you because he believed the quality of Avermore's writing has deteriorated and that the man needed to face the truth about it. Marlowe knew you would tell the truth, no holds barred. Quite discerning of him, if you ask me."

Daisy remained unconvinced. "Perhaps, but—"

"And," Lucy interrupted, "Marlowe agreed with your subsequent strategy to hold Avermore's feet to the fire by using his contract as leverage, a strategy that worked. And when you informed him that you acquired a manuscript from Avermore but that it was not the new one he was hoping for, he gave you full authority to edit it as you saw fit and work with Avermore to revise it. So far, I would say your success speaks for itself."

"Thank you, but—"

"Furthermore, the fact that you can see in Avermore's work what you cannot see in your own demonstrates exactly why Marlowe is right. You and the earl can help each other."

"It was his face," Daisy blurted out.

"What?" Lucy blinked, uncomprehending. "Marlowe's face?"

She shook her head. "No, Avermore's. As I was walking out with the manuscript, I glanced back and saw his face. There was such weariness, such sadness in his expression. As if . . ." She paused, striving for a way to explain. "He looked as if his lover was leaving him."

"That's a terribly fanciful description. Perhaps you imagined it. You do have a vivid imagination, you know."

"No," she said, shaking her head. "I did not imagine it. I don't think he will ever write another book."

"If that's so, it is his choice, dearest."

"But what if I am partly to blame for it? When I critiqued his play, I didn't think he would be bothered by my opinion, but now, in hindsight, I appreciate that he was. I hurt him, and I berate myself for having been so cavalier. Rejected myself, I now appreciate how painful criticism can be. If I go back and tell him everything I think is wrong with his manuscript, what will that do to him? I don't want to hurt him again."

"So do you want to simply give Marlowe the manuscript as it is, collect your fee, and go on your way?"

Everything in her rebelled against such a course. Yet, when she thought of the agony in his face, she was afraid of making things worse. "I don't know what to do," she whispered. "I just don't know. And, again, what if I'm wrong?"

"Daisy Merrick, I can't believe what I'm hearing." Lucy slid off the chair, sinking down beside her on the rug. "We both know there isn't any being right or wrong about things like theater, art, and literature. There are only opinions, and others are free to agree or disagree. Marlowe believes that Sebastian Grant wants to write again, but that he needs help to do it. Marlowe hired you to be that help."

"If you were me, what would you do?"

Lucy thought about that for a moment, then she said, "I couldn't do it. I'd mark Sebastian Grant down as a lost cause without a second thought, turn the manuscript over to Marlowe, and happily collect my fee. But you are not me, Daisy. You hate giving up on people, and you would never forgive yourself if you didn't at least try to help him."

"Avermore doesn't want my help. He told me to get out of his sight and never come back."

Lucy reached out and brushed a loose lock of Daisy's hair back from her forehead. "Isn't that what people say when they need help the most?"

"Pass." Sebastian finished putting the cards dealt him in order as the bidding for whist went around, but he scarcely heard the voices of the other three men at the table. His mind was preoccupied with another voice, one that had been echoing through his mind for three days.

What will you do now?

Damn that woman. Her words had haunted him ever since he'd handed her the manuscript. In his mind's eye, he kept seeing her face, somber and unhappy. She'd accomplished her task and earned her five hundred pounds. What did she have to be unhappy about?

"Sebastian?"

The sound of his name jerked him out of his reverie. "Hmm?"

His partner, Baron Weston, gave him a puzzled frown from across the table. "It's your bid, old chap."

"Sorry." He glanced over his cards, but that was of little help, since he had only the vaguest idea of how the bidding had gone thus far. "Three diamonds."

Perhaps a change of scene would do him good. Nothing was keeping him here, after all. He thought again of Africa, but with reluctance, he discarded the notion. Even if he had the money, adventure was not really what he sought. He wanted . . . God help him, he didn't know what he wanted anymore.

Weston had just made a bid—spades, Sebastian thought—and he forced himself to concentrate. Whist was a game at which he and his partner excelled and there was a hundred quid in it for him if they won the rubber. He glanced over his hand again, noting that he could support spades. "Seven spades."

The moment he said it, he knew he'd made a mistake. To his left, Lord Faulkner challenged him with a double, and Weston gave a heavy sigh. Ten minutes later, Faulkner and his partner took the game and the rubber, forcing Sebastian to add another two hundred quid to his already sizable debts.

"Spades?" Weston muttered as they stood outside waiting for Sebastian's carriage. "Why spades? What were you thinking?"

"I thought you called for spades."

"I don't know how you could have thought that, since I said five diamonds. I was following your lead. Living abroad has clearly ruined your skill at whist." Weston gave him a dubious look. "Are you all right?"

"Of course," he lied at once. "I was a bit distracted tonight, that's all."

There was a pause, then Weston said, "I heard about your play. Hard lines, my friend."

"It doesn't matter." He felt an overwhelming need to get away. Turning his head, he peered down the street, but his carriage was nowhere in sight. "I think I'll walk home."

"Home? I thought we were going to Laverton's supper party."

He'd forgotten that, too. What was wrong with him? He rubbed a hand across his forehead. "I believe I'll give Laverton's a miss, Wes, if you don't mind." Improvising, he added, "I've the devil of a headache. Feel free to take my carriage for the rest of the evening."

He started down the street, leaving his bewildered friend staring after him.

What will you do now?

Perhaps Miss Merrick's question bothered him because he'd never had to answer it before. All his life, he'd had only one ambition, only one obsession. He was a writer. He'd never imagined doing anything else. Even the title and estate had never been all that important to him, much to his father's dismay. Only writing had ever mattered. Now that he had finally accepted that he was finished with writing forever, he felt as unanchored as a piece of driftwood.

He wanted . . . again Sebastian tried to grasp at a new purpose for himself. What did he want, damn it all?

Contentment. The word came so suddenly, he stopped

on the sidewalk. He wanted to be content. And he had no idea how to achieve that state, for never in all the thirty-seven years of his life had he ever been content.

He resumed walking, turned onto South Audley Street and ascended the steps to the front door of his flat. He let himself in and dropped his latchkey onto the table by the door, then tucked his hat under one arm and pulled off his gloves, noting that the evening post had arrived.

Wilton came into the foyer, and Sebastian handed over his hat and gloves, then he picked up his letters. He sorted through them as he went upstairs, and upon entering his study, the bills went into the wastepaper basket. No point in keeping them since he couldn't pay them. A letter from his tiresome second cousin Charlotte followed the bills, leaving only a quarterly report from his land agent and a letter from Aunt Mathilda.

Smiling, he set aside the envelope from Auntie and opened the report from Mr. Cummings first. His land agent informed him that the estate had managed—barely—to pay its own expenses from March to June, although the death duties imposed following his father's demise eighteen months earlier still remained unpaid. The wealthy American tenants leasing Avermore had vacated, having decided Dartmoor was too remote for their tastes, and had decamped for Torquay, the fashionable center of English social life in summer. The rent was paid through September, however, and Lady

Mathilda wished to move from the summerhouse into the main house until new tenants could be found.

No surprise, that. Auntie understood the economic realities of owning land nowadays, but she found it hard to see strangers living in the house where she'd grown up. She had always loved Avermore, so much so that she'd come to town only once since Sebastian's return to England. She had stayed long enough to welcome him home and present him with a furnished flat and a handful of servants before promptly returning to Devonshire.

He set aside the letter from Mr. Cummings and opened the one from Auntie. Sure enough, Mathilda was asking his permission to move back into the main house. She also suggested he take up residence there for the summer, a suggestion she had made many times before, and one he had always refused; but this time, Sebastian found himself actually considering it.

If a man sought contentment and peace of mind, surely there was no better place to find it than the English countryside. He'd never felt much contentment at Avermore, but his father had been alive then, and that had made all the difference. Wherever the old man had happened to be, Sebastian had always been happy to be someplace else. Auntie had been the only thing worth coming home for during holidays when he was a boy.

But now, his father was dead, and avoiding home was

no longer necessary. He thought of Avermore, with its thatched cottages and farms, its wild woods and mossy dells, its streams filled with trout and its lakes filled with tench, its meandering canals and *ha-ha*s shaded by weeping willows, and he decided a trip home might be just the tonic he needed.

If all that wasn't persuasion enough, Devonshire was far enough away from London to spare him any further visits from Miss Merrick. Sebastian pulled out notepaper and a quill, and for the first time in years, he told Auntie he was coming home.

Four days later, Sebastian was at Avermore, comfortably ensconced in a hammock by a millpond, a basket containing the remains of a picnic on the grass beside him, and a bottle of ale in his hand. The sun was shining, the spring breeze brushed over his skin, and the hammock in which he lay swayed gently back and forth. If contentment was what he sought, this was as good a place to find it as any.

No more novels. No more burdensome deadlines. No more expectations—from others or from himself. No more frustrating afternoons at his typewriting machine, trying to find something worth writing down. No more striving to find the right word, the perfect sentence, the flawless story. No more of his own obsessive demands for perfection, and no more cocaine required to silence those demands. He'd come full circle, it seemed. Had his father been alive to see this day, the old earl would have crowed with satisfaction to know his son had given up that silly writing nonsense at last.

Sebastian frowned, feeling a ripple of uneasiness as his father's disdainful voice echoed back to him from his boyhood.

Idling away your holidays, writing stories? What is wrong with you, boy? I despair of you, I do indeed, engaging in such worthless pursuits.

Sebastian felt his pleasant mood slipping, and he forced aside thoughts of his father. He focused his mind instead on the groan of the waterwheel, the drone of the bees, and the breeze that stirred the leaves overhead, and his momentary uneasiness faded away. It was good, he thought, to be home.

"Lord Avermore?"

Oh, God. Any shred of Sebastian's hard-won contentment dissolved at the sound of that familiar voice, and he opened his eyes, turning in the hammock so abruptly that he almost fell out of it, dismayed to find Daisy Merrick standing ten feet away.

"You again?" He groaned. "What are you doing here?"

"I have read your manuscript, my lord."

He glanced over her rumpled green traveling suit, and it was then that he noticed the yellowed sheaf of papers tucked in the crook of her arm. He lifted his

gaze again to her freckled face and the determined cast
of her countenance did not bode well for his purpose in
coming to the country.

"Bully for you, love. That makes one of us. I haven't
read the thing since I wrote it." He lifted his bottle of
ale in salute and took a swallow. "Did you happen to
bring a cheque?"

"No."

"Of course not. That would have made your presence
useful for a change." He fell back into the hammock
with a resigned sigh. "So, what brings you to Devonshire?" he asked, sure he was going to regret the question. "Have family in the neighborhood?"

"I've come to discuss the manuscript with you."

A feeling of dread settled in Sebastian's guts. Desperate, he closed his eyes. Maybe if he ignored her,
she'd go away.

"The basis of your story is solid, and it has a powerful premise," she offered, as if he'd asked for her opinion. "It reminds me of your earliest works. Since it's an
older manuscript, that makes sense, of course."

She fell silent, as if waiting for him to respond. He
didn't.

"That being said," she went on, "I'm afraid there are
problems with it. You'll need to do some substantial
revisions in order to make this novel suitable for publication."

Damned if he would. "I'm not doing any revision."

He kept his eyes stubbornly closed. "I'm not changing a word."

"My lord, I'm afraid you don't have a choice. I cannot accept this as written. You must revise it."

He couldn't let that pass. He just couldn't. He opened his eyes and turned his head, scowling at her. "Who the devil are you," he demanded, bristling, "to tell me what I must do?"

"I am your editor."

"What?" he scoffed, refusing to believe it. "That's absurd. Marlowe is my editor."

"Not anymore." She walked to the side of the hammock, pulled a folded sheet of paper from the top of the sheaf bundled in the crook of her arm, and held it out to him. Sebastian set aside his ale, then snatched the paper from her hand, unfolded it, and scanned the transcripted lines of a telegram.

MISS MERRICK COMMA I APPOINT YOU AVERMORE'S EDITOR STOP EDIT MS AS YOU SEE FIT STOP AVERMORE NOT PAID UNTIL MS REVISED TO YOUR SATISFACTION STOP MARLOWE

"Damn Harry! This passes all bounds!" He sat up and wadded the telegram into a ball. Leaning sideways, he hurled it as hard as he could. It sailed past the trunk of the willow but missed the pond, landing on the bank several inches from the water's edge. He swung his legs over the side of the hammock and stood up, forcing her back a step. "I refuse to accept you as my editor."

Those brilliant eyes did not waver. "You have to," she said quietly. "If you wish to be paid, you have no choice."

"Why are you doing this?" he asked, feeling a hint of despair. "What possible difference does it make to you if the book is any good or not? Why do you care?"

"I care because you were once a fine writer, one of the finest I've ever read, and Marlowe has employed me to help you be a fine writer again." She pulled the sheaf of papers from the crook of her arm and held it up. "This manuscript is capable of greatness if you revise it."

"No, it's not!" he roared, his voice loud enough to echo across the water and into the hills beyond. "For God's sake, why isn't anyone listening to me? I can't do what you want."

"Yes, you can. If you wish to be paid, you must." She held the manuscript out to him, but when he folded his arms and did not take it, she dropped it onto the grass. "I have included a letter outlining the problems I have with the story, and various suggestions for how you might resolve them. After you complete the revisions to my satisfaction, I will approve the manuscript for publication and you will receive your money."

"I'm not revising a word," he said again. "Accept it as is, or not at all."

She sighed. "Do I really need to quote from your contract again? Your editor—" She broke off and pointed a finger toward her chest. "That would now be me," she reminded him, as if he could forget such an appalling fact. "Your editor has to approve your completed manuscript before you can be paid. I am not approving this until you revise it."

"Of all the idiotic—" He broke off with a muttered oath and bent to retrieve the bundle of papers. On top was a typewritten letter, and he yanked it out from beneath the twine. The moment he did, he appreciated the thickness of it. Tucking the manuscript under one arm, he unfolded the letter. Without reading it, he flipped through it, counting pages, and after a moment, he returned his attention to her, appalled. "Good God, what revisions are you asking for that require a twelve-page letter to explain them? Woman, don't you know *anything* about writing? In composition, brevity is a virtue."

"Quite so." She didn't even blink. "I was as brief as possible."

He sucked in his breath, and returned to the first page. The letter began with the usual polite salutations— thank you for your manuscript, Marlowe Publishing is honored to receive it . . . Sebastian skimmed past those. He also cast only a cursory glance over her flattering opening remarks about the book—how the premise was unique and intriguing, the characters vivid, and the story thoroughly engrossing. Instead, Sebastian cut to the chase.

He flipped to the second page, and there, he found a numbered list of points she felt he needed to address. He got as far as the first one and stopped. "No dedication?" he muttered and looked at her. "That's your most important criticism? That there's no dedication?"

"I did not list my comments in order of importance. I listed them in order of chronology. I felt that would make your revisions easier."

"Revisions are never easy, Miss Merrick. They are a pain in the arse."

She didn't even blink at his crudeness. "And," she went on, "not all the comments in my list are criticisms. My comment about the dedication, for instance, was merely an observation. I thought you might simply have forgotten to include one."

"I didn't forget," he assured her, feeling nettled and defensive, and not knowing quite why, since he didn't care what she thought. "I never put dedications in my books. And since you seem to be quite an authority on my writing, Miss Merrick, you should already know that."

She pressed her lips together as if suppressing a tart rejoinder. After a moment, she said, "I merely thought to give you the opportunity to provide a dedication should you wish to do so."

"Well, I don't. Dedications are silly, pointless, and

smack of sentimentality. Lady novelists use them, I daresay," he added, being deliberately provoking, "but no serious writer would."

"Quite," she answered at once. "Herman Melville was a silly lady novelist, and *Moby-Dick* a frivolous book."

Sebastian decided he'd had enough. He folded the letter, pulled the manuscript from beneath his arm, and shoved the letter back in its place beneath the twine. "I won't do this," he said and dropped the manuscript onto the grass. "I can't."

She ignored that, of course. "You only have one hundred and thirteen days remaining of your extension," she informed him, "and you have a great deal of work to do. I suggest you begin as soon as possible."

She turned and walked away without another word, and as Sebastian watched her go, he knew he'd been right about her all along. She had been sent by the devil to make his life hell. So far, she was succeeding admirably.

Chapter 8

My God, this novel makes me break out in a cold sweat.

Gustave Flaubert

"You must be in need of tea." Lady Mathilda reached for the teapot, a delicate porcelain thing of painted pink roses from an earlier era. "Facing down Avermore can be a rather intimidating business," she said as she poured pale China tea into a delicate matching cup. "Especially if he doesn't want to do a thing. Anyone would need sustenance afterward. Sugar?"

She held up the sugar tongs in an inquiring manner, and Daisy nodded. "Yes, please. Two lumps. And lemon."

Lady Mathilda added the requested ingredients to Daisy's cup. She stirred the tea with a tiny silver spoon. "I hope my nephew wasn't terribly rude?"

"Not rude, no. Though it was clear he wasn't happy to see me. Thank you, by the way," she added, taking the teacup, "for sending your carriage to meet my train. Lord Marlowe had already informed you of the situation, I understand?"

The older woman nodded. "Marlowe's at Torquay, and he and his wife called upon me a few days ago. I understand you are a friend of the viscountess?"

"Yes, ma'am. Lady Marlowe and I have been acquainted for many years."

"An excellent woman, and a fine writer. Her second novel has just been published, you know. I understand you are an aspiring writer as well, Miss Merrick?"

"Yes, ma'am." She paused, then added, "Is there a room in the house where I could work? I could use my bedroom, but—"

"Your bedroom? Oh, no, my dear, that won't do. There isn't a writing desk in there, only a dressing table. I would suggest you make use of the library." She waved a hand toward the adjoining room behind Daisy. "It's just through there, and it has several nice large desks. Plenty of light, too."

Daisy turned to look over her shoulder, but the pair of tall walnut doors behind her were closed, blocking any view of the room beyond. She returned her attention to her hostess. "Your nephew doesn't use that room himself?"

"For his writing, you mean? Oh, no. Sebastian has

his own private study, not that he has ever done much writing at Avermore. His father, my late nephew, never looked kindly upon having a son with literary ambitions. Writing was all very well as a hobby, but he felt Sebastian's main concern ought to have been his position as the future Earl of Avermore. Sebastian, however, was not content to write simply as a recreation. He wanted his books to be published, and the two men had countless rows about it."

Daisy nodded in understanding. "My sister is rather like that. Very concerned with the practicalities."

"Ah, yes, Marlowe mentioned you have a sister. She must be worried about you journeying across the country alone and staying with strangers."

Lucy's concerns had been mainly centered upon the fact that her younger sister would be sharing a house with a man of Sebastian Grant's notorious reputation, but she decided it would be best not to say so. "Once Lady Marlowe had assured my sister you were willing to act as chaperone during my stay, her worries on my behalf were assuaged," Daisy said instead, and was rather proud of her tact.

"I am happy to do it, my dear. I can only hope that Marlowe is right and that you can help my nephew with his work. I don't envy you your task, I must say. Sebastian is a dear boy, but he is also temperamental and often quite intractable where his work is concerned. He is an artist. Very much like his grandfather, my brother. Henry was a poet, and he had the same qualities."

Daisy wasn't certain she agreed with Lady Mathilda's description of Avermore as a dear boy, but the adjectives temperamental and intractable seem apposite.

"Sebastian," Lady Mathilda continued, "has always insisted upon doing things his own way, and it's exceedingly difficult for him to accept help from anyone, even when he needs it. He's always been that way. Devilishly proud. And most particular about his books, too." She laughed. "I remember the very first story he wrote that he allowed me to read—he was eleven, I think—and oh, the fuss when I suggested perhaps the main character in the story should be an ordinary boy instead of a warlock! Why, I believe he spent a week telling me all the reasons that wouldn't work. You could have knocked me over with a feather when I discovered he'd taken my advice to heart and he'd rewritten the story using my suggestion."

"Do you have any advice for me, ma'am?"

She considered that for a moment. "Marlowe feels Sebastian's last few books have not matched the caliber of his previous works. He feels they lacked heart. I understand you agree with that assessment?"

"Yes, I do."

"So do I." She paused for a moment, then went on, "Marlowe feels that you bring a certain insight to Sebastian's writing that neither he nor I can claim. Being only recently acquainted with Sebastian, you can be more objective than either of us."

"I hope so, Lady Mathilda."

"I have a great deal of affection for my nephew, Miss Merrick, and I have been worried about him for a long time. He changed when he went abroad. I don't know why. He began writing at a breakneck pace, and produced a substantial body of work as a result, but the quality of the work did suffer. His letters home became less and less frequent, and when he stopped writing altogether, I knew something was terribly wrong, though I did not know what. I'd been hearing gossip from Italy for years, of course, but—" She stopped. "That's neither here nor there. You asked me for advice? My advice is to always give him your true opinion. Don't try to be kind and sugarcoat things for him. He'll see through that sort of nonsense in an instant."

"I have my flaws, ma'am," Daisy said ruefully, "but sugarcoating things is not one of them."

The old woman gave her a shrewd look. "No doubt that's why Marlowe chose you for this task. If my nephew respects your opinions, he will consider them, though he might argue with you to high heaven. But stick to your guns if you think you're right. Don't allow him to bully you or drive you away."

"He's already tried that. He hasn't succeeded."

"Good. You're made of strong mettle, I see." Lady Mathilda lifted her teacup, studying Daisy over the rim. "Still, it's best to batten down your hatches, my dear. I fear there are storms ahead."

Daisy thought of Avermore's eyes, the resentment that had darkened their color to the gunmetal gray of thunderclouds, and she couldn't help but agree.

Curiosity was a dangerous thing. It killed cats. It was probably what impelled moths to fly into flames and caused small children to fall into wells. It was what led a sane writer to do crazy things, like read reviews of his plays and revision letters for his books.

Sebastian stared at the twine-tied manuscript in the grass nearby, knowing he would regret it if he allowed his curiosity to get the better of him. And yet, he felt an overwhelming desire to know what Miss Merrick had said.

He leaned forward, causing the hammock in which he sat to tip precariously, but from this distance, he couldn't read her letter. He craned his neck and squinted, but even then, he couldn't quite make out the typewritten words. He sat back, aggrieved.

What did her opinion matter anyway? She was a rejected writer and an infuriating critic and probably an incompetent editor, too. He shouldn't care a jot what she had to say.

He leaned forward again, resting his elbows on his knees. She'd told him the story had a powerful premise, but that was hardly illuminating. Hell, he'd written the blasted thing twenty years ago. He couldn't even remember what the premise was. Still, he couldn't help but wonder what she wanted him to change.

He studied the manuscript, nibbling on one thumbnail, his curiosity battling with his good sense.

Best all around if he tossed the letter into the pond, told her to go to hell, and cabled Harry in Torquay that he wasn't changing a word.

But what would he do if Harry chose to be stubborn about this and continued to support Miss Merrick in her misguided attempts? Sebastian thought of all the revision letters Harry had sent to him in Italy, all the editorial suggestions he had refused to implement in the past, and all the concerns Harry had expressed about the deteriorating quality of his work. He thought of that day at Marlowe Publishing when Harry had heaped condemnations upon him, and he knew he had already pushed his publisher's tolerance to its limits.

Sebastian stared at the manuscript, a sick knot in his stomach. He could not afford a legal battle with Marlowe Publishing, and yet, he could not do what they asked of him. He could not go back. He could not force his books into being by sheer will. It was too hard, too painful, too exhausting.

Yet, what other choice did he have? In Italy, in the drug-induced haze of his life there, it had been easy to forget his obligations. In a remote part of the Swiss Alps, it had been simple to deny his responsibilities.

But here, in the home of his ancestors, with his aunt, whom he loved, close at hand, it was neither easy nor simple. He was pinned in a corner, no longer able to avoid the hard realities of his situation, and he wished he had never come home.

What will you do now?

Daisy Merrick's damnable question echoed through his mind again, and Sebastian looked up, gazing out across the water of the pond to the mill and then to the woods beyond.

His play had closed. If Marlowe chose not to pay him for this book, he would go further into debt. He would be reduced to borrowing from friends. Phillip, perhaps, or St. Cyres. His pride revolted at the thought of living off of them like some pathetic distant relation. There had to be another alternative.

Sebastian returned his attention to the sheaf of papers in the grass. It wouldn't hurt, he supposed, to at least read the letter. Perhaps the revisions she wanted were not as difficult as the length of her letter made out. Perhaps, despite her assurance of brevity, she had not been brief, but had rambled on for ten pages about only a few minor problems that could be easily fixed.

He walked over to the manuscript, sank down onto the grass, and pulled the letter from beneath the twine—all twelve pages of it. He was probably going to regret this, Sebastian thought, and began to read.

Five minutes later, he tossed the letter aside, his misgivings about Miss Merrick's abilities as an editor thoroughly justified. She was out of her mind if she expected him to make such substantive changes. She might just as well have demanded an entirely new book.

An image of her face, with its pretty golden freckles and teal-blue eyes, came into his mind. Somehow, he had to convince her to give up on this silly revision business, publish the book in its present condition, and pay him his money. But how?

He could make an attempt at bribery, he supposed, offer her a share of the money if she'd let the manuscript stand. But the moment he thought of that idea, he rejected it. If money motivated her, she'd have approved his book and collected her fee already.

He could make himself as uncooperative and disagreeable as possible, but he suspected that wouldn't work either. Miss Merrick was no timid little rabbit. She was stubborn enough to withstand even his most belligerent attempts to drive her away.

In the distance, the church bells rang, bringing Sebastian out of his contemplations. There was no point in speculating about this now. Before he could determine the best way to bring Miss Merrick around to his way of thinking, he had to become better acquainted with her, and tonight was the perfect opportunity. Sebastian picked up the manuscript and started back toward the house to dress for dinner.

* * *

Had Daisy envisioned an earl's country house as the setting for a novel, it would not have looked like Avermore House. She would have imagined something opulent, with gilded ceilings, flocked wallpapers, and every piece of furniture swathed in ball-fringed velvet. But Avermore was nothing like that.

It was a solidly built three-story affair of prosaic red brick and gray stone, with furnishings that were more comfortable than ornate. The marble chimneypieces were simply carved, the walls were adorned with plain papers, white moldings, and gold-framed landscapes, and there wasn't a scrap of ball fringe in sight. It was a charming house, elegant but unpretentious, and not at all in keeping with Daisy's notions of the aristocracy. But then, being the daughter of a bankrupt Northumberland squire who'd lost his lands before her thirteenth birthday due to his profound love of cards and his abysmal lack of skill with them and to his even more profound love of drink, Daisy had grown up without much knowledge of country-house life.

What the house lacked in opulence, however, was more than made up for by the vibrancy of the gardens. June, in all its beauty, could be enjoyed from any window, including her own. The view from her bedroom was an island of flowers surrounded by an enormous expanse of green turf. In the evening twilight, the magenta roses, blue delphinium spires, chartreuse sprays of lady's mantle, and the white petals of her namesake seemed especially vivid.

Her gaze moved past the lawn. In the distance, she could see the mill, with its stone walls and thatched roof. She could also see the pond and the willow trees. She could even see the hammock, but not the man she'd left standing beside it, and for perhaps the tenth time since she'd returned to the house, Daisy hoped she'd done the right thing.

After her conversation with Lucy a week ago, she had thought long and hard about what her next step should be. Though in the end, she had been forced to the conclusion that her first duty was to Marlowe as her employer, and her second duty was to herself and her personal sense of integrity, she had also begun to appreciate that she had a duty to her fellow author. It was, she supposed, rather like the duty of a physician, for it required that above all, she do no harm. She was aware that she may have already violated that duty by her scathing review of his play. While she did not regret the opinions she had expressed, she acknowledged that she should have been more aware of the impact her words would have on a fellow author. Daisy stared out at the mill, and she hoped that forcing his hand today had not done more harm than good.

Too late to have doubts now, she supposed. If he called her bluff, if he refused to revise his book, that was his choice, and Marlowe would be the one to agree or refuse to publish the manuscript in its present state. She would be compensated either way. Marlowe had already assured her of that. In her letter, she had given her honest opinions as tactfully as possible. If Avermore refused to make the changes, her duty was discharged, and she could go home, knowing she'd done her best.

Why won't you people leave me alone?

His desperate, angry voice echoed back to her, and the knowledge that she'd done her best was not much consolation.

The scratch on her door forced Daisy's attention away from the window as a severe-looking maid in a gray print dress and a starched apron and cap came into the bedroom, carrying a pitcher of steaming water and an armful of snowy-white towels.

"I am Allyson, miss, upstairs maid," the servant told her as she set down the towels and poured hot water into the bowl on Daisy's malachite-topped washstand. "Her ladyship has asked me to do for you, since you've not brought your own maid up from London."

"Oh, but—" Daisy stopped, biting back just in time the confession that she'd never had a lady's maid in her entire life. There was no need, she reminded herself, to confess such things to a woman she barely knew. "Thank you, Miss Allyson," she said instead. "I appreciate your giving service."

If the maid thought the situation odd, she was too

well trained to show it. "I've unpacked your things, miss. Your blue silk I've sent down to the laundry to be pressed, and your skirts I've hung in the wardrobe. I hope that's all right?"

"Yes, of course." Daisy turned her head, eying the mentioned wardrobe in bemusement. It was a piece of furniture from an earlier era, when ladies wore crinolines and it took sixteen yards of fabric to make a dress. Her three skirts of thin summer wool and half dozen shirtwaists seemed woefully inadequate to the yawning vastness of the armoire.

"The rest of your things are in the dressing table," Allyson went on, bringing Daisy's attention back to her. "And I've put your little leather case just beside it. When your evening gown is ready, I will bring it up to you straightaway. In the meantime, if there is anything else you need, miss, just ring for me. The bell pull is beside the bed."

Daisy glanced at the tasseled rope of gold silk that hung beside the unadorned cherrywood four-poster and nodded. "I see. When is dinner served?"

"Eight o'clock, miss. The first gong sounds one half hour beforehand so that guests may begin gathering in the drawing room."

Rather like Little Russell Street. She smiled at that thought, for in every other way, she seemed far removed from the prosaic, shabbily genteel confines of the lodging house in Holborn. "And breakfast?"

"Warming dishes on the sideboard in the dining room at eight o'clock, and guests may help themselves. Unless you'd like breakfast in your room? The ladies often prefer it that way."

"No, thank you, Allyson. I shall come down for breakfast."

"Yes, miss." The maid dipped a curtsy and departed, closing the door behind her.

Daisy availed herself of the hot water to wash away the dust of travel, donned fresh underclothes and stockings, and sat down at the dressing table, where the maid had already laid out her tortoiseshell brush, comb, and mirror. She took down her hair and brushed it, then she coiled and pinned the thick, unruly strands into a chignon at the back of her head, but she studied her reflection in the mirror without satisfaction. Too bad one couldn't wear a hat to dinner, she thought, making a face. A hat ought to be allowed if one had hair the color of carrots.

I think you're a delicious little morsel with pretty hair, a shapely bum, and a deuced supply of impudence.

Sebastian Grant's acerbic voice echoed back to her, and though she knew the man had no business noticing her bum, she couldn't seem to work up the proper outrage about his comments. She touched a hand to her hair, curling a stray tendril around her finger. He'd said her hair was pretty.

She remembered with painful clarity the relentless

teasing of her girlhood, how other children had called her "beanpole" and "freckle face" and "carrot-head." She knew Sebastian Grant was an arrogant, bullheaded man with far more pride than was good for him, and she shouldn't set any store by his opinions on anything. It wasn't as if his remark had been intended as a compliment. Nonetheless, in her entire life, no one else had ever told Daisy that her hair was pretty.

He'd almost kissed her that day, she remembered. What if he had? What if he had swept her up in those strong arms of his and pressed his lips to hers? Imagining it, Daisy felt a delicious little thrill. Always under her sister's watchful eye, she'd only been kissed once in her entire life, a quick, moist, most disappointing press of lips with the village fishmonger's son when she was fourteen. She pressed her fingers to her mouth, and she suspected a kiss from Sebastian Grant would be something quite different. The man didn't have a wicked reputation with women for no reason.

The return of the maid brought Daisy out of her reverie with a guilty start. She jerked her hand down as Allyson came bustling in with her freshly pressed evening gown of blue-black silk. The maid tightened her stays and assisted her into the close-fitting gown, buttoning up the back and adjusting the enormous, elbow-length puff sleeves. Daisy slid her feet into her black kid slippers, and was just pulling on her long white silk gloves when the gong sounded.

"Perfect timing, Allyson," she said to the maid. "Thank you."

The poker-faced servant didn't smile, but Daisy fancied she was gratified by the compliment just the same. "Doesn't do to be late for dinner, miss," she said, gave Daisy's sleeve a final tug, and nodded as if satisfied. "The soup goes cold."

Daisy started out of her room, then stopped. She had a quarter of an hour before dinner. She might as well take her writing things to the library and arrange them for tomorrow.

She caught up her leather dispatch case and made her way back down to the elegant crimson-and-green drawing room on the ground floor where she'd had tea earlier with Lady Mathilda and found that she seemed to be the first one down for dinner, for the drawing room was empty. The double doors to the library had been opened and through the doorway, she could see walls filled with shelves of books. How wonderful to write surrounded by the works of other writers. What could be more inspiring?

Daisy entered the library, and at once her gaze fell on a beautiful, intricately carved rosewood *secretaire* in the center of the sun-yellow room. That, she knew at once, would be her desk. She placed her dispatch case atop the blotter that rested on its polished surface, opened the case, and removed her manuscript and a sheaf of fresh notepaper. There was an inkstand on the desk, she noted, with a filled inkwell and two elaborate ostrich quills. She eyed them for a moment, tempted, even pulling one out of its silver stand for a closer inspection, but in the end, she decided she preferred her own. She removed the wooden box containing her plain goose quills and nibs and placed it on the blotter. Closing the case, she set it on the floor and ran her fingers over the desk's sleek surface with a happy sigh. She couldn't wait to begin work.

A slight cough behind her made Daisy realize she was not alone in the room. She whirled around to find Lord Avermore had arrived before her. Dressed for dinner in a black evening suit and white linen shirt, he was standing by one of the recessed bookshelves, an open book in his hands. The light from the gas jet overhead gleamed on his black hair and caught the glint of silver cuff links at his wrists as he marked his place with one finger, closed the book, and bowed to her. "Good evening, Miss Merrick," he said with a smile.

The smile took her back, rather. She started toward him, studying his face as she approached, but she could discern nothing in his expression but pleasant, gentlemanly politeness, and she wondered if he'd even read her revision letter. She wanted to inquire on the subject, but with an effort, she curbed her curiosity. "What are you reading?" she asked instead as she halted in front of him.

He held up the small volume so that she could read the print on the plain cloth cover.

"*A Shropshire Lad*," she murmured, "by A. E. Housman." She looked up. "I've not heard mention of this book. Is it a novel?"

He shook his head. "No. Poetry."

Daisy looked at him askance. "You read poetry?"

"You needn't sound so surprised, Miss Merrick. All English boys study poetry at school."

"But they don't all like it," she countered. "And," she added, studying him, "if anyone had asked me when I first saw you if you were the sort of man to read poetry, I'd have said no. In fact, I didn't even think you looked like a writer."

"What occupation should I have had?"

She laughed. "I thought you ought to be navigating your way along the Ganges River or exploring Antarctica, or something equally adventurous."

"I spent one summer in Great St. Bernard Pass with the Augustine friars, climbing the Valais Alps. We slept in tents, and carted food and water on our backs. Does that signify?"

"Heavens, did you cart your typewriting machine on your back as well?"

Something flickered in his gray eyes, something dangerous that marred his easy politeness. "There was no need," he answered. "I did no writing in the Valais."

Looking into his eyes, Daisy decided it might be wise to change the direction of the conversation. "You read poetry, but have you written any?"

"God, no," he answered, sounding so appalled by the idea, she couldn't help but laugh. He laughed as well, and the dark moment passed. "I much prefer reading it to writing it," he confessed. "The public, I'm sure, is grateful for my preference. Do you like poetry?"

"I don't know," she confessed. "I've always preferred novels. I've never read much poetry."

"That's a crime." He lifted the book in his hands, and his dark lashes lowered as he transferred his gaze to the page. " 'With rue my heart is laden, for golden friends I had, for many a rose-lipt maiden and many a lightfoot lad. By brooks too broad for leaping, the lightfoot boys are laid. The rose-lipt girls are sleeping in fields where roses fade.' "

"How terribly sad. Still, it is a beautiful verse."

"Well, if you think that, tell Marlowe. Perhaps he'll buy the fellow's next set of poems. Housman published this collection at his own expense, I understand, after several publishers turned it down."

"Really? Why was it rejected, do you suppose?"

"Who can say?" He closed the book and turned to put it in its proper place on the shelf. "There's no point in speculating why one is rejected. It doesn't matter."

"Doesn't matter?" Daisy couldn't believe what she was

hearing. "As an author, how can you say that? When you have been rejected, haven't you wanted to know why?"

"Not particularly."

"But wouldn't knowing the reason for the rejection be beneficial?"

He turned toward her. "In what respect?"

"So that one could do better the next time, of course. So that one could improve."

"Ah, we're back to that again."

His voice, indulgent and a bit amused, frustrated her. "I like to believe we are all capable of improvement," she said with a pointed glance at him.

"What if one doesn't want to improve? What if one is quite contented with oneself as one is?"

She sniffed, unimpressed. "A person should never be content. One should always strive to be better."

His gaze roamed over her face with an openness she found unnerving. "God," he murmured, smiling a little, "how young you are."

"Young? I'm twenty-eight!"

"Oh, well, in that case, you're only a decade or so behind me. Clearly in your dotage. My mistake." His smile widened, marking laugh lines at the corners of his eyes. "It was those freckles of yours which led me astray."

She gave an aggravated sigh. "Don't tease me about my freckles! I hate them. I wish there was some sort of cosmetic that would make them disappear. Or at least hide them."

"What?" He stared at her as if appalled. "Why, in heaven's name would you want to hide them? That's like wanting to hide an adorable nose or pretty feet!"

She frowned, bewildered, for he was looking at her as if she'd lost her mind, when it was obvious he was the crazy one. "But no one likes freckles. They aren't pretty."

"Nonsense. It's clear you haven't a clue about feminine beauty. I suppose you wish you had baby-blue eyes, too," he added with a sound of derision, "and golden hair, and a mouth like a rosebud."

She thought wistfully of her sister. "Yes," she admitted. "I do, rather."

"Then you don't know what you're saying. Which doesn't surprise me," he added, returning his attention to the books. "You usually don't. One day, you'll talk sense about something, and I shall keel over from the shock."

Daisy studied his profile, uncertain whether she should be flattered or insulted. "You really are the most exasperating person!" she cried. "One minute you compliment me, and the next, you insult me."

"Women hiding their freckles." He shook his head, still staring at the bookshelf before them. "Lord deliver us. What's next? Marxist government?"

"Goodness, Sebastian," said a voice from the doorway. "Discussing Marxism? You know one never talks politics before dinner."

They both turned as Lady Mathilda came bustling into the library, her black silk taffeta rustling. She stopped halfway into the room, eying her nephew in dismay. "And haven't you poured Miss Merrick a sherry yet? Really, where are your manners?"

She turned to Daisy as Avermore bowed and started back to the drawing room in search of sherry. "My nephew isn't usually so uncivil, my dear. You must forgive him."

Daisy touched her fingertips to her cheek, still a bit stunned by the idea that he thought her freckles were pretty. "There's nothing to forgive," she murmured. "Nothing at all."

Chapter 9

If one cannot confound one's critics, one must seduce them.

Sebastian Grant

$\mathcal{S}$ebastian had never been a man who believed all that nonsense about women being less intelligent than men. However, there were times when the fair sex seemed to defy all sense of logic.

Why would any woman wish to hide one of her most charming assets? He pondered that question over dinner, studying Miss Merrick's face covertly from his place at the head of the table, but by the time they had adjourned to the drawing room afterward to read, he was forced to confess himself baffled. Why, when a woman was lovely in her own unique way, would she prefer to look like one of the wax-faced dolls that lined the shelves of Harrod's toy department?

Of course, women often did sacrifice their most appealing features for the sake of fashion. They distorted their luscious bodies with hopelessly uncomfortable corsets and shadowed their faces with enormous hats, so Miss Merrick's wish to hide her unfashionable freckles wasn't out of the common way, he supposed. But as a man, he found it incomprehensible. Contrary to what she believed, the freckles across her nose and cheeks were not unattractive. Quite the opposite, in fact, for they gave her face a touch of whimsical magic, as if some pixy had taken a fancy to her and blessed her with a sprinkling of gold dust.

Sebastian reached for the glass of cognac at his elbow, giving her another covert glance over the top of his book. Seated beside his aunt on the settee opposite him, her head was bent over her own book, and the soft lamplight shone on her hair, making it seem like burnished fire. As he had the first time he'd ever seen her, he pictured all that hair tumbled down around her, only this time, he pictured it in candlelight, and as he did, arousal began spreading through his body. He imagined standing behind her, pulling her hair back so that he could kiss all the freckles on her bare shoulders.

This wasn't the first time he'd thought of kissing her. He'd almost done it that afternoon at his flat in London, but then she'd started talking about critiquing his work, or being his assistant, or some other bit of nonsense, and ruined what to Sebastian's mind could have been a most delightful afternoon.

He took another sip of cognac, still watching her as he thought about that afternoon in London. He'd commented, most inappropriately, on the luscious shape of her bum. She should have slapped his face for that, but she hadn't. She'd looked shocked, of course, but also disbelieving—a similar expression to the one on her face earlier this evening when he'd assured her that freckles were pretty. She'd pursed her lips, staring at him with a puzzled little crinkle between her brows, as if his sanity was in question.

It was clear Daisy Merrick had a modest and wholly inaccurate opinion of her own attractiveness. There were many ways he could show her he had a different opinion on the matter, and as he imagined some of them, the desire within him deepened and spread.

He tried to suppress it, and with an effort, he returned his gaze to his book. As pleasurable as these erotic fantasies were, they were not helping him achieve his objective, unless he intended to seduce her to get his way.

That, now, was an idea worth considering. Sebastian's hand tightened around his glass as he contemplated seduction as a way out of this mess. Not only was it a delicious notion, it might actually work.

There were drawbacks, of course. Daisy Merrick was a desirable woman, true, but she was also respectable, and probably innocent as well. He was a gentleman, and taking her innocence would be a most dishonorable thing to do. He'd lived a wild life and the reputation he'd acquired in Italy was well earned, but even he had never seduced a virgin.

On the other hand, he was desperate, and her intractability was leaving him with few options.

Sebastian stared down at the lines of Housman's poetry with unseeing eyes as his mind struggled for an honorable solution, but there was none. This would all be so simple, he thought with a hint of cynicism, if they were lovers. A woman could always be counted upon to justify a man's weaknesses if he was her lover.

On the other hand, was it necessary to take things that far? If he jollied her along for a bit, pretended to cooperate with the plan she and Harry had cooked up, she'd soon see for herself what writing was like for him. If he threw in a bit of seduction, stole a kiss or two, she'd start to soften, begin to see his side. From there, it should be easy to convince her to publish his manuscript as it was and pay him.

Sebastian lifted his gaze from his book to glance at her, and once again an image of her with her hair loose around her bare shoulders came into his mind. Seducing her without actually bedding her might be the only option he had, but he had the uneasy feeling it was also going to be agony.

* * *

He was staring at her again. Daisy looked up from her book as she turned a page to find him watching her across the small gilt table that separated them. He was lounging back on the crimson velvet sofa opposite, his head tilted to one side, that half smile curving one corner of his mouth, a glass of cognac in his hand. Open in his other hand was a book, the same book of poetry he'd been perusing earlier, but he didn't seem at all interested in reading it, for it seemed as if every time she looked up, she found him watching her. She found it quite unnerving. This thoughtful, assessing study was strangely intimate, almost like a touch.

With that thought, Daisy felt her face coloring up, and she hastily lowered her gaze, but she was too flustered to give the book on her lap her full attention. She could still feel Avermore's gaze on her, and she found her eyes skimming the same sentences over and over without reading them.

The house was quiet, for the servants had gone to bed, and the only sound was the pendulum of the clock, ticking as it swung back and forth, counting off the seconds. A soft thud had Daisy glancing sideways, and she observed that Lady Mathilda's book had slid off her lap and her head had lolled sideways, indicating she had fallen asleep.

Daisy returned her attention to her own book. Realizing she had already read this page, she turned to the next, but as she did so, she again caught Avermore watching her, and she couldn't stand it anymore. He was up to something, and she wanted to know what. When Mathilda began to snore softly beside her, she closed her book and stood up.

Avermore followed suit at once, also rising to his feet. "Miss Merrick? You're not depriving us of your company yet this evening, I hope?"

"Oh, no," she answered, "It's just that . . ." She paused, searching for an excuse that would enable her to speak with him alone. "I'm finding this book a bit dull, that's all. I thought I would search your library for a more interesting one." She glanced at the snoring Lady Mathilda, then returned her attention to Avermore. "Are there any books you could recommend, my lord?"

"Of course." He set aside his book and walked with her into the library. "Several arrived from London in yesterday's post, including some recent fictional works. Shall I show you?"

She allowed him to put his hand on her elbow and guide her toward one side of the room, where recessed bookshelves flanked the fireplace. He brought her to a halt on the left of the fireplace and began scanning the leather- and cloth-bound volumes directly in front of them. "This one, for instance," he said as he pulled out a particular book.

She took it from him. "*The Damnation of Theron Ware*," she read the title.

"It has some brilliant characters, including an especially fascinating one named Svengali. But if that's not to your liking, there's also this one." He pulled out another volume and handed it to her as well. "*The Heart of Princess Osra*. It's by the same fellow who wrote *The Prisoner of Zenda*. It's set in Ruritania as well, but earlier. It's a sort of prequel to *Zenda*."

Another time, Daisy might have been interested, for *The Prisoner of Zenda* was among her favorite novels, but at this moment, she had other things on her mind. "Why do you keep staring at me?" she whispered.

He turned his head to look at her. "Was I staring?" he whispered back.

"Yes. I wish you'd stop. It isn't polite."

"Forgive me. But you have presented me with a puzzle, Miss Merrick, and I am attempting to resolve it."

"What about me do you find puzzling?"

"I am trying to comprehend why a woman would think something as pretty as her freckles ought to be hidden."

Daisy frowned, giving him a dubious look. "Do you feel all right this evening?"

"I'm perfectly well. Why do you ask?"

"You're being *nice*."

He chuckled. "You make it sound like an accusation. I can be nice on occasion, you know. I only regret that you have not seen that aspect of my character before now."

Daisy made a sound of skepticism. His manner was

not at all in keeping with what she'd come to expect from him, and she found all this amiability highly suspicious. "It isn't a bit like you, especially in regard to me. The only explanation I can find is that you're not feeling well." She paused, her eyes narrowing. "Or perhaps," she added, "your consideration and your compliments have an ulterior motive?"

"Maybe I'm simply tired of fighting with you, and I'm attempting to call a truce."

"Truce, my eye," she muttered. "I think you're being nice and giving me compliments because you don't want to do those revisions, and you're hoping to sweet talk your way out of it."

"What a splendid idea." He gave her a wide smile. "Is it working?"

Daisy caught her breath at the dazzling sight of his smile. She'd never seen him smile like that, and perhaps because it was so rare and unexpected, its impact was devastating. It softened the strong planes of his face and made him seem not only handsome, but also boyishly charming. More than ever, Daisy felt as if she were navigating uncharted waters. "All this flattery won't change a thing. If you wish to be paid, you will still have to revise your manuscript."

"Oh, very well," he said with a sigh. "If you're going to be stubborn about it, I suppose I've no choice. But I wasn't lying."

"Lying?"

"About the freckles." Any trace of humor in his face vanished. His lashes lowered. "I meant every word."

When he lifted his hand and cupped her cheek, Daisy suddenly couldn't breathe. When he touched his thumb to her lips, her stomach quivered, and a wave of warmth came over her, spreading through her entire body. *Oh heavens*, she thought, *I'm in the suds now.*

She'd come to Devonshire prepared for him to be his usual irascible self. She'd expected him to fight her tooth and nail at every turn. She hadn't expected him to be charming. Even more surprising to Daisy was the effect this change in his demeanor was having on her. The light caress of his thumb against her mouth seemed to be robbing her of the ability to think straight, her knees seemed strangely weak and wobbly, and her heart was racing.

What if he did kiss her? What would it be like to have his lips touch hers, to have him put his arms around her and press his body against her own? When he moved, bending his head as if to answer those questions, sliding his hand to the back of her neck and pressing his thumb beneath her chin to lift her face, the pleasurable warmth inside her grew to a burning anticipation that was unlike anything she'd ever felt before.

Lady Mathilda was in the very next room, Daisy reminded herself, struggling to come to her senses. The woman could awaken at any moment, and all she had to do was look over her shoulder to see them through the doorway. Daisy would not dream of disgracing herself by being caught in such a compromising situation. And she had an obligation to fulfill. She was here to assist Avermore with his work, and romantic attentions from him were the last thing she needed. She'd worked for wages long enough to see plenty of that sort of nonsense, and it never turned out well. Besides, she was no fool. She knew perfectly well why he was making advances, and she wasn't going to let him.

When he bent his head closer, she flattened her palm against his chest. "That won't work either."

He straightened, looking at her with a schoolboy sort of innocence that didn't deceive her for a moment. "I don't know what you mean."

"Of course you don't. Kissing me is just your way of calling a truce, I suppose?"

To her chagrin, he laughed. "It's one way."

The sound of his laughter had Daisy casting an uneasy glance to the open doorway, but to her relief, Lady Mathilda was still fast asleep, her head tilted back as she snored at the ceiling. Daisy returned her attention to the man before her and realized he was still touching her. She lifted her hand from the hard wall of his chest, grasped his wrist, and shoved away his hand, but the moment she did so, she felt an immediate need to erect some sort of barrier between them. She lifted the books he'd given her, hugging them to her chest. "So, if this is your way of calling a truce, then you do intend to revise the manuscript?"

"Well, I don't want to write an entirely new novel. That's far too much work, and I'm terribly lazy. You've left me few options, you know."

The ambiguity of that answer didn't escape her, but he gave her no chance to clarify it.

"Since you've placed your writing things in here," he said, glancing around, "I assume you've decided we shall work in this room?"

"We?" she echoed in surprise. "You intend to write here, too? But Lady Mathilda informed me you have a private study."

"So I have, but I'm afraid that room won't do."

"Why not?"

He leaned closer to her in a confidential sort of way. "It's beside my bedroom," he explained, smiling as she colored up. "I never know when inspiration might strike, so I've always found it convenient to have where I write close to where I sleep."

An image flashed through her mind of him awakening in the night, inspired by a sudden idea, and rising naked from his bed, the skin of his bare chest gleaming like marble in the moonlight.

Daisy drew a deep breath, trying to force aside these somewhat salacious contemplations. "I don't see what that has to do with me."

"We're supposed to work together," he reminded her. "Help each other. Remember?"

"Oh. Yes, quite." Her words sounded strangled to her

own ears, images of him without his clothes still in her mind. Desperate, she strove to regain her self-possession. "I don't see why our situation requires us to work in the same room."

"What if I need you? Or you need me? Deuced inconvenient if we are in utterly separate wings of the house, don't you think?" Without waiting for an answer, he glanced around and pointed to a substantial teakwood desk directly opposite the secretaire she had chosen. "I'll use that."

"I'm not sure working in such close proximity would be conducive to our efforts. Wouldn't it be too distracting?"

"Quite the opposite, I think. I've no discipline anymore, you see. I need you to watch over me, make sure I keep my nose to the grindstone."

Given that he'd just tried to kiss her, Daisy had every reason to be skeptical of such virtuous-sounding motives. On the other hand, if he was under her eye, she could at least ensure he did some work each day. She capitulated. "Very well, then. We'll begin first thing tomorrow. Nine o'clock."

"Nine o'clock?" He groaned. "I can't remember the last time I rose at such an ungodly hour. "You're a slave driver, Miss Merrick."

"Not yet." She turned away. "That starts tomorrow."

Chapter 10

I am a galley slave to pen and ink.
Honore de Balzac

"Sir?"

Sebastian felt Abercrombie's hand on his shoulder, but he did not even open his eyes. "Hmm?" he grunted.

"Sir, it is half past seven."

Sebastian couldn't remember the last time he'd been awakened at such an ungodly hour of the morning. With the monks, perhaps. He shrugged, trying to shake off his valet's hand, but if he thought that would make Abercrombie go away, he was mistaken.

"Sir, you wished to bathe, dress, and breakfast before nine. Remember? You are starting work on your book today."

Work on a book? Sebastian's sleep-clogged mind scoffed at that. He didn't write anymore. He gave a protesting grunt and rolled over, thinking that turning his back would do the trick and Abercrombie would leave him in peace. But when his valet gave a cough and once again shook his shoulder, he realized he had underestimated the persistence of servants who were owed back wages.

"My apologies, sir, but you were most emphatic about being awakened at this hour. You said Miss Merrick would no doubt appreciate promptness."

Miss Merrick? Ah, yes. At once, images of her began drifting through his mind—of her slender body, of small, plump breasts and a shapely backside, of luminous skin and golden freckles. She thought freckles should be hidden. Silly woman. He'd love to kiss every freckle she had. Every . . . single . . . one.

With these erotic notions going through his head, he burrowed deeper into the pillow and imagined touching her, gliding his fingertips across her collarbone and down to the peak of her breast—

"Sir, your bath has already been prepared. If you don't rise soon, the water will grow cold."

Sebastian groaned at this domestic intrusion on what could have been a deuced fine fantasy. Reminding himself it wasn't a fantasy he could act upon, he forced down his arousal and got out of bed.

As he bathed and shaved, Sebastian considered his plans in light of what had happened last night. He remembered the velvety feel of her lips against his thumb and the rather dazed way she'd looked up at him, and he'd been sure a kiss was in the offing. But she'd seen right through him, clever girl, and stopped him cold. There'd been a glint of determination in those lovely eyes of hers, something with which he was becoming quite familiar, and he realized winning her over would require more ingenuity then he'd first thought.

When his valet brought out the old, well-worn clothing he'd always favored when writing, Sebastian eyed the comfortable gray flannel trousers and ink-stained white linen shirt with approval. If a man was trying to impress a woman, it was better to dress well, but in this case, the opposite would probably be more effective. He was trying to show her he was a tortured writer in the throes of creative agony. Best to dress the part.

Once he'd donned the flannels, Sebastian leaned closer to the mirror above his dressing table and rubbed a hand over his freshly shaved cheek. He might have to stop shaving for a few days and go on a drinking binge. Nothing made a man look more wildly artistic and tortured than beard stubble and a hangover.

He ventured downstairs just as the clock was striking half past eight, and he expected to find Miss Merrick at breakfast, but to his surprise, she was not in the dining room. Aunt Mathilda was there, however, drinking tea and opening her letters. Miss Merrick, Auntie informed him, had already breakfasted and was in the library hard at work. Sensing a hint of reproof in his great-aunt's eyes that he was not doing the same, Sebastian hastily gulped down a cup of tea and a plate of bacon and kidneys, rolled back the cuffs of his shirt to demonstrate an earnest willingness to do his best, and informed his aunt that he and Miss Merrick wished to write undisturbed until luncheon. Having eliminated any inconvenient interruptions from servants or his aunt for at least the next four hours, he departed for the library.

He found her seated at her desk, scribbling away with quill and ink. In profile to him, with the sunshine from the window flowing over her body and lighting all the coppery glints in her hair, she reminded him of a Renoir painting. Sebastian paused in the doorway and leaned one shoulder against the doorjamb. She hadn't observed his arrival, and he was content for the moment to watch her unnoticed and enjoy the view. Over the years, he'd become quite adept at finding distractions from writing, but Daisy Merrick could prove the most delightful distraction from work he'd ever had.

Her hair was piled up in a mass of soft twists and curls that he liked, for it looked as if it would come tumbling down at any moment. He turned, leaning a bit to one side, appreciating the slender line of her neck and the winsome curve of her cheek above the prim white collar of her shirtwaist. He imagined leaning down, kissing the soft skin of her ear.

Lost in these delightful contemplations, it took him a

moment to notice that as she wrote, she did not stop or hesitate, but composed line after line without reservation. Unless he was flying high on cocaine, he'd never managed to write like that. Plagued by his constant doubts, he'd always been wont to stop and reexamine his sentences, but she seemed to have no such qualms. Her nib made scratching sounds as she moved it quickly across the page, and the only time she stopped was to ink her quill. He watched her with a hint of envy. How could anyone write like that? he wondered.

She reached the bottom of the page, set the quill back in its stand and blotted the sheet. As she turned to set it on the pile of manuscript pages, she perceived him in the doorway.

"You've caught me staring again, I fear," he said, straightening away from the doorjamb, "but you seemed lost in creative composition, and I didn't want to intrude on the moment. Besides," he added as he entered the room, "you make a deuced pretty picture sitting there. It was like looking at a Renoir."

She didn't seem impressed. "I already told you, buttering me up with compliments won't help you."

"Perhaps it won't help me," he said as he crossed the room to her desk, "but I don't think it will hurt either. Besides, as I told you last night, I don't give compliments I don't mean."

She didn't debate the matter. Instead, she pointed with the quill to the teakwood desk behind him. "Your valet was down earlier. He brought your writing materials and arranged them for you."

Sebastian glanced over his shoulder at the teakwood desk. His Crandall had been placed neatly atop the blotter in the center. Above it on the desk stood a brass inkstand containing two quills and a penknife. To the left of the typewriting machine was his old, yellowed manuscript and a supply of fresh paper. He stared at the pristine white stack and the yellowed old one and felt a shimmer of apprehension.

"I noticed you have a Crandall."

Her voice brought him out of his apprehensions. "Yes," he answered, reminding himself that this was all a charade. He wasn't here to write, but to find a way out of writing. "I've had it for years. It's a battered old thing, but it still works." He glanced across her desk, noting for the first time that she had no typewriting machine. "I thought you were an accomplished typist. But you write your manuscripts in longhand?"

"I have a typewriting machine at home, but I never use it. The keys stick, and it's an upstrike machine, so I can't see when I've made a mistake. I find it easier to write in longhand." She glanced past him. "If I had a Crandall," she added, sounding envious, "I wouldn't hesitate to give up my quill. It's a beautiful machine."

"Like you, I like being able to see what I'm typing. Also the Crandall is light. I've always traveled a great deal, and I can take it anywhere."

She tilted her head to one side. "But not through the Valais Alps," she murmured.

Her curiosity was evident, but he had no intention of enlightening her. He was here to show her how impossible writing was for him, play the tortured artist, but he bloody well wasn't going to bare his soul. "No," he answered abruptly and turned away. "Not in the Valais."

He circled his own desk and pulled out the chair. He sat down, and as he stared at the polished black iron and gleaming steel of the Crandall, a feeling of dread settled like a stone in his stomach.

He drew a deep breath, shoved aside his apprehensions, and reached for a blank sheet of notepaper. For his plan to succeed, he had to make some show of working. He rolled the sheet of paper into the Crandall, but the moment he put his fingers on the keys, he felt a jolt of pure, unreasoning panic. He jerked his hands back.

"Is something wrong?"

He glanced across the desks to find she was watching him with a hint of concern.

"Not a thing," he lied, even though the truth would have served his purpose better. "Why do you ask?"

"You seem . . . restless."

"I'm perfectly well."

Satisfied, she returned her attention to her work. He once again put his hands on the keys and froze, paralyzed. The white sheet of paper loomed before him like a frozen Arctic wasteland. He closed his eyes, but that only made things worse, for he could feel the insidious craving for cocaine seeping into his bloodstream.

He couldn't do this. He couldn't even pretend to try. His hands slid away from the typewriter, punctuated this time by a muttered oath.

"My lord?"

He looked up again, and watched her give a little cough. "Before you attempt to revise your manuscript," she said gently, "perhaps you should read it?"

"Read it?" He seized on that with profound relief. Reading, even if it was his own prose, was far better than pretending to write. "Yes, of course. That's an excellent first step."

Shoving aside her revision letter, which lay atop the manuscript, he grabbed a handful of the yellowed pages, leaned back in his chair, and assumed what he hoped was a properly conscientious expression. He could feel her thoughtful, somewhat puzzled gaze on him, but he ignored it, and forced himself to begin reading the handwritten lines he'd penned so long ago.

It was torture. By the end of the first chapter, he wondered how on earth, at seventeen, he'd had the conceit to think he had any talent. By the end of the second, he wondered how Harry could ever have had the bad taste to publish any of his work. By the end of the third, he knew he'd exercised excellent judgment in never submitting this novel all those years ago. It was rubbish.

Throughout the morning, he slogged along, but by the time he had reached the end of chapter nine, the manuscript had become so unbearably dull and hackneyed, he simply had to stop.

Opposite him, Miss Merrick was still immersed in her own work, scribbling away, and he wondered again how she could write like that. She'd been at it for several hours now, lost in that magical writer's world where nothing mattered but the story.

Ah, to be like that, to be able to forget everything and everyone and become immersed in the work. What a blessing when that happened. Before the cocaine, such moments had been rare for him, but he could still recall what it was like when they came—the exhilaration when the words just flowed, the joy of composing an eloquent, perfect sentence, the satisfaction of a pivotal scene done right, the relief of penning those two most beloved words, *The End*.

But Sebastian remembered the dark side, too, and that was why he envied her. For she was fresh and naive, so eager for it all, wanting it so much. He'd been like her once, years ago, at the very beginning. The words poured out of her now, with an ease that was natural and unfettered by the inevitable doubts and disappointments and the biting criticisms. Those would come, and year by year, book by book, writing would become harder for her. Instead of pouring out, the words would start to come in dribbles, and then in precious drops. Desperation would set in, then panic. She might try cocaine, absinthe, or maybe gin, but regardless of what she tried, in the end, she would become like him. Empty, with no stories left to tell. All writers came to that in the end.

As if to banish these gloomy speculations for him, the sun came out from behind a cloud. It flooded through the window behind her and filled the room with light, making the outline of her upper body plainly visible and brightening his spirits at once.

She was wearing a corset, he noticed, for he could see the tiny puffed sleeves of what was unmistakably a corset cover silhouetted beneath the leg o'mutton sleeves of her shirtwaist. His conscience might not allow him to bed her in reality, but he could imagine it all he wanted. He'd remove her clothes for her, layer by layer, starting with that prim, starched shirtwaist.

She moved, but that did not interrupt Sebastian's torrid imaginings, for she closed her eyes and tilted her head back with a groan, exposing the tender skin of her throat and jaw, which only served to add fuel to the fire in his body. She squeezed her shoulder blades together, a move that pushed her breasts forward, and his arousal blazed into hot, powerful lust. In his mind, she was suddenly naked and he was cupping her breasts in his palms.

"You are doing it again."

This abrupt return to reality was painful. He stirred

in his chair and forced his gaze up to meet hers. "I beg your pardon?"

"You're staring at me."

He glanced down at chapter seven, then back at her, and decided he just couldn't take any more. He needed a distraction. "Sorry. I was wondering how you manage to write like that."

The disapproval in her expression changed to bewilderment. "What's wrong with how I write?"

"I didn't say anything was wrong with it. It's just that you write without any hesitation, and it intrigues me."

These observations seemed to take her back. "Well, there isn't much need to pause at this point. It's just a draft, after all."

"Yes, but don't you ever pause and reflect?"

She seemed even more bewildered. "Not really, no. As I said, it's a draft. At this stage, I simply write as fast as I can, trying to end each day with at least ten new pages."

He'd been able to do that for a while. One shot of cocaine and four of espresso, he thought with a hint of nostalgia, and he'd been able to compose pages and pages without stopping. He glanced at the lines of script she'd penned so quickly, then at the blank sheet of paper in his typewriting machine, and felt his envy deepen into despair. He'd never write like that again. He'd never write like her.

"How much do you write each day?"

Her voice broke into his thoughts, and Sebastian

forced aside memories of Italy. He lifted a blank sheet of notepaper with a wry face. "That's typical of my daily output every time I try to write nowadays. Give or take a sentence or two."

"Every time? You're exaggerating."

"No, petal, I'm not. Which is why I stopped." He tossed the sheet down on the desk beside the Crandall with a sigh and rubbed his fingertips over his eyes. "It's too damned hard."

"It's hard, yes. Sometimes."

He lowered his hand and glared at her, resenting her and her enthusiasm and her damned ten pages a day with a vehemence that surprised him. He'd thought he didn't care anymore.

"It can also be very satisfying," she said gently. "You must know that. You have produced an extensive body of work. Without finding some sense of satisfaction and accomplishment, why would you have kept doing it?"

"Insanity?"

She did not seem to give that suggestion the seriousness it deserved. "You must have found something rewarding in it."

"Perhaps," he acknowledged, "but most of the time, it's torture. It's like climbing a jagged mountain on your hands and knees. Naked," he added for good measure. "With your muse whispering to you the whole time that you'll never reach the top and you must be insane to try."

She studied him without replying, her pretty, freckled face filled with compassion.

He couldn't stand it. Jerking to his feet, he walked to one of the French windows that led onto the terrace. He started to open the door, thinking only of escape, but her voice stopped him.

"What if you could view it differently?"

He paused, his hand on the door handle. "What do you mean?"

"See it as an amusement rather than a torture."

"An amusement?" he echoed with scorn and turned to look at her over his shoulder. "You're not serious?"

But she was. He could tell by the earnestness in her face. "I think believing that would help you," she said.

"No, it wouldn't. It's a lie, and a lie is never a help to anyone."

She set down her quill with a sound of exasperation and stood up. "Changing the way we choose to look at a thing is not lying!" she said, coming to stand beside him at the French window. "There's nothing wrong or false about keeping a positive outlook."

"The glass is half full, is that the idea?" He shot her a wry glance. "Are you always like this?"

"Like what?"

"All sweetness and light? All sunshine and good cheer?"

She didn't become angry. Unexpectedly, she smiled.

"I am, rather," she confessed. "I'm afraid it quite irritates my sister."

"Really? I can't imagine why."

She made a face at him. "Mock me if you like, but I don't care. I choose to think writing is fun. You don't, and that's why you find it so hard."

She had such a simplistic view. "Writing isn't fun. It's an obsession. It's an addiction. It can be rewarding, I suppose, perhaps even cathartic. I know I've always felt an overwhelming sense of relief whenever I've finished a book, but only because the obsession that enslaves me has passed. Writing is many things, but it is not fun. How you can think it is baffles me."

"I use my imagination to make it so. Every time I sit down to work, I imagine I'm embarking on a wondrous journey, and my story is a place filled with fascinating people, mysterious alleyways, and hidden treasures."

It took everything he had, but Sebastian managed not to roll his eyes.

"And I try not to disparage my first attempts," she went on. "That's why I write a first draft as quickly as I can. It's hard, but I try to save critical analysis for later, when I can be more objective."

A sensible idea, he supposed. And one he'd never been able to master. But then, he didn't write multiple drafts. He wrote one draft, and only one. He always had. "But what if the pages you've dashed off with such speed are drivel? You've wasted your time."

"Better to waste time writing something," she shot back in exasperation, "than to waste time writing nothing!"

The impact of those words was like a physical blow. He turned his head, looking out the window. "True enough," he murmured and rested his forehead against the glass. "True enough."

Silence fell between them. They both returned to their desks, where she resumed writing, and he once again picked up his manuscript. But her words continued to echo through his mind, and he found it impossible to resume reading.

Writing fun? He felt an odd glimmer of emotion. It was an old, old feeling, faint and musty and wholly unexpected.

Longing.

He tried to shove it away, scoffing at her absurd notions. Telling oneself something over and over did not make it true. And he didn't want it to be true. Yet, the results she achieved spoke for themselves. Or did they?

With that question, he realized he knew nothing of her writing, and he felt a sudden, overwhelming curiosity to read what she'd been scribbling with such rapidity and ease, see for himself if such work was any good, if she had any real talent. It wasn't as if he didn't have the right to read her work. He was expected to do so. The situation Marlowe had arranged worked both ways.

It occurred to him that mentoring her could help his cause. He'd read her work, flatter her, reassure her that she was doing splendidly on her own and she didn't need any help from a has-been like him.

He glanced up to find her once again bent over her desk, scribbling away. Her writing had to be god-awful, he thought. No one could compose decent prose at that pace. He grimaced. There was no activity more painful than reading bad prose, but if it succeeded in getting him out of this mess without having to write anything, it would be worth every dreadful word.

Chapter 11

The trade of authorship is a violent and indestructible obsession.

George Sand

*H*e hated to write. Daisy found that difficult to comprehend. The moments she spent inventing stories were some of the happiest moments of her day. And he was Sebastian Grant, the most prolific and acclaimed writer of their generation. How could he be so accomplished at something he hated?

That afternoon, she sat at her desk, pretending to read over her last few chapters, as she studied him covertly and tried to understand. The hostility in his voice when he'd talked about writing was undeniable, and it explained why he hadn't supplied Marlowe Publishing with a manuscript for three years, and why he was fighting her tooth and nail, but how could she help him overcome his animosity? If he hated his work, if he didn't want to do it anymore, what could she say or do to change that? The little suggestions she'd provided earlier seemed woefully inadequate. What more could she do?

Probably nothing, she acknowledged with uncharacteristic pessimism. After all, one person couldn't force another to like something.

But what had caused this aversion to his work? And how could it be overcome?

She took another peek at him, watching him read his manuscript. As he scribbled something along the side of one sheet, a lock of his black hair fell over his forehead. He brushed it back in an absent-minded gesture, then reached for her letter. His finger moved down the page as if he were searching for something, and when he stopped at a particular paragraph, she saw a frown knit his dark brows. He tapped it with his fingertip, his frown deepening.

Was he displeased by something she'd said? Angry? Perplexed?

Before she could decide, he set down the letter, inked his quill, and scribbled another note in the margin. "Turnabout is fair play, I assume?" he asked without looking up.

Daisy blinked. "I beg your pardon?"

"You chided me for staring at you," he said, his gaze still focused on the pages spread out before him. "Yet you've been watching me all afternoon."

"Nonsense." She lowered her gaze. "You aren't that fascinating."

He chuckled. "Then to deserve such intense observation, I must have a spot of blackberry sauce from lunch on my chin and you are secretly laughing at me."

She sighed, wishing she were a more accomplished liar. Setting down her quill, she plunked her elbows on the desk, then entwined her fingers and rested her chin on them. "All right, then," she said as she watched him scribble another note in the margin of his manuscript, "Why do you hate writing?"

He did not pause. "If that question is what's had you watching me all afternoon instead of working, why didn't you just ask me?"

And she thought he'd been too absorbed in his own work to notice her observations. "Because it would be pointless. You'd just say it's none of my business, and tell me to keep my impertinent questions to myself."

"I might," he acknowledged, "but I wouldn't have thought you'd be daunted by that." He looked up, giving her a wry glance. "Not much seems to daunt you, Miss Merrick. Even writing doesn't appear to hold any fears for you."

"Why should it? What is there to be afraid of?"

"That is the question, isn't it?" he countered lightly. "There are so many bogeymen under that particular bed, how does one begin to list them all?"

"What do you mean?" She stared at him as realization

dawned. "That's the reason you don't write anymore," she murmured. "You hate it because you're afraid."

His lips tightened and he didn't confirm her supposition, but he didn't have to. The truth was in his face.

"But why?" she cried. "There's nothing for *you* to fear. You're a brilliant writer."

He smiled a little. "When I'm not being a second-rate Oscar Wilde, you mean?"

"Oh, how I wish you wouldn't bring up that review! If I had known—"

She stopped, but it was too late. His smile vanished and an implacable hardness came into his expression. Yet when he spoke, his voice was soft. "If you'd known, then what, petal?" he asked and set down his quill. "If you'd known that the sight of a blank sheet of paper fills me with panic, you wouldn't have told the truth about my play?"

"I'm sorry." Daisy stared at him, feeling awful. "But surely, criticism, even if it's unfavorable, doesn't make one afraid?"

"No. It's much more complicated than that."

"And criticism can be an elucidating thing. It can," she added, insisting upon it even though she was less sure of that notion than she had been. "You don't believe that, I know."

"But you do. Because of that . . ." His voice trailed off, and he stood up. "I think it's time this situation became more equitable."

She blinked. "I beg your pardon?"

"Marlowe wanted us to work together," he reminded her. "We are to critique each other, help each other. If I'm to do that for you, I need to read your work."

Daisy felt a sudden pang of misgiving. "I don't think that's really necessary right now," she heard herself saying. "You shouldn't be worrying about me. Your attention should be on your novel. You only have one hundred twelve days."

He waved aside that obligation with a shrug of his wide shoulders. "I doubt a few hours spent reading your work would have an impact on my deadline."

Daisy stared at him with a sinking feeling in the pit of her stomach, a feeling she didn't understand at all. She had agreed to this plan with enthusiasm, thinking herself eager to hear the opinions of her fellow writer. Yet, now that she was expected to hand her work over to him, she felt a strange, inexplicable reluctance.

"It's hardly worth your time," she said, gathering the pages of her partial manuscript into a tidy stack. "I only have two hundred pages completed. I'm less than halfway."

"An excellent start," he said with affable approval. "I can give you my opinions before you've gone too far. Much easier to make changes if you haven't yet reached the halfway mark. Trust me on that. I've written myself into enough corners to know."

It suddenly seemed imperative to procrastinate. "It might perhaps be better to wait."

He made a sound of amusement. "Wait for what? Hell to freeze over?"

Waiting that long seemed quite reasonable at the moment, but she refrained from saying so.

"Are those the pages?" he asked, gesturing to the pile in front of her. He stood up, and came around his desk as if to take them, and Daisy felt a wave of pure panic.

She moved as well, grabbing the pages before he could. "But it's a draft. I haven't revised it."

"But that's perfect, then. You'll be able to do your revisions later with my opinions in mind."

Very sound logic, but Daisy still couldn't quite bear to give in. "I think I should polish it a bit first."

"I don't think so." He circled her desk to stand beside her. He started to take the pages from her, but she turned away, hugging the pages of her precious manuscript to her chest.

He put his hands on her shoulders. "What's wrong, Daisy?" he asked softly, close to her ear.

She stiffened, sensing she'd just been trapped. "You've made your point," she said with chagrin and turned her head to look at him over her shoulder. "It's much easier to criticize than to be criticized. Tomorrow, no doubt, you'll tear me to bits in the name of literary criticism and tell me I must take it in the proper spirit."

He didn't deny it. His hands tightened on her shoulders and he turned her around. She forced herself to look up at him, but to her surprise, there was no glimmer of satisfaction in his expression. Nor did he seem inclined to mock her or laugh at her. His expression was grave, with a hint of understanding, and something else, something she couldn't quite define. "There's no need for you to be afraid," he said, and began pulling the pages from her grasp.

With reluctance, Daisy capitulated and let him have the manuscript. "Just don't expect too much," she said in an agonized whisper. "It's rubbish, really."

He chuckled as he walked away with her precious pages. "All writers say that."

The clock was striking midnight and everyone else had gone to bed by the time Sebastian finished reading Daisy's partially completed draft. He set aside the last page, and leaned back in his chair, staring at the stack of handwritten sheets with chagrin. This wasn't going to be easy at all.

In wresting these pages from her, he'd thought to use them as a tool to soften her up and extricate him from this business. But after reading her work, he realized his plan had a fatal flaw: his conscience. He couldn't utter flattering lies about someone else's writing. It violated his sense of ethics, a sense he hadn't really known he still possessed until now.

It wasn't that she was talentless. Quite the contrary. The envious side of his nature had rather hoped her writing methods resulted in horrible prose, but that petty hope had been set aside by the time he'd read the third page. She had the ability to tell a story, and her style had charm and a certain measure of wit. On the other hand, Sebastian understood why Harry had rejected her work. Her prose was raw, painfully so. It was also fraught with melodrama, and her most important characters were often too selfless and heroic to seem real. Still, despite all that, he'd read two hundred pages without being bored. That said a great deal about her ability. All she needed was practice. And perhaps a bit of guidance.

He picked up a quill, reached for a fresh sheet of notepaper, and started making a list of points she needed to consider regarding her story. That romantic scene in chapter seven between Ingrid and Dalton, for instance, was too treacly for words. It was clear Miss Merrick had little experience with love affairs, for no man with a beautiful woman in his arms would ever think in such self-sacrificing terms. The scene would have to be redone without all the high-blown senti-ment. And saving the dog in chapter twelve was out of the question . . .

He scribbled until he reached the bottom of the page, but when he started to continue on a second sheet of notepaper, he suddenly realized what he was doing. He stopped and tossed down the quill with an oath, appre-ciating for the first time why Harry had put Daisy Mer-rick in his path and devised this little scheme. Harry had been able to see what he had not—that he and the girl had something in common. They each possessed an artist's conscience, the sort of conscience that demanded the truth about their work. Harry hoped, of course, that this common ground would have the happy result of two talented authors producing novels for Marlowe Publishing. Sebastian leaned back in his chair with a sigh. He wished it could be that simple.

Staring at his notes, he knew he should just send her back to Harry right now. Giving her a true and thoughtful critique would only encourage her, make her determined to reciprocate by helping him. It would drag the whole business out that much longer. And yet, he couldn't tell her pretty lies either. He might be a tortured writer with no qualms about using a bit of seduction or playing on her sympathy, but he couldn't butter her up with undeserved praise about her work. The worst part was that he found himself wanting to help her. An irony, that—since he had never believed anyone else's opinion could help a writer improve. Still, he reflected, staring at the notes he'd written, it didn't hurt to tell her what he thought. Hell, perhaps he would find solace in mentoring her, since he could do nothing for himself. And if Harry published her book as a result, that might be some consolation to her for being unable to help him.

Sebastian picked up his quill to finish summarizing his comments. As he dipped the quill in the inkwell, he glanced through the library doorway to the drawing room and saw her. She was seated beside Auntie, her back to him, reading.

He smiled to himself. He liked the notion of playing mentor to a pretty protégé. It was a cliché, and he usually deplored clichés, but in this case, he didn't mind. Mentoring Daisy gave him plenty of opportunities to employ a bit of seduction, and as far as Sebastian was concerned, there was nothing wrong with that.

Daisy didn't sleep well. Throughout the night, she stared at the ceiling, thinking of all the flaws in her story, all the things with which Sebastian was sure to thrash her. She went down to breakfast the following morning filled with apprehension, convinced that he was going to be as merciless with her as she had been with him.

Though prepared for the worst, she couldn't completely dispel her innate optimism. He could take this opportunity for revenge, but despite his resentment for this entire venture, he didn't seem a spiteful sort of man. And it was possible—unlikely, but possible—that he'd like the manuscript. In the past, she'd often read her work to the ladies of Little Russell Street, and they had always seemed to enjoy it.

Sebastian Grant, however, was a far different proposition from the girl-bachelors of Little Russell Street. Most of the time, he was impatient, cynical, and terribly pessimistic. And if he didn't like her writing, he'd have no compunction about saying so, for he wasn't any more tactful that she was, and he had far less consideration for the feelings of others. Yet, last night, she'd caught a glimpse beneath his blunt, irascible exterior.

Daisy's hands paused in the act of spreading jam on her toast as she recalled how he'd looked when he'd taken her manuscript out of her hands. There had been a hint of understanding in his expression, along with something else, something she couldn't quite define.

He didn't come down to breakfast, which only added to her suspense. She went into the library and tried to work, but it was a futile effort. She couldn't seem to concentrate.

It was half past eleven before he finally came in with her manuscript in his hand, but she could read no indications of his opinion of it in his expression. As he crossed the library, she felt impelled to pretend she was hard at work. She inked her quill and wrote several nonsensical notes in the margin of her draft, hoping she seemed wholly unconcerned by what he might have to say. Nonetheless, when he paused before her desk, she couldn't keep up the act. She froze, her fingers clenching tight around her quill, and raised her gaze a notch. From this vantage point, all she could see were his strong fingers curled around the pages into which she'd poured her hopes and dreams. Would he condemn it, she wondered, or praise it?

In the end, he did neither. What he did say was the last thing in the world she would have expected.

"You have to kill the dog."

Daisy looked up, astonished. "I beg your pardon?"

"The dog, the one that belongs to little Gemma." He made a gesture of impatience with his free hand as she continued to stare at him. "The one that goes missing in chapter twelve. Dalton goes looking for it, saves its life. Remember?"

He was talking about the dog? Daisy shook her head, and she almost laughed with relief. He might still shred her work, but at least a blunt pronouncement that she had no talent wasn't the first thing out of his mouth.

She worked to recover her poise. "Yes, of course I remember the dog. It's just that . . . that wasn't at all what I thought you'd say. I thought you were going to tell me I was a terrible writer and helping me would be a waste of time."

"Nonsense. You're a tolerable writer. You might even become a great writer one day, if you could curb your fondness for metaphors and stop the excessive melo-drama."

"Thank you."

He grinned at the acerbic note in her voice and set the manuscript on the desk beside her inkstand, then he leaned back comfortably against his own desk and folded his arms across his chest. "Marlowe was right. You have talent. Your pacing's off, but your story isn't bad. On the other hand," he went on before she could savor that speck of praise, "your prose is quite raw. It's a draft, I know, but still, you need to work on a smoother flow. Also you tend to overwrite, using far too many adjectives and adverbs, and you go on too long about inconsequential details. Pare down your descriptions to just the essentials, and for heaven's sake, stop the metaphors. You're no good with them."

When he paused, she drew a deep breath and dared to ask, "Is that all?"

"No. You have a more serious flaw, one which cannot be overcome merely by judicious editing."

That did not bode well. Daisy braced herself. "What is this flaw?"

"Your writing is too sweet, and far too sentimental."

"I see," she murmured, though she really didn't.

"Don't worry, though," he went on. "All's not lost. You can dilute the sweetness and make your story much more powerful and authentic by doing one simple thing. Kill the dog."

Her creative instincts were outraged by such a barbaric suggestion. "I can't kill the dog!" she cried, dropping her quill and jumping to her feet. "No one ever kills the dog!"

He returned her appalled stare with one of patient gravity. "You have to. The way you have it now, when he saves the dog and brings it home to the little girl, it's all so nauseating and treacly, it'll give your readers a stomachache."

"But the dog is what brings the lovers together!"

"What better way to bring the lovers together than through a shared tragedy? Listen to me," he added as she made a sound of dissent. "It's bad enough that Dalton saves the dog by miraculous and quite unbelievable means, but when he brings it home to Gemma and Ingrid, the story degenerates into a sticky, gooey mess. Unless you're writing a book for children, of course, in which case you should leave saving the dog until the end—"

"Or perhaps you're just so jaded and cynical," she interrupted, "that it's impossible for you to believe in warm, happy moments."

He shrugged. "Fine. Don't kill the dog. Turn your characters into one-dimensional paper dolls and the story into a silly farce. It's your book."

That sparked Daisy's temper. "Just because I chose to save the dog, that does not make my characters one-dimensional or my story a silly farce!"

"Yes, it does, and it's your fault. As the author, you set the stage for a moment of crisis, led the reader to that point rather skillfully, in fact. Killing the dog was the perfect thing to do." He gave her a shrewd look across the desk. "But when the moment came, you couldn't bear to do it, could you? You had made the dog a character in himself, one you cared about. You felt impelled to save it, so you twisted the story in an impossible way, and thereby lost a perfect chance to affect the reader's emotions in a powerful, wrenching scene. You chose instead to turn your story into unbelievable, sentimental hogwash."

Daisy pressed her lips together and looked away. He was right. When the moment had come to kill the dog, she hadn't been able to do it. She had worked for days, struggling to find a plausible way to save the animal, but even she had known the result strained credibility. The dog had to die, she'd known it all along, but having it confirmed by someone else, someone whose work she respected, gave her a sickening lurch in the pit of her stomach.

She looked at him again. "Isn't there some way . . ." Her voice trailed off, and she swallowed hard. "Isn't there some way I could save it?"

It wasn't possible, she knew, and when he shook his head, she capitulated. "Oh, very well," she muttered, feeling wretched. "I'll kill the dog. But if this book is ever published, some people will be very upset with me."

His gray eyes were hard, his reply merciless. "You cannot allow the feelings of yourself or your audience to dictate what happens in your book. You must be true to the story. The story is the only thing that matters. The story trumps all."

She nodded. That was what made him good, she realized. He put the story first, ahead of all personal feelings. That was something she needed to learn. She lifted her head and tried to rally her spirits. "All right, but when I've dispatched the dog, I intend to give myself a very nice reward! Chocolate, I think, for I fear I shall be quite depressed."

The hardness in his face vanished, and he gave an unexpected chuckle. "No doubt. Killing a dog can ruin a writer's whole day." He tilted his head to one side, still smiling, arms still folded across his chest. "Do you often give yourself rewards?"

"Yes. Whenever I have to do something difficult, I find it encouraging to know there's a treat waiting for me when I've accomplished it." A thought struck her, and she added, "You might try that technique and see if it helps you."

"Another way to make writing fun?"

"Yes." She made a face. "Laugh at me if you like."

His smile vanished. "I'm not laughing at you."

She saw it again, that hint of something in his eyes. She'd been unable to define it last night, but at this moment when she looked at him, she realized what it was. Tenderness.

Her throat went dry, and she could only stare at him, powerless to look away. The big grandfather clock, its ponderous chimes booming from the drawing room, which finally broke the spell.

She gave a little cough. "Is there anything else I should know?"

"Yes. You haven't a clue how to write romance."

"What?" Daisy made a sound of indignation, and any

warm feeling she'd been harboring toward him began to evaporate. "That's ridiculous."

"It's clear you want to write stories of romantic adventure," he went on as if she hadn't spoken. "You do all right with the adventurous aspects, though you do sometimes stretch credibility. Dalton saving the dog from the quicksand on Morcambe Bay at just the right moment, for example. But when it comes to writing about love affairs, petal, I think you might be a bit out of your depth."

That stung, but it was no less than the truth. Sheltered and protected by her sister and the respectable maiden ladies of Little Russell Street since she was sixteen, she knew little about romance. A quick, furtive kiss from the village fishmonger's son behind the church. The desperate groping of an old man in a supply closet. These and one or two similar, equally disappointing incidents were the extent of Daisy's romantic experience.

Not that her circumstances were a complete explanation. Daisy was painfully aware that her tall, thin frame, her carroty hair, and her freckles were attributes that had never inspired much romantic attention from the opposite sex.

Sebastian Grant, she suspected, wouldn't know how that felt. With his stunning good looks, impressive physique, aristocratic lineage, and widespread fame, women probably flung themselves at him everywhere he went. If his reputation was anything to go by, he'd had dozens of love affairs. She'd had none.

Daisy ducked her head, staring down at the sheets of paper spread across her desk. Now she understood why she always had so much trouble with the romantic moments in her books. She didn't have the knowledge. "You're right, of course," she mumbled. "I can't write what I don't know, can I?"

"I could help you with that."

"Yes," she agreed with a painful little laugh, "I'm sure you could. You've probably helped dozens of other aspiring female writers. Made love to most of them, too, I daresay."

"Believe it or not, I've never had a protégé before." He stirred, straightening away from his desk, and picked up the sheaf of papers she'd given him to read. He came around the secretaire to stand beside her. Laying the manuscript on her desk, he began flipping through the pages. "Here," he said, pausing to tap his finger against a particular paragraph where he'd scrawled some notes along the margin. "This is an example of what I'm talking about. This scene where Dalton declares his love to Ingrid. It doesn't work."

Daisy leaned forward, frowning at the page he indicated. "What's wrong with it?"

"Dalton. He's so noble and so kind, I just can't swallow it. He's ready to give up everything, and why? For Ingrid's love."

The disdain with which he uttered the last few words was too much to bear. "Oh, for heaven's sake," she cried, turning toward him, "I'm not the only one who has characters sacrifice for love. I read that sort of thing in books all the time. Other writers do it."

"In Chapter Two?"

That rather took the wind out of her sails. "Perhaps not," she was forced to admit. "Is that what you meant when you said my pacing was off?"

"Yes. If you had started your story with him already in love with her, pining away, it might be different, but they meet in Chapter One, and after one conversation, he's ready to sacrifice everything? I don't believe it. Besides," he added before she could debate the point, "I don't give a damn what other writers do. And neither should you. You're a better writer than most."

She blinked, startled by the compliment, but after a moment, pleasure began seeping through as if she'd just been wrapped in a warm blanket. "I am? Truly?"

"Well, you could be." He saw her smile, and added, "But for God's sake, stop making your hero so damned self-sacrificing. When they meet, he knows she's in love with someone else, and that she doesn't want him, but he's going to risk everything simply for her happiness?" He made a sound of derision. "Men are not nearly as noble as you seem to think, unless they are stupid."

"Or heroic."

"You say heroic, I say stupid. Either way," he added before she could argue further, "Dalton's behavior is unbelievable. Men do not behave this way."

"There are men willing to sacrifice everything because of unrequited love for a woman! There are," she insisted as he made a skeptical sound through his teeth.

"I've never met any."

She folded her arms, glaring at him. "Again, this opinion could stem from your jaded perspective. Perhaps you are just more selfish than other men."

"I hate to be the one to tell you this, but I am a fairly typical example of the masculine mind."

"Somehow, I find that a disquieting thought."

He grinned. "Sorry to spoil your idealistic notions about my sex, but there it is. Men are selfish. When Dalton first meets Ingrid, self-sacrifice is not going to be what's going through his mind."

"It isn't?"

"No." Sebastian lifted his hands to cup her face, and Daisy sucked in a surprised breath as his warm palms cupped her cheeks.

"What—" She paused, moistening her lips with the tip of her tongue. "What is going through his mind?" she whispered.

His eyes gleamed like molten silver as his thumbs pressed upward beneath her jaw to tilt her head back. "This," he said, and kissed her.

Chapter 12

Writers write for fame, wealth, power and the love of women.

Sigmund Freud

The moment he touched his mouth to hers, Sebastian knew he'd been wrong, terribly wrong, to think stealing a few kisses from Daisy Merrick would be harmless, that a bit of seduction would be enough. Her lips were just as soft as he'd imagined, their taste just as sweet, but what he hadn't imagined was the affect her kiss would have on him.

The contact of her mouth against his brought waves of pleasure so acute it was almost like pain. His heart wrenched in his chest, and arousal instantly began coursing through his body. He felt as if he were a green youth of sixteen, kissing a girl for the first time. The taste of her eclipsed any sensation he'd felt before, making one word hammer through his brain and pulse through his blood.

More.

He parted her lips with his, and his tongue entered her mouth. The aggressive move shocked her, he could tell, for she made a faint, smothered sound, and her hands opened, flattening against his chest as if to push him away. In some dim part of his mind, he perceived her shock and knew it stemmed from inexperience, but his need was powerful and desperate, and he was powerless to stop. When he touched his tongue to hers, she made a tiny movement as if she might break away, and he couldn't bear it. He slid his hands to the back of her head to keep her there, and kissed her even more deeply than before.

The effect on his body was immediate and dizzying. Euphoria flooded him in an instant, intoxicating rush, and instead of being satisfied, he was filled with an even deeper craving for more.

He pulled back only long enough to suck in a breath of air, then he tilted his head the other way and kissed her again. As he tasted her, as his tongue explored her mouth, awareness beyond the kiss itself began seeping into his consciousness. The hairs at her nape tickled the backs of his fingers. The prim, high collar of her shirtwaist felt crisp against his palms. The skin of her cheeks was like warm satin beneath his thumbs. Her neck was slender, delicate, as fragile in his hands as the stem of a flower. He cradled it with care, striving to contain his moves.

Once again he pulled back, thinking to stem the violent tide of his own desire before it drowned them both.

But unexpectedly, she opposed him. Her arms came up around his neck, and she pulled him close again, her mouth seeking his with an awkwardness that spoke of her inexperience but with a hunger that matched his own.

Her parted lips grazed his, and the lust within him surged up higher than before—more fuel heaped on an already blazing fire—and he realized—too late—that instead of being liberated by her kiss, he was captured by it. He wanted even more.

Greedy with need, Sebastian slanted his mouth over hers in a kiss that was open and lush. Still cupping her delicate neck against one of his palms, he used his other hand to tug at an end of the grosgrain ribbon that adorned her throat, untying the bow. He unfastened the top three buttons of her shirtwaist and spread the edges apart with his fingers. He tore his lips from hers because he wanted to see what he had exposed, and one peek at the toffee-gold freckles that dotted her skin above the lacy pink edge of her underclothes threatened to drive him mad. His hand clenched around the placket, shaking with the effort of holding back, fighting the barbaric urge to rip the shirtwaist all the way apart and see more.

Slowly, ever so slowly, he lowered his head, nuzzling the V of her open collar, inhaling the fresh garden scent and feminine warmth that emanated from her skin. When he pressed his lips to the base of her throat, the hammering thrum of her pulse against his mouth made him dizzy. "My God," he breathed. "How lovely you are."

Wanting still more, he shifted his hand, embracing the small, round shape of her breast through the layers of clothing, and he knew in an instant he had gone too far.

Her body jerked in reaction, and she pushed at his chest to shove him away. "Good Lord," she gasped, her breath coming in little pants between her kiss-plumped lips. "What are we doing?"

"Making writing fun?" he suggested and bent his head, hoping to recapture her mouth.

"Stop." The heel of her hand lifted to cup his chin, her fingers pressed against his face, blocking his move. He lowered his gaze as she pushed his head back, and between her fingers, he could see her eyes narrow.

"If you think for one minute that I intend to let you get by with this," she breathed, "you are sadly mistaken!"

With renewed force, she pushed at him, expecting him to step back and release her, but Sebastian couldn't quite accept such an abrupt withdrawal. Desire for her was still humming through him, and he was too caught up in it to let her go.

She didn't seem inclined to wait for him to regain his equilibrium. She flung out her arms, pushing his aside to break free, and took a step back. "You really are a devil," she accused. "A clever, manipulating devil."

Without her in his arms, he felt oddly bereft, but when he reached for her again, she jumped back, her palm flattening against his chest to stop his advance. "Don't insult me any further."

"Insult you? What are you talking about?"

"Did you really think making love to me would persuade me to let you out of your obligation?"

"That isn't why I kissed you," he muttered, trying to think. "I just . . . you're so lovely, I couldn't help myself."

The moment he said it, his artistic instincts were outraged. No writer with an ounce of talent, he thought in self- disgust, would compose a hackneyed line like that. Never before had he seduced a woman with anything that lame. But at this moment, his head was still spinning, his body was still on fire, and he just couldn't explain things any better.

Daisy, understandably, did not believe him. "You must think me such a silly little fool."

"No, I don't. You're a bit naïve, perhaps, but—" He stopped, for it occurred to him saying things like that was probably not a good idea. "I have never thought you a fool. In fact—"

"I can just imagine how you envisioned it," she cut in. " 'You're so lovely, Daisy,' and, 'I just can't help myself, Daisy.' " She paused, rolling her eyes and making a sound of derision. "I assume I was supposed to fall right into your arms like a swooning featherbrain? At which point, you'd move in for the kill with, 'Oh, by the way, darling, I don't really need to do those revisions, do I?' "

That particular strategy seemed rather out the window now. "Something like that," he admitted with a sigh.

"Of all the conceit! To think your advances would be so appealing to me that I would forget my duty to my employer! Not to mention my virtue and my self-respect."

That nettled him. "A few kisses wouldn't put either your virtue or your self-respect in jeopardy! And in my defense," he added, "I'd like to point out that you weren't exactly fighting me off."

"I shouldn't have had to!" she countered. "I should never have been subjected to your unwelcome attentions in the first place."

"Unwelcome? Ah, so that explains why you wrapped your arms around my neck and kissed me back."

"I did no such thing!"

"Liar."

She folded her arms, glaring at him. "You are the one who lied," she countered, refusing to be put on the defensive. "You never had any intention of doing those revisions, did you?"

"Intentions have nothing to do with it. The changes you want are so substantive and that manuscript so raw, I'd have to start at the first page and rewrite the entire book. I can't do it."

"You mean you won't."

"Phrase it anyway you like. Writing has become unbearable for me, but it's not by choice. I can't explain it any better than that because you wouldn't understand."

She took a deep breath. "I might. Explain it to me."

Caught, he tilted his head back, staring at the ceiling. How the hell could he explain without giving chapter and verse? "Writing is first a desire," he began. "The desire to express oneself, the desire to be heard, the conviction one has things to say." He lowered his head to look into her eyes. "You know what I mean."

"Yes. Go on."

"Then one is published, and writing becomes a compulsion, a need—the need not only to be heard, but also to be admired, even adored. The more attention you receive, the more you crave. There's no satiating it. But now everyone has expectations—your publisher, your family and friends, the public—and you know you will disappoint them and lose their admiration, possibly their respect. So you work harder, write more, burning your candle at both ends. Desperation begins to creep in, because deep down, you know you're fighting a losing battle. The struggle to live up to your own and everyone else's expectations is exhausting, and one day, you . . ." He paused, treading carefully. "You reach a moment when you just can't tolerate any more, when you're exhausted and uninspired and there are no stories left to tell. You're empty. You're finished."

"For someone who's too exhausted and uninspired to write, you seem to spend a great deal of time and effort inventing ways to avoid it."

He looked away. "I have my reasons," he muttered. "Reasons that are none of your business. The point is, I have no desire to write another word. Ever."

"What if we could make you want it? For once, don't argue with me," she added as he tried to speak. "Just play along for a moment. What if we could find a way to make you want to write again?"

"For God's sake, woman, don't you ever accept facts? And I don't understand why it matters to you one way or the other. Your task was to see I gave Marlowe a book. I've done that. Why should you care if the book is good or bad?"

"You are a gifted writer, and I refuse to allow your talent to be wasted!"

"That's your reason?" He couldn't help a laugh. "You're doing this out of a sense of artistic altruism?"

"No, damn you!" she shot back. Her hands clenched into fists. "I'm doing this because I want to succeed at something! I want to become a great writer, and you're going to help me do it!"

Sebastian stared at her, and in her eyes, he could see not only anger, but also hope. He exhaled a sharp sigh. "I told you before, there's nothing I can teach you."

"This isn't just about my writing. It's also about my obligation to Lord Marlowe. He hired me to help you write again. He did not hire me to accept a mediocre manuscript you wrote years ago just so that you could fulfill a contract."

"It's over!" he roared back, hating that she was pinning her hopes and dreams and ambitions on him. He didn't want that sort of responsibility. "I haven't a shred of inspiration left inside of me. I have nothing left to say."

"You always have plenty of things to say to me, most of which are rude. And you may be the rudest, most temperamental man I've ever met, but you're not empty. You're not finished. I refuse to believe it."

"Why? Because you write pages and pages every day without stopping? Because if you can deny this drought has happened to me, you can convince yourself it won't ever happen to you?"

He thought he saw a glimmer of his own fear reflected in her eyes, but it was gone before he could be sure, and her former determination returned. "We need to find a way to bring back your creative instincts."

"I don't want to bring them back. I burned my candle at both ends for many years, petal, to satisfy my creative instincts. I've roamed all over the damned world. I've a reputation as a man of excesses, and it's well earned. I've brawled and drank and gambled my way through some of the bawdiest taverns you could imagine. I've taken—" He broke off, startled and dismayed to realize he'd almost confessed his darkest, most insidious excess of all. "Do you want to know why I've done all those things? Because I've always been afraid, that's why!"

"Afraid of what?"

"That one day I'd run out of things to write about."
He gave a bitter laugh. "Now, look at me. I am living
the very thing I spent most of my life running from. An
irony, wouldn't you say? One of God's little jests. My
father would be so damned smug if he knew."

"Your father?"

"He didn't want me to write. He deemed it a silly,
pointless preoccupation, and whenever he caught me at
it, he would become enraged. I was to be the next Earl
of Avermore, he'd often say. I was destined for nobler
things than pegging away at a typewriting machine
like a clerk. Though why he thought spending money
without any means of earning it was a noble thing, I've
never understood. He threatened to disown me when I
refused to have my first book published under a pseudonym. And he actually did disown me when I refused
to marry the American heiress he'd chosen for me.
That's when I left England. I didn't even consider returning until after his death."

"That sounds like a fine basis for a novel."

"Does it? Then why don't you write it and leave me
alone?"

He might as well have been talking to the air. "There
must be something that would motivate you, inspire
you, stir your senses."

"Well, there's you," he said without thinking. "You
stir my senses beyond belief."

"I'm serious."

"So am I," he said with feeling. "Kissing you was the most delicious thing I've felt in a long, long time."

She didn't seem flattered. She fell silent, studying him with a thoughtful frown, her head tilted to one side. If he were to guess her thoughts at this moment, he would have predicted them to be a condemnation of some sort, but Daisy, not for the first time, surprised him.

"All right, then." She squared her shoulders and lifted her chin a notch, meeting his gaze with a touch of defiance. "How many of my kisses would inspire you to revise that damned manuscript?"

Daisy stared at Sebastian, stunned by her own outrageous proposition. She was mad to have made such an offer, yet she could not bear to take it back. Her pulses were racing, and she felt almost giddy with excitement.

Sebastian, however, did not seem to share this heady feeling. "A delightful notion, petal," he drawled, "offering me your kisses as motivation. But I don't think you quite know what you're doing."

It was mad, she knew—mad, wicked, and dangerous. The risks were enormous, the consequences grave if they were caught, especially for her. She met his gaze, her heart in her throat, and shoved doubts out of her mind.

"I know exactly what I'm doing," she assured him with all the bravado she could muster. "It's like you said. I can't very well write romantic moments in my books if I've never experienced them. You can help me and I can help you. That's the whole reason I'm here, isn't it?"

"Excellent point." He unfolded his arms, and reaching out, he touched her face, tracing his fingers along her cheekbones. Then he cupped her cheeks and leaned closer. Her heart shivered in her breast when he brushed her lips lightly with his own. "But somehow," he murmured against her mouth, "I don't think this is the sort of help Marlowe had in mind."

"You're being so damned stubborn," she whispered back, "I'm forced to improvise."

"I'm stubborn?" He laughed against her lips. "Pot, meet kettle."

His fingers tightened against the back of her head as if he intended to kiss her again, but Daisy had no illusions about his motives. She ducked her head and moved out of his grasp. "Not so fast," she reproved, putting herself at a safer distance by circling her desk to stand on the other side. With that substantial rosewood barrier between them she felt much more capable of further discussion on the subject of kisses. "If this . . . this exchange is going to work, we have to establish some rules."

"Rules?" He smiled and her stomach dipped with a strange, weightless sensation, as if she had just jumped off a cliff.

"Yes, rules," she said firmly. She paused and took a deep breath, trying to steady her jangled nerves and think of how to make this crazy notion work. "The first rule," she said after a moment, "is that you can't have kisses any time you want them."

"Why not?"

"This is a means of providing you with motivation and reward," she reminded dryly, "not distraction."

"It's beginning to sound like torture."

She wasn't sympathetic. "You've already had one kiss, and that should be sufficient inspiration for the time being."

"I don't think so." He leaned over the secretaire, smiling, a hint of mischief in his eyes. "I still feel a bit stale."

"Too bad. If you want another kiss, you have to work for it."

"How?"

She leaned closer. She heard him catch his breath, and the sound gave her an exhilarating sense of power she'd never felt in her life before. She lowered her gaze to the hard, sensuous line of his mouth. He wanted her kisses, but did he want them enough? She waited, making him wait, too, as she pretended to consider. "When you've revised one hundred pages of manuscript," she finally said, "you may have another kiss."

"One hundred pages? You're joking."

"I told you, I don't make jokes."

"Petal, be reasonable," he murmured, trying to cajole.

"At that rate, I'll be having a kiss from you around Michaelmas, if I'm lucky."

"That's not true. You only have one hundred and twelve days to revise the entire manuscript. To make that deadline, you'll have to have one hundred pages revised well before Michaelmas."

"You don't seriously intend to hold me to such a strict deadline, do you? That manuscript is five hundred pages. You've seen how difficult this sort of thing is for me. Be reasonable."

"One hundred and twelve days."

His lashes lowered. "If I'm going to rewrite the entire book in that amount of time, I'll need lots of incentive." He once again looked into her eyes. "I want a kiss every fifty pages."

She couldn't relent. For every inch she gave, he'd try to take a mile. If she did have power over him, she had to hold on to it, use it now, while she had it. "One hundred pages," she repeated. "And I choose the time and place. And I approve the revisions to each one hundred pages before I give you your next kiss."

He didn't speak, and for a moment, she feared she'd pushed him too far, demanded too much. Though they were not touching and the desk was between them, she could sense the tension in his body, feel the rebellion in him. Any moment now, he'd tell her to go to the devil.

He let out his breath in a slow sigh. "All right," he

agreed. "It's a bargain, then. One hundred pages for a kiss."

Daisy felt a flash of triumph and relief, but he gave her no chance to savor it.

"But," he went on, making her tense, "I insist upon some rules of my own."

"What?" She straightened away from the desk, staring at him. "Not a chance."

"I'm not the only one who receives benefit from this little game," he reminded her. "We are supposed to teach each other, remember? Learn from each other. Help each other." He smiled. "Quid pro quo, Miss Merrick. We both benefit, so we are both allowed to make some of the rules."

She studied that smile of his, wary, sensing a trap. "What rules do you have in mind?"

He tilted his head as if thinking it over. "I don't know," he said at last. "I have to think about it. I reserve the right to bring my rules in later."

"That is absurd! I won't agree to anything that ambiguous!"

He folded his arms. "Then I won't revise."

"Then you won't be paid."

"Fine. You'll have to face Marlowe and tell him you failed."

Daisy sucked in a sharp breath. Clever bastard, she thought, glaring at him, seeing the glimmer of satisfaction in his eyes. He knew he'd found a vulnerability in her, and there was no pretending otherwise. And she realized with chagrin that when it came to using power, she was only a novice. He was a master.

"Oh, very well," she agreed crossly. "One might as well argue with a bull as argue with you. You may add a rule of your own."

"Three rules," he countered at once. "You made three. I'm entitled to make three."

She should have known he wouldn't agree to being allowed only one. "All right, all right! But," she added before he could crow about his victory, "no rule you enact can negate an already established one. No changing one hundred pages to fifty or one kiss to two."

"I would never do anything like that," he said with such innocence in his expression that she knew she'd been right.

"It's exactly what you'd have done," she said. "I could read your mind like a book."

He didn't deny it. Instead, he held out his hand. "Are we agreed?"

Daisy lowered her gaze to his outstretched hand—the long, strong fingers that had caressed her face and wide palm that had touched her so sweetly through her clothing. What rules would he come up with? Doubt once again whispered in her ear, doubt and caution, but she refused to listen. Instead, she reached out and clasped his larger hand in her smaller one to seal their bargain. "Agreed."

Chapter 13

Fill your paper with the breathing of your heart.

William Wordsworth

$\mathcal{D}$aisy could not sleep. Her outrageous proposition reverberated through her head like the blaring of trumpets, making sleep impossible.

How many of my kisses would you need to revise that manuscript?

What on earth had she been thinking? She was no bawd. She was a virtuous woman, properly brought up. Whatever had possessed her? Lucy, she knew, would never have done such a thing. But, then, she wasn't Lucy. Try as she might, she'd never been able to master tact or restraint.

She sighed into the dark. Tonight, there had been nothing restrained about her. Any other woman would have gasped in maidenly outrage and slapped his face for what he'd done. Not her, though. Oh, no. She'd done the very opposite. She'd proposed that he give her more.

Perhaps she was out of her mind. That might explain it.

Daisy plumped her pillow and rolled onto her back, pondering the matter of her sanity as she stared at the intricate white swirls of plasterwork and the darker lines of their shadows on the ceiling of her room. It was past midnight and the house was silent, but she was wide awake. Despite the cool spring breeze that floated through the room, she felt much too warm, her body still tingling from Sebastian's kiss and the exhilarating aftermath.

She hadn't lost her mind, she told herself. She'd invented that preposterous idea of kisses for a reason. She was hoping it would help him, that it would inspire him, spur him on to do those revisions.

Even as she told herself that, she knew it was a lie. Their bargain might save his literary career, it might motivate him to write again, but she couldn't even pretend to be altruistic about this. She hadn't done this for him. Daisy bit her lip. She hadn't done it for him at all.

Sebastian had been right about her. She'd had little experience with romance. Every story she'd ever written had a pair of lovers, but until today, she hadn't understood why she'd always had so much trouble describing their emotions and expressing their passions. Now she knew the reason was her own lack of experience. She had the chance to finally understand what lovers did in shadowy corners and what they talked about in whispers so chaperones could not hear. And then, once she knew how lovers behaved with each other and the romantic things they did, she could write about them with authenticity.

Yet, even as she acknowledged that motive, she knew it wasn't the true one either. It wasn't literary considerations for either of them that had impelled her to make such a reckless, imprudent proposition to the most notorious man she'd ever met.

She'd been wondering what his kiss would be like, yes, and she'd been sure it would be nothing like her first kiss all those years ago, yes, but the touch of his mouth against hers had gone beyond anything she could have imagined. It was the most extraordinary thing she'd ever felt in her life. And, shameless as it was, she wanted to feel that way again.

She'd always thought a kiss was sweet, poignant, blissful. But now she knew it wasn't like that at all. It was a lush, lavish, shocking exchange, with open mouths and tongues that touched. It evoked the strangest sensations—an aching warmth, and a hungry, desperate need for more. She remembered how he'd unbuttoned her shirtwaist and pressed his lips to the base of her throat, and how that had made her feel—as if she were melting into a puddle on the floor.

And he hadn't only kissed her either, she remembered, blushing in the dark. He'd touched her, too.

Oh, heavens, what had she done?

Daisy turned onto her side, pressing her hot cheek against her pillow at the edge where the cotton was cool. The memory of how his palm had cupped her breast, how his touch had seemed to scorch her right through her clothes, was still so vivid in her mind, that even now, she could feel again the pulse and flex of her own body in response.

She flung back the covers and sat up in bed with a groan as her own words came echoing back once again.

How many of my kisses would inspire you to revise that manuscript?

An image of him came into her mind and she closed her eyes, leaning back with her weight on her arms, thinking of his lips pressed to the base of her throat. How long? she wondered, and anticipation unfurled within her, anticipation so keen, it banished any regrets or apprehensions. How long before he kissed her again?

This, she thought, was romance. And she wanted it—wanted it so badly, she could hardly stand it. It might be wicked and sinful and just plain wrong, but Daisy couldn't find it in her heart to regret the bargain she'd made. Even if it was a bargain with a devil.

* * *

A man with sense would have said no. A man with sense would have ushered Daisy Merrick's shapely bum and delicious offer right out the door yesterday and put her on the first train back to London. But if Sebastian had ever had any sense, he would never have become a writer.

Hands on his typewriter, he stared down at the sheet of paper in the roller and the two words he'd typed on it. The Crandall still worked, and he still remembered how to use it. He'd managed to tap out the words, "CHAPTER ONE," without any trouble whatsoever, but immediately after that, he'd run into difficulties.

He pulled his hands back from the machine, staring at the Crandall with anguish and hostility, feeling cocaine's lure like an insidious serpent. It whispered in his ear and slithered through his bloodstream, beckoning him, tempting him, trying to distract him at every turn.

He didn't have to do this, he reminded himself. He could walk away. Sebastian exhaled a sigh and picked up Daisy's revision letter. He'd already read it a dozen times, but he read it again, just so he would have something to do besides give up.

"The opening is too staid," he murmured under his breath. "It reads like a description out of Baedeker."

She was right, of course. The hero's journey across the Channel, his train ride from Calais to Paris, a description of the Gare Saint Lazare, did read like a snippet from a Baedeker travel guide.

Sebastian straightened in his chair, set the letter aside, and once more put his fingers on the Crandall's keys. He tried to think of a new opening line for the book, something with emotion and life. "Samuel Ridgeway," he muttered as he typed, "was a young man with prospects."

No, too passive. He X'd that line out and tried again. "When Samuel Ridgeway stepped off the train, the Gare Saint Lazare was teeming with activity."

He stopped and rolled his eyes. Of course it teemed with activity. It was a train station, for God's sake. Once more, he crossed words out, and as he watched X's popping up over each letter he'd typed, Sebastian felt a twinge of despair. How the hell could he rewrite an entire manuscript when he couldn't even compose a decent opening line?

There's an easier way, his mind whispered. *You know what it is.*

Desperate, he shut out the serpent hissing in his ear by focusing his mind on an entirely different desire, a desire far more delightful than any drug.

He eased back in his chair and closed his eyes. At once, an image of her came into his mind, an image of creamy skin and toffee freckles, of frothy pink lace, white nainsook, and brown ribbon. He imagined the inviting swell of her breast against his hand,

and lust flooded through him. He inhaled sharply in reaction and almost caught her delicate, floral scent. Imagining her in this way, he could almost taste the sweetness of her mouth, he could almost feel her arms tightening around his neck and pulling him closer. Almost.

He groaned aloud and opened his eyes. It was bad enough that, somehow, he had agreed to rewrite the damned book. But now he also had to play the delicious dance of seduction with a woman too innocent for the real thing. When she'd offered up her kisses as inspiration, he'd hardly been able to believe his luck, but now, staring at the rows of X'd out text in his typewriter, he wondered how lucky he'd been. He felt rather like a condemned man staring up at heaven from the depths of hell.

Sebastian tried to look on the bright side. At least this was revision; he didn't have to write an entire book from scratch. And every hundred pages he received a delicious reward for his efforts.

He could also up the stakes, he realized, remembering that he could add three rules to this game she's concocted.

What should his first rule be? He ran the tip of his finger idly along the edge of her revision letter as he contemplated that delightful question. It couldn't be anything too shocking. The last thing he needed was to do all this work only to have it come to naught, so whatever rule he came up with had to be satisfying enough to reward him for his hard work, and yet romantic enough to satisfy her innocent expectations. That was going to be a bit tricky.

The sun came up over the horizon, and morning light poured into the library through the French windows. He blinked a few times against the sudden brightness, and stretched out one arm toward the lamp on his desk. As he turned the brass knob to extinguish the lamplight, a ray of sunshine hit the fabric shade, shooting brightness through the tasseled fringe. Sebastian turned his hand, idly fingering one of the tassels, and as he watched the morning light shimmer on the brightly colored strands of orange, gold, and brown, he suddenly knew what his first rule was going to be.

Smiling, he lowered his hand and returned his attention to the sheet of paper in the typewriting machine before him. An idea flitted through his mind, vague and shadowy but unmistakable. His smile vanished, and he straightened in his chair, suddenly alert.

Without any real awareness of what he was doing, he put his hands on the keys and with quick, hammering strikes, he typed out a sentence. He contemplated it for a moment, and then, with deliberation and intent, he typed another sentence. And then another. Slowly, from deep down inside him, came a faint glimmer of hope.

* * *

When Daisy came down to the library, she found that Sebastian had arrived before her and was already hard at work. He was tapping out words on his typewriting machine at a rapid pace, and she hesitated by the door, not sure she should go in, for she didn't wish to distract him.

From this angle, she could see most of his face. Though his brows were furrowed in concentration, he was smiling a little as he typed, and she felt a profound sense of satisfaction. For the first time since she'd met him, he looked content. As a writer, she appreciated the meaning of that. The work was going well. She moved to depart, but at the sound of his voice, she stopped again.

"And where do you think you're scurrying off to?" he asked without pausing in his task.

"I didn't wish to interrupt your spurt of creativity."

"Hmm, that sounds like an excuse to me."

He stopped typing and gave her a look of mock sternness, tapping one forefinger on the top of his typewriter. "If I have to work, you have to work."

"Is that to be your first rule?"

"No, petal." His pretense of sternness dissolved away. His gaze traveled down her body and back again to her face, so slowly that it was almost a caress. "I shall reserve my rules for the important things."

A tingle ran up her spine, a delicious tingle of anticipation. To hide it, she pretended to be affronted. "You don't think ensuring I write my book is important?" she asked as she entered the library and crossed to her desk.

"I didn't say that," he replied as she sat down opposite him. He leaned closer, his chest brushing the top of his typewriter. "But in this game, there are other things I value more than your book."

"What things?" she blurted out, and then wanted to bite her tongue off.

He laughed. "You'll have to wait and see."

During the two weeks that followed, Daisy did plenty of waiting, and plenty of wondering, too, but she was gratified to note that her outrageous game seemed to have the desired effect on him.

Sebastian had made it clear to the servants and to his aunt that they were not to be disturbed in their work. With doors shut and interruptions eliminated, they spent every morning and most afternoons hard at work.

At least, Sebastian did. It was Daisy, strangely enough, who now found writing a difficult endeavor. She managed to kill off the dog, and just as he'd assured her it would, that change made the story much more powerful. But it also prompted a series of other corrections and presented a whole slew of new and unforeseen obstacles, obstacles she found herself wholly unprepared to deal with, especially since she couldn't seem to concentrate for more than five minutes at a time.

She found her mind wandering to their bargain dozens of times a day, and each time renewed her anticipation. She would often observe him during their hours together in the library, and though it was gratifying to see him working so hard, she found it far more gratifying that he was doing that work to gain kisses from her. It was the most romantic thing she could imagine.

As she studied him covertly during their hours together, she began to see him in a way she never had before. When he paused to read what he had typed, with his elbow on the desk and his chin in his hand, she noticed the line and sinew of muscle in his strong forearm below the rolled cuffs of his sleeve. When she watched him drum his fingers on the desk, she remembered how those fingertips had touched her face. When he stared thoughtfully out the window, the sensuous line of his mouth would evoke the memory of that stirring kiss and make her long for it again.

But none of that was helping her with her work. Daisy tried to force herself back to it, but when she read the last sentence she had written, she realized it made no sense. She crossed it out, and saw that she had a full page of crossed-out sentences. When she turned the page over, she discovered the other side was the same—not a single usable line on the entire sheet.

With a discouraged sigh, she wadded up the used notepaper and tossed it into the wastepaper basket beside her chair. She inked her quill and began again.

She wrote two sentences, then stopped, dissatisfied, and crossed everything out. She wrote a little more, and stopped again, realizing in horror that Dalton had just swept Ingrid up into his strong, manly arms and kissed her.

That was not something she could put in her book! Dalton and Ingrid were not even married. And even if she were so bold as to describe such an erotic moment, she certainly couldn't use such explicit terms. Why, she'd actually written the words *passionate kiss*. Heavens, what would the ladies of Little Russell Street say if they read that?

Making a sound of exasperation, Daisy ran a line through the entire paragraph and began to fear she'd made a serious mistake. While the kiss she and Sebastian had shared seemed to be helping his creative instincts, it was not helping hers at all. She wanted to write better, more authentic romantic moments, but she did not want to write pornography!

The sight of yet another crossed-out paragraph was so discouraging, she looked up, and found that Sebastian was watching her.

"Having a problem?" he asked innocently, but she could see an unmistakable glint of humor in his eyes.

Daisy felt a damnable blush rising in her cheeks. Reminding herself that there was no way he could know the content of what she had just written, she shoved a loose tendril of hair behind her ear and donned a dignified air. "No problem," she denied. "No problem at all."

"I'm glad to hear it."

He resumed work, and she tried to do the same, but within an hour, she was wadding up yet another sheet of used paper.

Sebastian seemed to take this as a plea for assistance. "All right," he said and stopped typing. "It's clear you're having trouble. Let me see if I can help."

He started to rise, as if thinking to come around and read what she'd written, and she hastily forestalled that, holding up one hand to stop him, her other hand clenching protectively around the wadded-up paper. "No, no, it's quite all right, really."

To her relief, he sat back down, but he did not let the matter drop. "Daisy, you've used up at least a dozen sheets already this morning. And when you're not crossing out your sentences or wadding up paper, you're sighing, tapping your fingers, shifting around in your chair, and staring at your manuscript with a frown on your face. It's clear you're having difficulties. Let me help you."

"No, no, that won't be necessary," she assured him and shoved the chapter she'd been working on in her dispatch case. "I'm not accustomed to writing for such long periods, day in and day out. I believe I just need a respite."

He glanced at the clock, then back at her, looking doubtful. "But it's not even time for lunch," he pointed out as she stood up. "You are stopping for the day? You? The slave driver?"

She made a face at him. "I do wish you'd stop using that expression. I am not a slave driver." She glanced at the window. "It's a lovely day. I think I'll go for a walk."

"If you're not a slave driver, you can prove it by allowing me to accompany you."

"Very well. But only if you show me the prettiest spots."

After securing a picnic hamper from the kitchens, Sebastian led her out through the kitchen garden, past a walled fruit garden, and across a wide expanse of green turf. They stepped over a stile and followed a footpath that meandered into a dense grove of beech and oak. It was a beautiful summer morning, and it felt good to leave work behind on such a day as this.

"It's nice to be in the country," she remarked as they walked. "London air is so foul."

"Yes, and it seems to become more so with each passing year. I was a bit shocked when I came home from Italy, for it seemed as if there was twice as much coal dust in London as when I departed."

"Italy has no coal dust?"

He shook his head. "It's much warmer there, you see.

Not so much need for coal. And of course, they don't have that cursed English dampness to keep the soot hanging overhead like a black cloud."

"I should love to see Italy. My friend Emma—she's Lord Marlowe's wife—she and Marlowe went to Italy on their honeymoon and she brought back some lovely photographs and drawings. Did they visit you there?"

"No. I did not see them." He paused, then added, "I'd gone to Switzerland by then. I didn't know the viscountess was your friend."

"Oh, yes. I've known Emma since I was sixteen." She found herself telling him all about the lodging house in Little Russell Street, and all of her friends there.

"I didn't realize we had friends in common," he commented. "Three of your friends have married men of my acquaintance. Marlowe, the Marquess of Kayne, and the Duke of St. Cyres are all friends of mine."

She laughed. "Mrs. Morris says Little Russell Street is a magnet for potential husbands. Miranda, who is my dearest friend, wishes that were so. She wants more than anything to be married and have a big brood of children. She's seen so many of our friends marry, but she is still unwed, and that has caused her no end of consternation."

He laughed. "And you? Why do you not use your connections to secure a husband? Any other woman would, in your place."

"My friends have offered to introduce me into society, of course. But—" She paused, thinking of a way to explain. "But we're a proud, independent lot, we Merricks. My sister," she added, "has become quite a woman of business. She owns an employment agency, securing domestics for wealthy matrons, typists for solicitors' offices, things like that. She does very well."

He seemed to perceive her inner feelings. "You envy her, don't you?"

Her steps faltered, and she stopped walking. "Yes," she admitted before she could stop herself. "Does that make me sound horrible?"

"No, petal," he said gently, stopping beside her. "It makes you human."

Daisy looked up into his face. "My sister is the accomplished one," she found herself saying. "She's the one who always says the right thing, does the right thing. She's successful at everything she tries. She's beautiful, too. I'm too tall and too thin and I've got all these freckles and hair the color of carrots. Lucy doesn't look a bit like me. She has the golden hair you mentioned, and the baby blue eyes, and the mouth like a rosebud. She's beautiful. She's also tactful and lady-like. She manages a successful business, but she's also had three marriage proposals. Three!"

He opened his mouth as if to speak, but she went on, "I haven't her head for business, more's the pity. And I'm twenty eight, without a single marriage proposal to my name. I've never even had a suitor."

No woman with sense would confess such a thing, particularly to a man, and yet, Daisy couldn't stop the words from pouring out of her like a flood. "You were correct when you said I can't write about romantic things because I don't know how. And it's not as if I'm accomplished. I can't sew, and I can't play the piano. I can't dance or draw or sing, and I'm too blunt and too outspoken for clever conversation."

As she unburdened herself, Daisy began to feel a sense of relief she'd never felt in her life before. No wonder it was said that confession was good for the soul. "I've had dozens of posts," she went on. "I've been a governess, a typist, a telephone operator, a dressmaker's assistant—but I've been sacked from every post I've ever had because I can't learn to hold my tongue. That's why I'm here, doing all this. Marlowe hired me to help you, and I refuse to let him down. I refuse to fail at yet another job."

She pressed a hand to her chest. "And if I become a great writer, Marlowe will publish my novel. If he does, I'll have something that's mine, wholly mine, an accomplishment I can hold in my hands and say, 'Yes, I did this.' That's why I'm pushing you so hard to write your book and for you to teach me everything you know so that I can become a great writer like you. For once in my life, I want to succeed at something."

He dropped the picnic hamper and caught her up by the arms, hauling her against him with enough force that she sucked in a breath of shock. "That is the biggest load of codswallop I've ever heard," he said savagely. "Like I told you before, you're a deuced pretty woman. God, do you think I'd ever agree to write again if all I got for my trouble were the kisses of an ugly woman? Give me a bit of credit for my taste in women, would you?"

She opened her mouth, but he gave her no chance to speak. "If I hear you disparage yourself for those luscious freckles of yours or that gorgeous hair one more time," he went on, "I'll go off and pound my head into a wall. Not to belittle your sister's charms, but I'd guess those marriage proposals were not in spite of her successful business, but because of it. Most men, as I said before, are selfish, and some, I'm sorry to say, also happen to be greedy and lazy. There's many a man out there who'd be happy to take over a successful business through marriage rather than hard work."

He paused just long enough to take a breath, then went on, "As for accomplishments, I've known dozens of accomplished women. I've been surrounded by 'em all my life, and yes, they can sew and sing and draw, but the amount of intelligent conversation most of them have to offer would fit in a thimble! Furthermore, you've been living in a ladies' lodging house, earning your living and writing your books. Governess? Dressmaker's assistant? The reason you don't have a line of suitors out your door is simple. You don't meet any men. Being an author won't change that, by the way, so best to stop grousing about it. You'll spend most of your time alone. And while we're on that subject, let me add that you're already a fine writer, and you don't need some publisher to bind your words up in a leather cover to prove it. But if you feel you need to be published in order to be a truly accomplished woman, don't worry. Talent aside, a writer only needs two things to become published: tenacity and gumption. Believe me, petal, you've got both of those qualities in abundance!"

With that, he stopped, but Daisy was so astonished that she couldn't think of anything to say. Sebastian had just described her and her situation in a way she'd never considered, and it took her several seconds to think of a reply. "Thank you," she finally managed.

He let go of her, seeming almost embarrassed by his outburst. "You're welcome."

He picked up the hamper and started walking again, but she didn't move. Instead, she stared after him, and slowly, she began to smile, happiness welling up inside her like sunshine. Lucy, for all her accomplishments, successes, and suitors, had never been the recipient of a speech like that. Daisy found a great deal of satisfaction in that.

Chapter 14

It is not enough to conquer.
One must also know how to seduce.
Voltaire

Sebastian walked down the path at a rapid clip, his boot heels crunching on the gravel, Daisy's words still ringing in his ears.

So that I can become a great writer like you.

The knowledge that she was pinning such high hopes on him and the success of this venture scared the hell out of him. God, if he could teach her anything, it was that writing was not worth such grand expectations. It was a capricious, ruthless, unpredictable occupation, not at all the sort of thing on which to pin one's hopes or one's self-worth. And it angered him beyond belief to hear her talk about herself as if she had nothing of value outside of being a writer. As if there was nothing worthwhile about her honesty and her optimism and her blithe disregard for obstacles. What would happen to her if writing was allowed to kill all of that? What would happen to her if she became like him? It hurt, somehow, to look down the road and imagine Daisy as the world-weary, cynical has-been he'd become. It would happen, if she didn't take care, if she didn't have some guidance.

He stopped walking and pressed the heels of his hands against his forehead with a sound of frustration. The whole mentoring thing had been a ploy. It wasn't supposed to become *real*.

The sound of crunching gravel caused Sebastian to lower his hands and glance over his shoulder, and as he watched her come around the bend in the path, with the sun shining on her bright hair, hair she didn't even think was pretty, he couldn't stand it.

"I was like you once," he said, turning toward her. "I thought writing was all there was to life. I thought it would prove to my father and to me that I was important in my own right, not because I was born into a certain class, not because I was destined to be the next Earl of Avermore, but because I could be great at something. Like you, I wanted something I could call my own. There was a sort of hole inside of me, and I thought writing would fill it." He took a deep breath. "But it didn't. It never will. It can't."

She started to speak, but he forestalled her. "If you want to be a writer, fair enough, but don't think it's more than it is. Do it to tell the story, and for no other reason. As for being great, that's an illusion. The moment you start thinking you're great, you begin sliding into mediocrity. Believe me, I know. Where do you think all that trivial pabulum you mentioned in your review came from? Because I thought I was great, when all I really was was cocky. Don't let writing do to you what it did to me. Don't let it become everything to you, because the moment it does, it slips away entirely and leaves you with nothing. Writing isn't enough to fill your life and make you whole. You need other things, too."

"What things?"

He smiled a little. "I don't know, petal. I'm still looking."

They ate their picnic beneath the shade of an immense oak tree, the largest and oldest tree at Avermore, Sebastian told her, planted by the first earl back in 1692, or something like that.

As they ate, they didn't talk much, for both of them seemed preoccupied with their own thoughts. She didn't know what was on Sebastian's mind, but for her part, she was thinking of her unaccountable admissions to him earlier. She'd never confessed such intimate feelings to anyone before, not even to Lucy. Especially not to Lucy, for her envy of her sister's beauty and accomplishments was a black and bitter feeling she'd always tried to suppress and deny.

But Sebastian had listened to her terrible admission without blinking an eye. In fact, he'd taken her feelings of envy as something perfectly understandable and natural.

Daisy couldn't help smiling at that. When she'd first met Sebastian Grant, she'd never have dreamed in a thousand years he could be easy to talk to. Why, there she'd stood, babbling on like an idiot, enumerating her most glaring flaws to the most attractive man she'd ever met, never dreaming he'd be angered by her opinion of herself.

If I hear you disparage yourself for those luscious freckles of yours or that gorgeous hair one more time, I'll go off and pound my head into a wall.

Daisy's smile widened into a grin, and her happiness bloomed again, staying with her all afternoon as Sebastian took her on a tour of the estate.

After leaving their picnic basket at the farm, they visited some of Sebastian's favorite boyhood haunts—the dilapidated treehouse he and his cousins had built when they were boys, the tors where they had played out their favorite sieges and battles, and the enormous boxwood maze. Though he hadn't been through it for years, he managed to guide her successfully amid the tall green hedges to the open space in the center, where, in the midst of a round pool, stood a fountain sculpture of nine women.

"The Muses," he explained with a grin. "My grandfather put this here. He wrote poetry, and this was one of his favorite places to work in summer. Probably because it was quiet." He gestured to a spot near where Daisy was standing. "He used to stretch himself out right there on the grass. He'd lie on his stomach, with his composition book in front of him, scribbling verses all afternoon. Sometimes, I'd come here, too, and we'd both write."

"Both of you hiding from your father?" she guessed.

"Rather," he agreed. "And from all the guests."

"Guests?"

"My father was very much the country gentleman. There were always house parties at Avermore in the summer, but here in the maze, no one could find us, and we could write in peace."

Something in the way he spoke made her curious. "You don't like parties?"

"Not particularly." Her confusion must have been evident, for he went on, "I'm well aware that I acquired quite a wild reputation in Italy, but that wasn't because I enjoyed that sort of thing. I mean . . ." He paused and looked away, staring into a tall green hedge. "Italy was a period of my life I'd prefer to forget. I became a different man there, and I spent three years in Switzerland trying to go back to being the man I'd been before. But one can't go back." He looked at her, and something in his eyes hurt her heart. "One can't ever go back."

He stirred, shifting his weight restlessly. "Let's go on, shall we?"

They left the maze, and Sebastian led her through thick groves of beech and oak trees to a wishing well, where he gave her a ha'penny to toss in. He didn't ask her what she wished for, but she told him anyway, and when she did, he sighed and shook his head, looking at her as if she were a hopeless pudding head. "Never wish for publication," he told her.

She made a face. "What should I have wished for?"

"Royalties, petal." He turned and started out of the woods. "Lots and lots of royalties. And serial rights."

She laughed, following him along a worn dirt path amid the trees and shrubbery. "Because if one is receiving those things, publication is already a given?"

"Just so." He stopped so abruptly, she almost cannoned into him from behind. "Hell's bells, I almost forgot to show you Osbourne's Bend. Of all the things to forget."

"What is Osbourne's Bend?"

"One of the finest spots at Avermore. Come on."

He changed direction, leading her through the woods until the beeches gave way to willows. They stopped by a sleepy, meandering stream. "This," he breathed with strange reverence in his voice she didn't understand, "is Osbourne's Bend."

Daisy stared doubtfully at the *U*-shaped bend in the stream before her. Sunlight dappled the water through the overhang of immense weeping willows, and on the other side, a battered old dock jutted out over the water from a thick growth of shrubbery. A punt was anchored at the end of the dock, its steering pole jutting upward off the stern.

"A very pretty spot," she commented, "but I don't see what's so special about it. It's just a bend in a stream."

"A bend in a stream? Woman, it's *Osbourne's* Bend, the best trout fishing hole in Dartmoor."

"Oh."

Her lack of enthusiasm for his favorite place made him sigh. "You obviously do not appreciate the importance of a good fishing hole."

"I'm sorry. Perhaps I might, if I knew how to fish." She looked past the water and the dock. To the right, sitting atop a slight knoll and backing up against another grove of beech trees, was a small round structure built of stone and capped by a dome. "What's that?" she asked, pointing to it.

"That's the folly. It wasn't called a folly when it was built, of course. It had a much grander name: the Temple of Apollo. My great-grandfather, William Grant, fourth Earl of Avermore, had it built when the grounds and gardens were redone in 1770. He wasn't a very original man, for he copied it from the one at Stourhead. It's identical in every detail, even down to the name. Rumor had it that Sir Henry Hoare, the owner of Stourhead, was livid about having his temple copied, but what could he do? Temples were quite the fashion then, you see. Every peer had one."

"I know, but why? Seems an awful lot of expense and trouble for something that serves no purpose."

"I'm only guessing, petal," he said with a grin, "but

I think that's why nowadays we call that sort of thing a folly."

She laughed, and he laughed with her. "Of course," she agreed, touching her fingers to her forehead in acknowledgement of her own obtuseness. "Quite so."

"It was supposed to be a place for quiet contemplation," he explained and leaned closer to murmur in her ear. "Though, if you want the truth, it's always been a favorite spot for conducting romantic rendezvous. I thought you ought to know," he added, donning an air of mock apology as she blushed. "For purposes of research."

"Thank you." She rallied, meeting the humor in his eyes with a dry look. "You're too kind."

She returned her attention to the view across the stream. Only a few hundred yards from the folly was another structure, one so different in style, form, and function that Daisy knew at once it was from a different, more recent generation. It was a house—a prim, doll-like house nestled amid the trees, painted white, with a shingled roof and a sloping veranda that overlooked the stream. Climbing roses along the front were in full bloom, a riot of apricot blossoms that twisted upward around the pillars and along the roof lines of the veranda.

"What a lovely cottage," she said, pointing to it.

"It is rather," he agreed. "That's the summerhouse."

"A summerhouse?" she echoed in surprise. "But it looks like a place one could actually live in."

He seemed surprised. "Well, yes, of course. My aunt usually does live there. The main house is leased most of the time, and when tenants are living there, Mathilda makes her home in the summerhouse. An American family had contracted to stay at Avermore through the autumn, but they decided to go to Torquay instead."

"Many peers lease their houses nowadays, don't they?" Daisy asked.

"It's rather a necessity. Estates are expensive to keep up. We have several properties that I don't believe I've ever lived in because they've always been leased, including a big sprawling mansion in London. Anyway, every time Avermore is vacant, Auntie moves back in until new tenants are found, because the summerhouse is a bit spartan."

"We had a summerhouse, too," she said, then amended at once, "Well, we called it a summerhouse, but it was really just a sort of open gazebo, made of wood. I was told that my great-grandmother served tea there on summer afternoons. We never did that, of course. It was practically falling down by the time Lucy and I were old enough to have anyone to tea. Not that we ever—"

She broke off, deciding that it was probably best not to mention that they'd never dared have guests to tea when she was a girl, since she and Lucy had never known if Papa would be sober. "Anyway, our summerhouse wasn't anything like that." She glanced around and spied a bridge a short distance away. "Might I have a look at it?"

"Of course, although we can't go inside the place. Since it's so far from the main house, my land agent keeps it locked when my aunt isn't in residence, and I haven't a key with me."

Sebastian led her over the bridge and up the short knoll. As they approached the house, he said, "I was under the impression that you come from Holborn, but I can't think where, amid the brick rowhouses of Holborn, there would be a summerhouse."

"I live in Holborn now," she clarified as they mounted the steps of the cottage. "My sister and I share a flat there. But we come from Northumberland, a village called Riverton." She paused in front of a window and leaned forward, cupping her hands against the glass so that she could see the cottage's interior. She was looking into a parlor, she realized, and though the furnishings were covered in white sheeting, the room was obviously of the same lavish comfort as the main house. The walls were papered with a pretty chenoiserie pattern, one corner of a thick Aubusson carpet peeked out from beneath the sheeting on the floor, and there was a stunning chimneypiece of green marble with a tall, gilt-framed mirror above it.

Daisy's mouth curved in a rueful smile. There'd been a mirror over the mantel of their drawing room in Northumberland, she remembered, although the gilt paint on theirs had long since begun to rub off.

She thought of her childhood home, with its shabby

chintz chairs, threadbare carpets and peeling gilt paint, and she couldn't help a laugh. Sebastian's idea of spartan and hers were very different.

Straightening away from the window, she caught the puzzled expression of the man behind her in the reflection of the glass, and she felt impelled to explain what she found amusing. "You describe this cottage as spartan," she said, turning around. "From what I can see, it's hardly that."

"I only meant that it has no bathrooms and no gas lighting. It's all candles, copper baths, and chamber pots down here. In terms of modern conveniences, the main house is much more up to snuff."

"I should hate to think what your opinion would be of the house I lived in when I was a girl," she told him, still smiling. "It was a big, tumbledown, ramshackle old place, practically falling to pieces. Most of the furniture was gone before I was ten."

"Your father was a man of property?"

She nodded. "He was a squire. But he had no money. He did, however, have a deep affection for cards."

"Ah."

"He gambled everything away by the time I was twelve. The house had to be sold to pay his debts. He died when I was thirteen." She paused, took a deep breath, and added, "He drank. Brandy. Quite a lot of brandy, actually."

"That must have been difficult for you and your sister. What about your mother?"

"I don't remember her. She died when I was barely five. Cholera." Hands behind her, Daisy leaned back against the window. "If she'd lived, things might have been different. My father might have been a different man."

Sebastian leaned one shoulder against the window frame. "I doubt it."

She felt a sudden flash of anger. "Do you always have to be so damned cynical?"

He shrugged. "I prefer to think of myself as a realist. People don't change, Daisy. If your mother had lived, your father would still have been the same man, with all the same weaknesses."

Her anger died as quickly as it had come. "You sound like my sister. When we lost our home, Lucy and I went to live with a cousin, and my father went to Manchester to find work. He promised he'd send for us when he was settled. He promised he'd take care of us, that he'd stop gambling and stop drinking. Lucy didn't believe him."

Sebastian leveled a shrewd glance at her. "But you did."

"Yes," she admitted. "I believed him. In fact, I never doubted him for a moment. I was absolutely sure he wouldn't let us down." A bitter wave rose up inside her. "I was such a fool."

"No. You just expected more than your father could give."

"It was my thirteenth birthday when I found out it

was all a lie. He'd been promising to come home for months, but he kept postponing it. I had said I wanted a birthday party, because if I had a birthday party, he'd come home. Lucy arranged it and wrote to Papa, but she warned me not to get my hopes up, that he might not be able to come, but I was sure he would."

"And he didn't."

"Oh, no," she contradicted, "he came. Right in the midst of things, he arrived, but he was drunk. I could smell the brandy from five feet away. So could everyone else. Needless to say," she added with a little laugh, "it was a short party. Everyone left, and he and Lucy had a flaming row. She told him to leave and never come back. He died a few weeks later, and we found out he had never stopped drinking and he'd never found employment in Manchester. He'd been living off of some woman."

She straightened away from the window, turning to face Sebastian with sudden desperation, wanting to understand. "Why?" she asked. "Why would my father do that?"

He looked away. "God," he muttered, "why ask me?"

"You've been a man of excesses, you told me. You've drunk and you've gambled." She felt a sudden grip of fear. "Are you like he was?"

He stiffened, and her fear deepened, but she persisted. "Are you? Would you lie to your family, ruin your life?"

"For drink? No. For another hand of cards? No. Would I be kept by a woman? God, no."

Relief washed over her in a powerful wave, and she closed her eyes.

"But," he added softly, "we all have our weaknesses, petal."

She opened her eyes and found him looking at her. She asked the question before she could stop herself. "What's your weakness?"

He straightened away from the side of the house, and she felt as if a wall had come between them. "It's probably close to teatime," he said. "We'd better go back."

She watched as he started across the veranda, and he was halfway down the steps before she spoke. "You aren't going to tell me, are you?"

He stopped to look at her over his shoulder, and she caught her breath, for she could see that hint of tenderness in his expression. "No," he said and continued on down the steps.

During the fortnight that followed, Sebastian continued to write like a man obsessed. He was usually in the library before Daisy came downstairs, and he often continued to work well into the evening, having his dinner brought to him on a tray. Mathilda expressed some concerns about how many hours he spent at his typewriter, but when she asked Daisy what had brought about this unaccountable change in him, Daisy could not very well enlighten her.

She couldn't tell his great-aunt about the game that she and Sebastian had concocted, and the fact that it was a secret made the whole thing much more thrilling. And it seemed to be working for him. Daisy, however, continued to struggle with her own writing, but strangely enough, she couldn't work up much regret about that. As she watched the stack of completed pages on his desk grow steadily taller, her sense of anticipation grew as well.

Questions constantly ran through her head. What would happen when he reached the one-hundredth page? How was this going to work? Would he want to talk about the revisions first? Or would he just hand her the pages, haul her into his arms, and kiss her? These questions and a dozen more richoeted wildly through her brain, ratcheting up her suspense with each passing day, until it was almost unbearable.

And then, one morning in mid-July, she knew some of her questions were about to be answered. When she came into the library to work, she found that for once Sebastian had not arrived before her. Instead, waiting for her on her desk was a tidy pile of manuscript pages tied with twine. With it was a note, tucked beneath the twine.

A pang of delicious excitement shot through her at the sight of that note. She snatched it up at once, broke the wax seal, and unfolded the single sheet.

It wasn't a note, she realized at once, it was a map. A map of the maze, with the route to the center clearly marked in red ink. At the center, also marked in red, he'd written the words *Four o'clock*.

She glanced at the clock and gave a cry of aggravation. It was only a little past nine. How would she ever manage to wait until four?

She lowered the note in her hands, and her gaze caught on the pages he'd left for her to read, reminding her that kissing him was not what she had come to Devonshire to do. Daisy forced herself back to reality and sat down at her desk. She folded the map and put it in her pocket, then she untied the twine and picked up her quill. Forcing herself to focus her attention on the pages in front of her, she began to read.

It was a little before four when Daisy took the map Sebastian had given her and made her way through the maze. When she arrived at the center, she found him already there, waiting for her. Daisy paused in the opening of the hedge and spied him on the other side of the Muses' fountain. In his hand was a small red book, but he didn't seem to be reading it, for the moment she stepped into the enclosure, he noticed her and shut the book, marking his place with his finger.

"Well?" he prompted before she had the chance to speak. "Did you read the pages?"

"Yes." She saw him tense, watched a wary expression

come into his face, an expression of vulnerability that she found terribly moving.

He took a deep breath. "And?"

"It's wonderful," she said and began to laugh as she saw the relief in his expression. "Truly wonderful."

"Thank God," he muttered, raking a hand through his hair. "I've been pacing here like a tiger in a cage for hours," he confessed. "I was afraid you'd say they were rubbish."

She smiled. "Isn't that what all writers are afraid of?" she asked, remembering when he'd taken her pages to read.

"Yes. So you like the way the story opens now?"

"Oh, yes! When he steps off the train and he literally runs into her, and he knows his life will never be the same—that's so much more exciting than before. And the part where he finds out she's married—oh, I can't quite pinpoint all the ways you changed it, but this time, when I read it, I was on tenterhooks, feeling the suspense. I wanted to keep reading and reading—" She broke off with a vexed sigh. "That's when I ran out of pages."

"I'll write more," he promised her. "But not now." He paused, and a look came into his face that made her remember why they were here. "Right now," he added, one corner of his mouth curving in that half smile of his, "I have something more important to do."

Daisy felt the suspense that had been haunting her all

week rise up again, and she tensed, waiting, expecting him to approach her. "You told me you've never read Byron," he said without moving, "but I'm not certain I believe you. It appears that you and he have the same ideas when it comes to inspiration."

He opened the book to the page he'd marked with his finger and began to read.

> " *'If Apollo should e'er his assistance refuse,*
> *Or the Nine be dispos'd from your service to rove,*
> *Invoke them no more, bid adieu to the Muse,*
> *And try the effect of the first kiss of love.'* "

Her breath caught in her throat at those words, and she struggled for a nonchalance she was far from feeling. "It seems to me," she said after a moment, "that Byron was a very intelligent man."

"I quite agree." He closed the book, but he still did not move. His gaze locked with hers. "Take your hair down."

She blinked at this abrupt transition, and her pretense of nonchalance dissolved in an instant. "I beg your pardon?"

"Your hair. Take it down."

She reached up, pressing a hand to the firmly pinned twist at the back of her head, feeling suddenly, terribly self-conscious. "My hair? Why?"

"That's my first rule. Your hair has to be down."

Daisy lowered her hand and clasped both hands

behind her back. She'd been in a lather of suspense for weeks, wondering how he intended to claim his reward, and what rules he would add to this game they'd concocted. She'd imagined all sorts of exciting things he might do, but taking down her hair, she thought with a jolt of panic, was not one of them.

He perceived her reluctance. "I've fulfilled my part of our bargain. Do you intend to renege on yours?"

She imagined her mop of orange corkscrew curls all hanging down in its usual hopeless tangle, and reneging was suddenly a very tempting idea. "I can't think why you'd want to see my hair down," she mumbled, looking away with a self-conscious laugh. Her mind strove for an excuse to refuse, but she could think of none. Meeting his eyes again, she told him the truth. "Boys teased me about my hair when I was a girl. 'Carrothead,' they called me."

"I won't tease you." He took a step toward her. "I want this, Daisy. I want to see your hair down, all loose and shining in the sun."

Agonized, she reached up to comply, keeping her gaze locked with his. Her hands were shaking, and she pressed one over the twist at the back of her head as she used the other to pull out hairpins. It wasn't until all the pins were gathered in her palm that she let her hair fall free.

She shook it back. "There," she said, feeling almost defiant as she shoved the pins in her pocket.

He circled the fountain, coming toward her, and with each step, her heart beat harder in her chest, and by the time he halted in front of her, she was sure he could hear the rapid, thudding sound. Never in her life had she felt more exposed, more vulnerable, than she did at this moment.

He didn't speak. The book fell from his hand to the grass, but he didn't embrace her or attempt to kiss her. Instead, he grasped a fistful of her hair, lifted his hand high, and let the long strands slowly fall from his fingers. He smoothed it down with his palm, and then grasped another handful and began again.

He was playing with her hair.

Daisy stood motionless, staring up at him in astonishment. He'd said her hair was pretty, but until this moment, she hadn't really believed him. Looking into his face, she believed him now. His gaze was riveted, as if he found her hair the most fascinating thing in the world. He looked . . . entranced. "Beautiful," he breathed as if to himself.

A warm glow started deep in her midsection and began rippling outward, a blissful glow that eased away her panic and brought a pleasure so profound, she couldn't help but smile.

That caught his attention, and he shifted his hand, tangling his fingers more deeply into her hair. Gently, he pulled her head back and leaned closer. "If you want to back out," he said, his voice a harsh rasp close to her lips, "do it now, because the rules are only going to get harder."

The warm glow in her body intensified at the light brush of his mouth, growing hotter and deeper. Tingles were running up and down her body. Heavens, he hadn't even kissed her yet, and she was in a state of such excitement she could hardly breathe.

He waited, his lips poised a hair's breadth from hers, and she knew he was waiting for her to decide whether to go forward or call a halt. "I don't want to back out," she whispered.

He gave her no chance to say more. His lips pressed fully to hers, and the rush of pleasure was so acute, the rush of joy so piercingly sweet, she cried out against his mouth.

His fingers were still tangled in her hair, and his free arm wrapped around her waist, lifting her onto her toes, pulling her fully against him. His lips parted hers the same way they had before, a lush feast for all her senses.

Her body felt vibrantly alive, as if every part of her—every cell and every nerve—existed only for this moment and this kiss. Nothing else mattered, nothing in the world.

Daisy breathed in the scent and taste of him. Her hands spread across his chest, feeling his hard muscles against her palms through the linen of his shirt, the rise and fall of his breathing, the beating of his heart.

Just as the first time he'd kissed her, Daisy felt as if she was no longer in control of her own actions. It was not conscious thought that caused her to press her body closer to his. Her mind did not tell her to wrap her arms around his neck or curl her leg around the back of his in a desperate attempt to bring him even closer. Her body did these things of their own accord. She was driven by something she'd never felt before. Carnality. She stirred, her hips against his, and all she wanted was to savor this odd, new sensation.

He didn't let her. With a groan, he tore his mouth from hers and turned his face away, breaking the kiss. His arm around her relaxed, easing her body back down until her feet touched the ground. He grasped her arms and pushed her back a fraction, separating their bodies even as he buried his face against her hair. She could feel his breathing, deep and ragged, against her temple.

Her own breathing was just as uneven. Her knees felt weak and she held on to him as the only solid thing in a world that was spinning. She was shocked by her own carnal appetite, something she'd never dreamed existed within her. Just as shocking was the awful pang she felt at his withdrawal, as if a tantalizing meal had been placed before her and then snatched away after she'd taken only one bite. When his hands fell to his sides and he began easing himself away, her arms tightened instinctively around his neck. She didn't want this moment to end.

"Don't tempt me," he groaned, pressing a kiss to her hair. "I have to let you go while I still can."

When he stepped back, she felt bereft, and still disoriented. He bent down, retrieving the book from where it had fallen into the grass. "Here," he said and held it out to her. "This is yours now."

"Thank you." She took it from his hand and when she opened it, she noticed something written on the flyleaf in his bold, black scrawl.

Every writer of romance needs her own copy of Byron. S. G., July 12, '96.

Daisy's happiness rose again, and she looked up, wanting to thank him, wanting to see those gray eyes watching her and that hard mouth softened by a smile, but he was already gone.

She didn't follow him. Instead, she wrapped her arms around herself, hugging her present to her chest, wanting to hold all these feelings in, to keep this blissful euphoria as long as possible, wishing she could hang on to it until he had completed another hundred pages.

"Write fast, Sebastian," she whispered. "Write very, very fast."

Chapter 15

I can resist anything but temptation.
Oscar Wilde

*H*e wrote about her. He called her Amelie, and gave her a husband, and described her hair as raven black, but in his mind, it was Daisy he saw.

He dreamed about her. About the rich, flaming color of her hair and the deep blue green of her eyes, and the soft, sweet yielding of her mouth, and he'd wake up with his body on fire and the scent of Pears' soap in his nostrils.

He thought about her. For perhaps the thousandth time in a week, he thought of her arms around his neck pulling him closer, her tongue tasting deeply of him, and the pressing of her body close to his. He recognized it for what it was—the awakening of her body to lust. And thinking about that only fanned the flames of his own desire.

He imagined her. He sat across from her day after day, half his mind on the work before him, the other half occupied with removing her clothes, tasting her mouth, seeing her smile. He typed words onto pages with hands he imagined were caressing her. And the more preoccupied he became with Daisy, the more pages he wrote about Amelie. Samuel Ridgeway's passion became his passion, and the story poured out of him onto the pages with an ease he hadn't felt since Italy.

He was playing a dangerous game with her. He knew it, but he could not stop. The waiting and the tension were almost unbearable, the pleasure of imagining himself with her again was too tempting to resist, and he found his mind returning to those moments alone with her again and again. In the weeks that followed that kiss in the maze, he worked, and he imagined. The novel he was revising took on a life of its own; it transformed into something completely different from the original. And it was good, damn good, some of the best writing he'd ever done in his life. Even he knew that—deep down, under all his damnable self-doubt, a part of him knew he was creating a story that was extraordinary.

He suspected Daisy was not finding it as easy as he to harness passion and form it into sentences, scenes, and chapters. Even he did not quite understand why he was able to do so—something was driving him, and though he did not understand it, he intended to take full advantage of it for as long as it lasted. Three weeks after the kiss in the maze, Sebastian hammered out one sentence on page two hundred, stopped typing, and whipped the sheet out of the typewriter.

Daisy looked up at the sound, and he heard her catch her breath. She knew. "Four o'clock in the maze?"

"No." He stood up, gathered the pages of manuscript, and circled around to stand before her desk. "The Temple of Apollo. Might as well use the thing for its proper purpose."

There was a smile at the corners of her mouth, but her eyes opened innocently wide. "Quiet contemplation?"

"No." He dropped the manuscript pages on her desk and gave her a grin in return. "A romantic rendezvous."

By four o'clock, Sebastian had conjured at least a dozen different erotic scenarios involving Daisy Merrick. For days, he had been both tormented and inspired by memories of the kiss they shared, but today, he intended to make a new memory and find new inspirations.

She came into the folly out of breath, as if she'd been running, her eyes sparkling with excitement, and her hair already down in a tumble of curls around her shoulders. Sebastian's throat went dry at the sight of her, for he knew she felt the same anticipation he did, the same hunger, the same need that was in him.

"Were the pages all right?" he asked as she paused just inside the doorway.

"Yes. I thought you did an excellent job. Do you—" she broke off, taking a deep breath. "Do you want to talk about it now?"

"No." He had no intention of wasting any of the precious time they had now on things they could talk about later. "I have a new rule."

"Yes," she answered in a steady voice. "I thought you might."

"Close the door, Daisy. Best to lock it, too."

He saw her eyes widen, but she complied, and the heavy wooden door swung shut. The sound ricocheted around the stone walls and the dome overhead. The bolt rattled, her fingers fumbling to shoot it across the latch. She clicked the bolt into place, turned around, and started toward him. "What is the new rule?"

Her voice, he noticed, wasn't quite so steady now. He shouldn't do this, he reminded himself as she approached him. No, he added with a glance down the length of her slender body, he really shouldn't. But he was going to. He just had to remember to keep his head. He brought his gaze back to hers. "You have to kiss me in your underclothes."

She stopped, still about a dozen feet away from where he stood, shock washing over her face. "I can't do that!"

"Yes, you can. It's rule number two."

She gave a tiny shake of her head as she lifted her hand to her throat. "It's not decent!" she whispered, fingering the button hidden beneath her blue silk collar ribbon.

"In your underclothes, Daisy."

Her cheeks were rosy pink. "But it's daylight!"

He decided now was not a good time to tell her people did all sorts of indecent things in daylight. "Rules are rules."

Their gazes locked. He knew he was pushing her beyond what her much more innocent mind had been envisioning, but he could not bear to relent. He wanted this too much. He needed it too much.

Under his unwavering gaze, she pulled at her collar ribbon, untying it. She got as far as the first two buttons of her shirtwaist, but then she stopped. "Oh, heavens," she mumbled and gave it up, looking away with a laugh he suspected stemmed not from humor but from nerves. "I can't do this."

"If you don't want to do it, then you should leave now." Even as he spoke, he was cursing himself for his sudden bout of chivalry. He counted the silence—one, two, three seconds, but she did not move to go.

"Do you want to do this, Daisy?"

She didn't look at him. "Yes," she answered, her voice so low he almost didn't hear it. She lifted her hands to the third button of her shirtwaist, but her hands began to shake as she tried to unfasten it.

"Let me help you." With a few quick strides, he was standing in front of her. As she let her hands fall to her sides, he pushed her hair back from her shoulders, then he began slipping her buttons free, one by one. She made a restless movement and closed her eyes, clearly agitated by what he was doing, but she did not stop him. As her shirtwaist opened, revealing the lace, nainsook, and ribbon of her corset cover, desire began overtaking him in a thick, hot wave. By the time his hands reached the belt at her waist, he was so aroused, he could barely breathe.

She was breathing hard enough for both of them, he noticed, quick little huffs between her parted lips, her face turned away, her cheeks suffused with color, her eyes shut tight. He didn't know if her reaction stemmed from arousal or fear. Probably both, he concluded, but it didn't stop him. He unfastened her belt and let it drop to the stone floor, then he pulled her shirtwaist free of her waistband and slid the garment from her shoulders.

The sight of her this way was intoxicating. The late afternoon sunshine reflected off the aged limestone walls, giving the room a soft, golden glow. In this light, her hair seemed incandescent, each strand a glint of brilliant fire. Her shoulders dotted with freckles, her demure white undergarments, the shape of her small, sweet breasts—all of these beckoned to the lust inside him, deepening it, spreading it through his limbs.

He leaned down, and the warmth of her radiated to

him as he breathed in her delicate, flowery scent. And then he moved one inch closer and touched his mouth to the crest of her breast above the narrow edge of lace, and the feel of her bare skin against his mouth brought a pleasure so great that he groaned aloud.

She felt it, too, for her body stirred in response to the touch of his mouth. "Oh, no, oh, no," she moaned softly, her hands flattening against his shirt as if to push him away, even as she tilted her head back. "We shouldn't be doing this. I'm sure we shouldn't!"

He was sure of that, too, but he had no intention of stopping. He'd worked too damned hard to get here to call a halt now. His lips pressed to the rounded swell of her breast, he slid his hand beneath her underclothes, and within the tight confines of her corset, his fingers brushed across her turgid nipple.

That was a touch too much for Daisy's already strained virginal sensibilities. With a cry, she cupped his chin and grasped his wrist and shoved him away, then she turned as if to flee.

"Don't go." He wrapped an arm around her waist and pulled her back against his chest. "Don't go, Daisy. I haven't had my kiss yet."

"Yes, you have." She jabbed one finger toward her chest. "You kissed me right there!"

He made a sound of dissent and pressed his lips to her shoulder beside the ruffled edge of her corset cover. "That wasn't a kiss."

"It was, it was," she wailed softly, her fingers closing in agitation around his forearm. "You kissed my . . . my . . ." Seeming too flustered to voice specifics, she amended, "You've kissed me in my undergarments. Now you have to let me go. Oh, don't!"

She jerked as he tasted her skin with his tongue. He could feel her embarrassment and her agitation giving way to panic, and he tried in desperation to think how to keep her here and prolong this moment. "That was not a kiss. A kiss is lips to lips."

"All right then." She turned in his arms, so abruptly he had no chance to react, and rose up on her toes, touching her mouth to his. It was over before he could even appreciate it had happened at all, and then, she was ducking under his arm and bending to snatch up her shirtwaist and belt from the floor. "Now we're done."

"No, we're not." Once again, he hauled her back. "Even if that was a kiss—and it was so quick, I can't really be sure—it was with you down to only half your underclothes. I think the skirt has to come off for it to count."

He reached for the button of her skirt, and she suddenly stopped struggling. Her slim body went still, her back against his chest, her body rigid in his arms. "C'mon, Daisy," he coaxed, nuzzling her ear. "You wanted this, too. Remember?"

She did not relax, and though it took everything he had, Sebastian forced himself to give her the choice.

He loosened his embrace enough that she could step out of his arms.

She didn't. She remained where she was, though he could feel her quivering in his light hold. Slowly, ever so slowly, he bent down, turned his head, and kissed the side of her neck. The tendons there were as taut as harp strings against his mouth, but she did not break free.

Deciding not to push his luck, he gave up on the notion of taking off her skirt. Instead, he gently tightened his arm around her, easing her body closer to his own, until her buttocks were pressed against his thighs and the undersides of her breasts brushed his forearm.

Sebastian closed his eyes, breathing in the radiant heat and fragrance of her. Her hair tickled his cheek as he kissed her ear. He felt the quivers that ran through her in response, and when he flicked his tongue against her earlobe, they intensified, until she was shivering in his arms.

He turned his hand to cup her breast, and made a sound of appreciation at the round, perfect shape of it against his palm. Any attempt to get her out of her corset would probably cause her to bolt, so Sebastian forced himself to be content with caressing her breast through her underclothes.

Gently, still kissing her neck and caressing her breast, he turned their bodies to the nearest wall. Then, one arm cupping her breast, he used his free hand to begin gathering up her skirt and petticoat, working to get his hand beneath them.

She made a faint sound and stirred. "This isn't in the rules."

It ought to be, in his opinion. But he knew what he was doing was far beyond the scope of any agreements or rules they had made. Nonetheless, he was driven to press on, driven by a force she did not yet understand. She soon would, he knew. Before they left this room, he wanted her to long for more, just as he did. "I'll stop in time," he promised, drawing her skirts higher. "Trust me."

That, he thought with a wry hint of humor, had to be the most clichéd, overused phrase mankind had ever used on womankind, but his body was on fire, his wits were slipping, and a trite, overused cliché was the best he could manage just now.

He dipped at the knees, pressing his groin to her buttocks, and when she moved against him in response, the pleasure of it was so great, it threatened to knock him off his feet and break the promise he'd just made.

Lust was roaring through his body. He was rock hard and aching, and he wanted to pull her down to the floor, take her here and now, just this way, with both of them on their knees, but he couldn't. He'd just told her to trust him, for God's sake. Besides, he hadn't brought any of the usual protections. And she was an innocent, hardly the sort to be ravished from behind on a stone floor. He had to be satisfied with pleasuring her.

Kissing her all along the curve of her neck and shoulder, he worked to get his hand underneath her skirts. He lifted them, jamming layers of blue wool and white muslin between their bodies, then he slid his hand beneath her buttocks, eased it slowly between her thighs, and cupped her mound through her damp knickers.

She cried out, her body jerking sharply with the sensation. She leaned forward as if to escape, but there was nowhere to go, and her hands splayed against the wall. She turned her head, pressing her flushed cheek to the stone, and moaned a few unintelligible words.

It sounded like his name and something about the daylight, but he had no intention of stopping for that sort of nonsense, not now, not when her body was moving in response to his touch. She was close, so close, to the bliss. Nothing would make him stop until he'd given her that.

He rocked his hand back and forth, using the friction of her damp knickers to arouse her further, take her higher. She was panting now, soft pants of desire and distress.

He could hear his own voice in response, a whisper harsh with the strain of keeping his own desire in check. "It's all right," he said, trying to both arouse and reassure her. "It's all right, petal. This is what you're supposed to feel. Just let it happen."

Even as he spoke, he felt her hips pumping faster, moving against his hand in awkward, frantic little jerks as she strove toward what she didn't even know was coming. Watching her, he suddenly wished he could turn her around, for her face was only in profile to him, her flushed cheek pressed to the smooth, cool limestone, but he couldn't stop to change their position now without ruining the moment entirely. He contented himself with the sight of her flushed cheek and all its pretty freckles and the riot of red curls that fell behind her ear, and even though he could only see the pleasure in half her face, when she finally came, it was still the sweetest thing he had ever seen in his life.

She collapsed against the wall, panting, but he waited for the last convulsive waves of her climax to stop before he withdrew his hand. He lowered her skirts, smoothing them back into place, striving not to think about the painful, aching need in his own body. He turned her around so that he could see her entire face, and when she opened her eyes to look at him, there was such wonder in her expression that Sebastian's chest went tight, and he felt a jolt of pleasure as intense as any sexual climax he'd ever experienced.

He tucked a loose tendril of her hair behind her ear and forced himself to let her go. "Now that," he said as he stepped back, "was the sort of kissing I had in mind."

* * *

That was not kissing. Daisy didn't know what had just happened to her, but she knew even the passionate kiss they'd shared in the maze, as wonderful as it had been, could not compare to this.

She stared up at Sebastian, stunned by the whirlwind of sensations she had just experienced. She still tingled even though he was no longer touching her. The sounds that had issued from her own throat still echoed in her ears, though the room was silent.

Sebastian turned away to retrieve the clothing he'd removed from her body earlier. A lifetime ago, it seemed. When he brought her things to her, she felt in no hurry to don them. Her earlier shyness was utterly gone. After what had happened, it didn't seem to matter much that she was standing half dressed before him in a light-filled room.

Her body was charged with euphoria, and yet filled with an odd lethargy. Part of her wanted nothing but to slide her arms around his neck and kiss him and linger here as long as possible, but Sebastian did not seem to share her desire to tarry. He assisted her into her shirtwaist and started to button the garment for her, but then he stopped and drew a deep breath. "I think you'd better do this part yourself," he said, his hands sliding away. "I don't think I can manage it just now."

He didn't explain further, but his voice was hoarse, strained. As he turned away, she happened to glance down, and when she noticed the hard bulge against his trousers, realization suddenly penetrated her dazed senses. "Are you all right?"

A caustic chuckle echoed through the room. "Not at the moment, no," he told her over his shoulder as he walked away. "But I'll survive."

Silence fell between them as Daisy finished dressing, and it wasn't until she walked to where he had paused by the door that either of them spoke.

"You should go back first," he said. "And in case my aunt or anyone else happens to encounter you along the way, you're just out for an afternoon stroll in the grounds. Try to act as if nothing's happened."

Daisy feared that was going to be impossible. After the extraordinary events of this afternoon, she feared she would never be the same again.

Chapter 16

*Those who restrain desire do so because
theirs is weak enough to be restrained.*
William Blake

The following morning, she found out he was gone. Unexpected business in London, Lady Mathilda told her at breakfast, but Daisy suspected it had more to do with what had happened the day before than any business he might need to transact in town.

Lady Mathilda was watching her as she imparted the news of her nephew's departure, and Daisy felt impelled to follow Sebastian's advice. She worked to maintain an indifferent expression, but she was no good at this sort of thing, and Lady Mathilda saw through her at once.

"It's disappointing, I daresay," the elderly woman said, "but you needn't look like a puppy that wasn't taken for a walk, my dear."

Daisy took a sip of her morning tea and hastily invented an excuse for the disappointment Mathilda had seen on her face. "I had wanted his lordship to read some of my new chapters, and give me his opinion," she said, striving for a brisk, businesslike tone. "I fear I shall have to carry on alone and hope I'm taking my story in the proper direction."

Mathilda let it go at that, but Daisy felt the older woman's shrewd blue gaze watching her through the remainder of the meal, and she suspected her explanation had been about as believable as Jules Verne's stories of rocket ships to the moon. Beneath such scrutiny, memories of the previous afternoon insisted upon running through her mind, making her feel as if she had an enormous scarlet *A* on her chest. She escaped the breakfast table as quickly as possible and closeted herself in the library, determined to set aside such wayward distractions and work.

But again, despite her best intentions, work proved impossible. Memories of the things Sebastian had done to her kept flashing through her mind. The feel of his hard body pressing hers to the wall, of his low voice murmuring in her ear, of the extraordinary way he had touched her, continued to plague her.

She leaned back in her chair with a sigh. Her hands fell away from her typewriter and she looked across the two desks to the empty chair opposite her. For weeks, they had been in here together every day, and it seemed so strange to not see him seated across from her, to not hear the rapid *click-clack* of his typewriting machine. He had taken his Crandall with him, and that ought to have consoled her, for at least he intended to work while he was away. But Daisy stared at his empty chair, and she did not feel consoled. In truth, she felt utterly bereft.

London in August was about as exciting as a Latin lecture. Parliament had long since adjourned, the season was over, and everyone remotely interesting was either at Torquay, Nice, or someone's country house. Sebastian, who had come to town hoping for distraction, remembered only after his arrival just how boring his homeland's largest city could be at this time of year.

It wasn't as if he'd done much in the way of thinking prior to his departure from Avermore. That afternoon with Daisy in the folly had haunted him throughout the night, leaving him unable to sleep. He'd lain in bed, torturing himself with memories of the erotic episode and imagining any number of variations on that particular theme. Desperate, knowing her to be lying in a bed only a few doors from his own, he'd gone down to the library and attempted to work. But that, too, had failed, for even with two floors between them, he was still too close to temptation.

Desperate, he'd given up at dawn, and had scoured the library for a Bradshaw. Upon discovering there was a seven o'clock train from Dartmoor to Victoria, he'd woken Abercrombie and ordered his valet to pack his things. He'd left a note for Auntie and departed the house, deeming London far enough away from Daisy Merrick to keep the girl's virtue intact.

Sebastian had the vague idea that he could somehow transmute lust into pages and chapters, but he quickly discovered that without her sitting opposite him, writing was well nigh impossible. He found himself looking up from his typewriter countless times, thinking to ask her a question, gain her opinion, or solicit her advice, only to remember he was no longer with her at Avermore.

Inevitably, he would have to stop and go in search of something, anything, to take his mind off of her. The bright side, if there was a bright side to hell, was that his need for Daisy, not his need for cocaine, was what had him abandoning his typewriter. Lusting for a woman, even if that lust remained perpetually unsatisfied, was preferable to a lust for cocaine. The problem, however, was that London in August wasn't exciting enough to distract a man from much of anything, especially not from erotic imaginings of a pretty redhead with perfect breasts, long legs, and a luscious bum. Sebastian soon got in the habit of taking very long walks and very cold baths.

But as the weeks passed and August gave way to September, he could not rid himself of his desire for her anywhere. Regardless of what he did or where he went, he found reminders of her. The leaves of the elms in Hyde Park, just beginning to turn, made him think of her flaming hair. An exhibition of Monet at the National Gallery brought images of her vivid blue-green eyes. Even a stroll along the shops of Bond Street couldn't allow him to escape her.

A glance in one particular shop window found Sebastian stopping in his tracks. He backed up a step, and one look at the window display caused him to groan in aggravation. Hell's bells, couldn't he even walk down a London street without being tormented by his craving for her?

Sebastian flattened his palms against the glass, staring through the shop window, but he could no longer see the display that had stopped him here. He couldn't see his own reflection in the window, nor the gilt letters naming the establishment that were painted on the glass. No, the only thing he could see was her face—her sweet, freckled, innocent face, flushed with the wonder and euphoria of her first orgasm. Christ almighty. He wanted to smash his head through the glass.

Sebastian looked away, rubbing a hand over his eyes. This could only end badly, he reminded himself. He knew what he was toying with—her virtue, her innocence, possibly her heart. And yet, cad that he was, he didn't care. Only because of her was he able to write again. He could not give that up. He couldn't give her up. Not yet. Not when his need for her clawed at him day and night and wouldn't leave him alone.

Why fight it?

With an oath, Sebastian jerked open the door of the shop and went inside.

Daisy tried not to count the days since Sebastian's departure, but she couldn't help it. She missed him. Every night, she stared dismally at the empty place at the head of the dining table. Every morning, she came downstairs, hoping to find him at his desk only to be disappointed. Every afternoon, she walked the grounds of Avermore, going back to the places they had been.

At the wishing well, she tossed in a ha'penny and wished for his return. At Osbourne's Bend, she tried to understand why anyone would think yanking poor defenseless trout out of their home was entertaining. She went through the maze, the poetry he'd quoted to her ringing in her ears. She was tormented by memories of what had happened in the folly, and a month after his departure, she found herself back there. As she stared at the stone wall where he had touched her in that extraordinary way, all the hunger and desperate need she'd felt then came rushing back, and she longed for him to come back and do those wanton things to her again.

The past month had seemed like an eternity, and there had been no hint of when he would come home.

He might never return. Mathilda had received one letter from him, reporting that he had found new tenants for Avermore and requesting she be moved back into the summerhouse by the end of November, but Daisy received no word from him at all.

Perhaps, she thought as she left the folly and returned to the house, she ought to write to him in town and ask him straight out when he intended to return. She could always mention his deadline, remind him he had fewer than thirty days left, and ask about his progress on the book. She had every right to inquire, she told herself as she crossed the terrace to the French doors that led into the library. After all, she was his editor.

Daisy entered the library and pulled off her straw boater and her gloves. It was an hour until teatime. She really must stop dawdling and set to work. Tossing her hat and gloves onto a nearby chair, she started toward her desk, then stopped, stunned by the sight of what was on top of her desk.

It was a Crandall—a beautiful, shiny black, absolutely smashing Crandall.

With a cry of delighted surprise, Daisy rushed to her desk, and she had to touch the typewriter to be wholly sure she wasn't seeing things. But the solid metal beneath her fingers confirmed it was not a figment of her imagination. Obviously new, it was a far more elaborate model than Sebastian's machine. Along with the mother-of-pearl inlay, there were painted red roses. It was beautiful.

But where had it come from? Who had—

Daisy looked up, noting that Sebastian's battered old typewriter was once again in its rightful place. He was back.

A burst of joy shot up inside her like a rocket. She took a step, thinking to go find him at once, but again, something she saw gave her cause to stop. Beside her new Crandall was a note with his coronet. She snatched it up, broke the seal, and opened it.

Midnight. The summerhouse.
S. G.

Her heart lifted and soared. How would she endure all the hours until midnight? she wondered, as she folded the note and put it in her pocket. Surely it would be agony.

And it was. The month without him seemed the blink of an eye compared to the eight hours that followed. Pleading a headache, she chose to forgo tea altogether, and she had dinner brought to her room on a tray, for she couldn't bear to dine with him under her chaperone's perceptive eye, knowing she was slipping out for a secret rendezvous with Sebastian under his aunt's very nose.

But the impropriety of the appointment did not pre-
vent her from going, and the illicit aspect of their game
only served to heighten her excitement.

A few minutes before the appointed time, Daisy
slipped out of the house through a little-used side door
and went to the summerhouse. It was a good thing
there was a full moon to light the path, for she ran the
entire way.

The cottage was dark when she arrived, but she
mounted the steps to the veranda, yanking out the
pins that caught up her hair. She thrust the pins in her
pocket and opened the door. Shaking back her now
loosened hair, she went inside and closed the door
behind her.

She blinked several times, for it was darker inside
the cottage than the moonlit outdoors had been. She
was in a foyer, and to her right was the parlor she'd
seen through the windows the day she and Sebastian
had come here, though she could discern little more
now than she had on her previous visit. The sheeting
had been removed from the furnishings, no doubt in
preparation for Mathilda's return here, but the darkness
prevented her from seeing any details about the room.
Ahead of her in the foyer, however, a faint light shone,
spilling through a doorway on the left. "Sebastian?"
she called softly. "Are you here?"

He appeared in the doorway before she'd even finished the question. In his hand was a single candle in a

holder, giving his white linen shirt a golden glow. "You came," he said.

That surprised her. "Did you think I wouldn't?"

"I didn't know. A midnight rendezvous presents certain undeniable risks to a woman."

She didn't want to think about risks. "I had to come. If nothing else, I had to thank you for the typewriter. It's the most perfect gift anyone's ever given me."

He shifted his weight and looked away, seeming almost embarrassed. "Yes, well, a great writer needs a typewriter worthy of her."

Daisy's breath caught. "Am I a great writer?"

"You will be."

The certainty with which he said those words made Daisy's spirits soar, but his next words sent them crashing back down.

"I haven't lived up to my part of our bargain, I fear, for I don't have a hundred pages to give you."

She swallowed hard, working to keep the disappointment she felt out of her voice, but the moment she spoke, she knew she hadn't succeeded. "If you don't have the pages, I can't kiss you," she said, sounding dismal.

But Sebastian gave an unexpected chuckle. "Strictly speaking, kissing isn't necessary. Not for men, anyway."

She didn't understand in the least what he meant. "Why are we here, then?"

"Because I had to see you." He lifted the candle as if to look at her, and though the light of the candle was dim, it was bright enough that she could see lines of weariness in his face.

"Heavens," she cried, moving closer, "you look exhausted. What have you been doing in London? You clearly haven't been sleeping. Have you been—" She stopped, unable to ask, uncertain she wanted to know.

"Living up to my reputation?" he finished for her as if reading her mind. "No."

She crossed the foyer to stand in front of him, eying his face with concern. "Sebastian, are you all right?"

"I'm afraid not." He lifted his free hand and touched her, brushing a tendril of hair back from her cheek. "I'm in the throes of a madness, petal. You're right that I haven't been sleeping, at least not very well. I can't think. I certainly can't write. That's why I don't have a hundred pages to give you. I have about ten at most." He set the candle on the silver card tray, then reached for her, cupping her cheeks. "I came back hoping that you would take pity on me and give me more of your unique inspiration."

Just his palms touching her face was enough to have her shivering with excitement, and she suddenly didn't care if he had lived up to his part of the bargain or not. He was back, and that was all that mattered. "You want to break the rules?"

"Yes, and if you have any sense, you'll tell me no and leave." When she didn't move, he bent his head closer to hers, but he did not kiss her.

"I tried to get clear of you," he said. "If I had stayed, I would not have been able to stop the inevitable from happening. But the past month has been hell, and I've given up the fight. Daisy, you have been like a ghost, haunting me. Everywhere I went, I found reminders of you. I tried to write, but without you near, I have been stymied at every turn. I became the man I was before I met you, uninspired and without purpose. I want you, and God help me, I cannot stop wanting you. That's why I came home and asked you to meet me here."

His words thrilled her to the very core. "It has been the same for me," she confessed. "That's really why I came."

"Best if you hadn't. If you stay . . ." He paused, his gaze roaming her face. "We'll become lovers, Daisy," he said, meeting her eyes again. "In every sense. No more kiss and run, no more games, no more rules." His hands tightened, his fingers curling at her nape, his lips so close to hers. "Do you understand what that means?"

She hadn't, not really. Until this moment, she hadn't appreciated just what this game they'd started was leading to. The extraordinary ways he'd touched her in the folly were as far as her imagination had gone. But now, here, in the middle of the night, alone in a house with him, she understood. This rendezvous was leading to what the ladies of Little Russell Street spoke of in whispered euphemisms, what in books was mentioned with such delicacy that one couldn't be certain if the lovers were occupying a bed together or playing piquet.

Daisy took a deep, steadying breath. "Yes, Sebastian, I understand what it means. You want—" Her voice failed her, and she strove to regain it, to say the words out loud. "You want to lie with me. Sleep with me."

His hands slid away. "It's more than being horizontal on a bed together taking a nap."

"I know that." At least, she was assuming that—although precisely what was involved, she couldn't say.

"You can't know," he said, as if reading her mind. "Not really. Not until it's happened to you. And innocence, once it's lost, is lost forever. You can't get it back."

Mrs. Morris's voice came to her, a low hiss of gossip to her friend Mrs. Inkberry about one of Daisy's fellow lodgers at Little Russell Street. *She says she's working these long hours at the shop, but I know better. The little tart is sleeping with that man.*

Daisy looked up into the handsome face of the man before her, and she did not feel in the least like a tart at the prospect of sleeping with Sebastian. She felt happy, excited, exhilarated.

"Everyone's innocence has to be lost sometime, I suppose," she said. "Sebastian, I'm twenty-eight years old, and until I met you, I'd never experienced romantic passion. I've tried to write about it, I've tried to understand it, but until you, it was impossible. As far back as I can remember, I've been surrounded by women who have cosseted me and protected me and sheltered me from anything they thought might be carnal, or stimulating, or painful, or difficult. I've been spoiled by it, and I've been smothered."

"It's been for your protection, no doubt."

"I understand that, and I'm not ungrateful for it. But every woman ought to know the thrill of romance in her life. And you said yourself that I don't have suitors because I don't know any men."

"I'm not your suitor," he said, his voice suddenly harsh. "I'm not that honorable."

She laid a hand on his cheek and smiled. "I don't need to be protected from you."

"That, petal, is what's known as famous last words. I'm the very thing they've been protecting you from."

"For someone who arranged this rendezvous, you certainly are doing your best to dissuade me from it." She rose up on her toes, bringing her mouth within a hair's breadth of his. "New rule," she whispered, sliding her arms around his neck. "The muse is allowed to provide inspirations of her choice at her discretion." With that, she pressed her lips to his.

He didn't move, but she felt a shudder run through his massive frame. "God damn us both for fools, then," he muttered against her mouth. And then, his arms came around her, and he parted her lips with his.

She closed her eyes, groaning into his mouth. How could she ever have thought to forget the pleasure of this? Why would she ever have wanted to forget it? Her arms tightened around his neck, and she tangled her fingers in the unruly strands of his hair, that hunger for his touch rising within her.

He made a rough sound in response and deepened the kiss, tasting her with his tongue, driving all the air from her lungs and making her dizzy. This kiss was not like the others—this one was raw, powerful, almost savage.

Without warning, he broke the kiss, pulling back to look at her, his breathing ragged. He started to speak, but he only got as far as her name, then he stopped and cupped her face in his hands. He kissed her again, more gently this time, a soft, slow, drugging kiss that spread aching warmth through her limbs. She felt weightless, boneless.

His hands came down and he wrapped one arm around her waist. He bent, hooking his other arm beneath her knees, and he lifted her from the floor. "Grab the candle," he told her as he turned toward the stairs with her in his arms.

Daisy obeyed, taking up the candle with one hand as she wrapped her free arm around his neck. He carried her up the stairs—another romantic thrill for her to savor—and along a corridor to a bedchamber about halfway.

As in the parlor downstairs, the wrappings had been removed from the furnishings, and when Sebastian set her on her feet, she could make out the gleaming brass of a bed to her right and the shadowy outlines of furnishings in other parts of the room. She set the candle on the piece of furniture nearest her—a marble-topped washstand.

When she turned back around, he was standing before her.

"You're sure about this?" he asked.

She smiled at the gravity of his expression. "Yes, Sebastian. I'm sure."

"All right, then." He pushed her hair back from her shoulders and smiled a little. "As beautiful as you look in candlelight, my sweet, I can't help wishing it was day. I love seeing the sunlight on your hair."

"A fact which never ceases to amaze me," she whispered and reached out to touch his chest. The feel of his hard muscles beneath her palms stirred fires within her, fires that she'd never known existed until four weeks ago. The fires of arousal.

He did not move, but she could feel his gaze on her face as she began to unbutton his shirt. Her hands were shaking with anticipation, excitement, and agonizing uncertainty, but when he moved as if to do it for her, she shook her head. "No, I want to do it."

"Very well." He assisted her by slipping the straps of his braces off his shoulders, unfastening his cuffs and pulling his shirttails from the waistband of his trousers.

When all the buttons were undone, she parted the edges and slipped the shirt from his shoulders. It fell behind him and she studied his chest in the glow of the candle, fascinated. She lifted one hand to touch him. "You're beautiful," she said in wonderment. "Like a statue."

He didn't move as she explored his powerful chest and arms, as her fingers traced lines of muscle and sinew, circled the dark flat disks of his nipples and traveled down to the edge of his trousers.

That was where he stopped her. "My turn," he said, grasping her wrists and gently shoving her hands aside, then he began undressing her as he had that afternoon in the folly. His fingers worked swiftly, slipping buttons free in a far more efficient fashion than her shaking hands had unfastened his shirt. He unbuttoned her corset cover just as quickly and as he slid both garments off her shoulders, he leaned forward, pressing kisses to the bare skin he had exposed.

Daisy drew a sharp breath, tilting her head back. No story in a book, this. This was real. As she felt his lips trace a line along her collarbone, her heart began to beat with such force, she heard its thud in her ears. Her body ached for his kiss and his touch, and she wanted him to do all the things he'd done to her that afternoon in the folly, but she couldn't seem to speak, couldn't bring herself to say that. She lowered her chin to look into his face, and wordless, she reached for his hand, lifted it in her own, and pressed it to her breast.

Sebastian opened his hand over her, and though the layers of her corset and chemise separated his skin from hers, she could feel the warmth of his hand against her breast. Desire began spreading through her body—she recognized it this time, appreciated just what it was. Like a wave of warm honey, desire spread over her as he shaped and cradled her breasts against his palms. Slowly, it deepened, heightened, until she couldn't stand it anymore.

She worked her hands between his, thinking to unfasten the hooks of her corset, but again he grasped her wrists and pulled her hands away. "I'm enjoying this, if you please," he told her with mock sternness. "Don't spoil my fun."

"Well, you might have your fun a bit more quickly, Sebastian," she said with a hint of exasperation.

He laughed softly under his breath. "I want you to enjoy this night as well," he told her, pressing a kiss to her nose. "I've no intention of hurrying, so cease this impatience. To be done properly, lovemaking ought to be done slowly." But even as he spoke, he was conceding to her wishes by freeing the hooks of her corset. "Lift your arms," he said as he dropped her corset to the floor.

She complied, and he grasped the hem of her chemise. He pulled the garment up her body and over her head, and when he did, Daisy was seized by an unexpected wave of shyness. At the realization that she was now naked from the waist up, her earlier desire began slipping away like an image in the mist, and she ducked her head, but the sight of her breasts, bare and dotted with freckles, only made her feel even more vulnerable than before, vulnerable in a way she hadn't a moment earlier. Suddenly she wanted to cover herself back up.

But when she looked at Sebastian again, his mouth was curved in that half smile that she loved. "You're so lovely," he murmured, his fingertips brushing her nipples, and Daisy's sudden shyness dissolved away. For the first time in her life, she believed she might truly be pretty after all.

He bent his head, and Daisy thought he was going to kiss her, but his lips merely brushed hers and then he moved his head lower. When he touched his lips to her breast, a moan broke from her, and she felt her knees giving way again. Frantically, she reached behind her, groping for the brass footboard of the bed to help her stay on her feet.

He followed her move, taking a step forward. He lifted his hand to cup her breast, and this time, his warm, smooth skin touched her with no layers of fabric between. He bent his head to her other breast again, but he didn't merely kiss her there this time. Instead, his lips parted and he took her nipple into his mouth. Sharp sensation speared her, and she gasped, arching toward him as her hands tightened on the footboard behind her.

He pulled her nipple gently with his lips, rolled it playfully against his tongue, toying with her. She shivered and moaned, clinging to the bed as hunger and need began to claw at her. It was the same need that she'd felt in the folly, but stronger this time, and more powerful because she knew what it meant, what it would lead to.

Her body arched toward him, wanting more, and as her hips brushed against his thigh, the contact sent shafts of pleasure through her body.

It seemed to spark something in him as well. He fumbled for the button of her skirt, found it, and unfastened it. The ties of her petticoat he freed as well, then he tugged both garments downward, sinking to his knees as he did so. Her skirts were disentangled from beneath her feet, and a moment later, he was yanking off her boots and tossing them over his shoulder.

"What happened to taking things slowly?" she teased, but her question ended in a startled gasp as his fingers slid beneath the hem of her knickers and inside her stockings to caress the backs of her knees. The contact sent delicious tingles up and down her legs. "What," she managed to add in a strangled whisper, "happened to patience?"

"It's disappearing fast, I'm afraid," he answered, his voice as ragged as hers as he unfastened her garters. He slid off her stockings, then reached up and untied her knickers. As the silky nainsook fabric slid down her legs, Daisy realized he was baring her entire body to his gaze. Never had she been fully unclothed in front of another person, and yet she could not drum up her former embarrassment. She was beyond that now.

She touched a hand to his hair, drew one thick lock through her fingers, then brushed it back. A wave of tenderness came over her in that moment, a fierce, sweet tenderness she'd never felt before. When he leaned forward and kissed her stomach, a hot, wet kiss against her navel, liquid heat pooled in her midsection and radiated outward from that kiss to every part of her body. Heavens, she thought in wonder as she gazed down at him, was this what lovers did?

She felt his palm glide up her bare thigh, and her tenderness gave way to something far more carnal, far more greedy. She leaned back with a moan of accord, knowing what was to come, welcoming it.

The brass felt cool against her backside, but his touch scorching hot as he touched her in the same place he had before. And just as before, the caress sent shards of indescribable pleasure through her.

He knew that, he knew what she felt and what she wanted, and he seemed to take great delight in tormenting her with that knowledge. "You like that, don't you?" he murmured against her stomach. "Don't you, petal?"

"Hmm, hmm," was the only reply she could manage, and she nodded frantically, just in case he didn't understand that her inarticulate answer was affirmative. Somehow, his teasing words and his hot breath against her stomach made the sensations even more intense, the pleasure even more acute. Her hips moved, sliding against his hand as that hungry, desperate need took over, rising within her, carrying her toward the same luscious peak she'd felt before.

He dipped a bit lower, his tongue gliding down her abdomen, and something within her guessed his intent. "Oh, no!" she gasped, shocked, her fingers clenching silky strands of hair. But he was undeterred, and when he kissed her most intimate place, something seemed to ignite within her, and her protests gave way to a wholly opposite reaction.

"Yes, oh, yes!" she cried, shocked by the sound of her own voice ringing out with such wanton abandonment. The pleasure of this carnal kiss was indescribable; it washed over her in waves, each more intense, more exquisite than the last, coming again and again, until she was beyond words, until she could only breathe in quick, hard pants and her body was jerking frantically against his mouth, until at last, she collapsed, all her strength dissolving into sweet oblivion.

He rose, catching her before she sank to her knees,

wrapping an arm around her. Once again he lifted her in his arms, and carried her around to the side of the bed, where he laid her down.

He stood over her, and with the candle on the washstand directly behind him, his body was only a silhouette against the dim glow as he began to undress, his broad frame a dark wall in front of her as he slid his shirt off his shoulders. With the draperies drawn at the windows blocking out the moonlight, she couldn't even see his face, and when she heard his boots hit the floor, she felt a sudden throb of doubt.

"Sebastian?" she whispered as he slid his trousers down his hips.

The sudden misgiving in her voice did not escape him, and he hastily removed his linen and joined her on the bed. "It's all right," he said, caressing her cheek with one hand as with the other, he reached down to the floor beneath the bed and found the silk envelope he'd placed there before her arrival. Pressing a kiss to her lips, he slipped a condom free of the envelope, but though his cock was rock hard and his body ached for surcease, he didn't put the condom on. Not yet. There were other things he needed to do first.

He rather shared Daisy's apprehension. He'd never bedded a virgin, but he was fairly certain most of them did not find their first time a transcendent experience. He wanted Daisy's first time to be different.

Kissing her and murmuring words of reassurance,

he kept the condom in one hand as he slid the other between her thighs. She was wet and ready, but he held back, sliding his finger up and down the warm, silken flesh of her opening, savoring her soft cries and the undulating push of her hips against his hand as he pleasured her a second time.

There was, however, only so much restraint a man could bear, and though he relished her second climax as much as he had her first, by the time it came, his own body was screaming for release.

He withdrew his hand, slid the condom over his shaft, and moved on top of her, easing his larger frame between her thighs. Even through the thin layer of vulcanized rubber, the brush of her feminine opening against the tip of his penis was pure torture, but he strove to wait one moment more.

"Daisy," he said, his voice a harsh whisper against her ear, "it's time for me to be inside you. Do you understand?" He didn't wait for her to answer, but quickly went on, "I don't want to hurt you, but I can't wait any longer."

"Sebastian?" Her voice held a quiver of panic as he began to enter her, and her hips bucked as if to unseat him. He slanted his mouth over hers, kissed her hard, and thrust deep.

The sound of her pain was smothered by his mouth, but her arms wrapped tight around his neck and her body went rigid beneath his. She tore her lips from his with a sob, and buried her face against his neck. He stilled, fighting the need that was fast overtaking him. "I'm sorry, petal," he managed through clenched teeth, "but you'll be all right. I promise."

Even as he spoke, he could feel the tension in her body easing. Hoping her pain was easing as well, he began to move inside her. As he did, he strove to be tender, touching her breasts, kissing her face, and murmuring words to arouse her, but the pleasure of her tight sheath around him, the convulsive clench of her muscles pulling him deeper, was irresistible, and Sebastian lost his head.

He increased the pace, each thrust harder, deeper, faster than the one before, as he drove toward climax, and when he went over the edge, everything within him shattered in a shower of white-hot sparks and settled into pure, blissful oblivion.

Chapter 17

A human being has a natural desire to have more of a good thing than he needs.
Mark Twain

She'd had no idea. If anyone had ever told her that sleeping with a man, lying with him, was like this, she'd never have believed it.

Sebastian's body gave a final shudder, then eased down onto her. He felt solidly heavy on top of her, but not uncomfortably so. He was still . . . inside of her, joined with her in that extraordinary way.

The pain, thankfully, had subsided, leaving only the slightest sensation of soreness, rather like a parched throat or chapped lips. Physically, Daisy could only conclude that she was unharmed. Emotionally, however, she felt utterly at sixes and sevens. This . . . coupling had been the most singular and astonishing moment of her life.

It had been wonderful at first, even more wonderful than their afternoon in the folly, especially when he had kissed her and stroked her and called her lovely. As she had felt before, there had been a rising, thickening pleasure at his touch, followed by those euphoric explosions. Even now, just thinking about that part stirred and aroused her. But the part when he'd pressed into her, the stinging pain of his invasion had smothered the previous sweet sensations as effectively as a bucket of water smothered a fire.

He'd tried to warn her, prepare her, but she doubted any words could prepare one for this sort of thing.

His breathing was warm and quick against her temple. She could feel his arms beneath her, cradling her. And when he pressed a kiss to her hair and breathed her name, she felt a fierce and sudden wave of tenderness wash over her. She reached up, wrapping her arms around him. She began to caress him, running her palms over the smooth, hard muscles of his back, relishing this sweet, new feeling. The pain receded to insignificance.

He stirred, elevating his body slightly above her so that he could look into her face. "Are you all right?" he asked, repositioning his body with his weight on his forearms.

"I think so." She drew a deep breath. "Is it always . . . like this?"

Something in her question or perhaps in the tone of

her voice as she'd asked it brought an expression of dismay to his face. "No, Daisy, no," he answered, pulling one arm from beneath her to touch her face. "It won't hurt again, I swear to you. It's only the first time that hurts."

"That's a bit reassuring," she murmured, and clenched her muscles around him, again amazed at the strange sensation of being joined with another person in such a literal way. "No one ever told me about any of this. I mean, I've seen animals—" She broke off and shook her head. "But I was certain it must be different for *people*."

"Alas, no. But if it's any comfort to you, very few men are told about this either. I learned when some upperclassmen at Eton took me to a brothel. I was fifteen. She had enormous breasts and bad breath. I was quite disillusioned by the experience."

Daisy couldn't help laughing a bit at that.

He laughed with her, his perfect white teeth flashing in the dark like a pirate. He pressed a kiss to her mouth, then he shifted his weight. "I must be getting heavy," he murmured, and she felt his hand slide between their bodies as he lifted himself free of her. He rolled away from her and rose from the bed, one fist closed as if he was concealing something in it.

"What's in your hand?" she asked, curious.

"I'll explain later." Leaning down, he kissed her nose. "I'll be right back." He left the room, and when he returned a few moments later, whatever had been in his fist was gone. Instead, he carried a bowl of water and a rag. He sat on the edge of the bed and placed the bowl on the floor.

"What are you doing?" she asked as she watched him dip the rag in the water and wring it out. He didn't answer, but when he nudged her legs apart, she saw dark smears of blood on her thighs. No wonder she'd felt pain, she thought, for she knew it wasn't the start of her monthly. He knew it, too, she realized, watching him as he gently wiped away the blood.

"I'm sorry," he told her. "I know it hurt."

"A little," she admitted. "It isn't—" She broke off, and gave a sigh. "It isn't very romantic, is it?" she said a bit wistfully.

"Not the first time, no." He stopped, his fist tightening around the rag. "I wish it could have been. For you, petal, I wish it could have been."

He resumed his task, and as she watched him, Daisy felt that fierce, sweet tenderness welling up within her again, a bubble of emotion that pressed up, up, up against her chest, making her heart ache with joy, and she realized suddenly what it was she felt.

"I love you," she blurted out.

His hand stilled, and she felt a throb of fear, though she didn't know what, precisely, she was afraid of. It seemed an eternity before he looked at her, and when he did, her fear ebbed away, for he was smiling a little.

"So, you don't think coupling is romantic, do you?" he asked, dropping the rag back into the bowl on the floor. He leaned over her. "Why don't I show you how wrong you are, hmm?"

A tiny voice at the back of her mind whispered to her, pointing out what he hadn't said, but when his lips touched hers, Daisy's moment of misgiving vanished as if it had never been there at all.

Still kissing her, he eased his body down beside hers, his hand drifting to her breast. He began to caress her, and desire flickered to life inside her. "Is this romantic?" he asked as his palm covered her breast.

Daisy stirred, her desire deepening. "I'm not sure," she demurred, trying to sound indifferent though she suspected her smile rather ruined the effect.

"Not sure?" He laughed, a low, throaty chuckle. "Perhaps you prefer this?" He began to toy with her nipple, rolling it gently between his fingers.

Her smile vanished, and she had to press her lips tight together to smother her moan of pleasure. "It feels nice," she said when she could manage to speak. "But romantic?" She considered, then shook her head. "No, I don't think so."

"Nice?" he echoed, sounding a bit nettled. "Hmm, I can see I have some work to do." His hand slid down, and his lips grazed her nipple. This time, she could not stop the moan that came from her throat, and she arched toward him, pretenses of indifference forgotten in the heat of these carnal kisses. When he pulled back, her moan became a plea.

He relented at once. His mouth opened over her breast, and she shivered, closing her eyes against the shameful excitement that ran through her as he took her nipple into his mouth.

He suckled her, his teeth and tongue closing over her nipple, teasing her, toying with her, drawing sensation from the very core of her. Again, she arched upward, and this time, he did not pull back. Instead, he suckled harder, and Daisy's excitement spread, grew deeper and hotter. Her hips stirred restlessly.

As if she had given him a signal, his fingertips danced lightly down her stomach—another tease—and she couldn't help the gasp of accord that tore from her throat. "Yes, oh, yes!"

This time, however, he did not give her what she wanted. Instead, he flattened his palm against her stomach with the tips of his fingers barely brushing the curls at the apex of her thighs.

"Sebastian," she pleaded.

"Hmm?" He lifted his head from her breast. "Yes?" His fingers stirred, but his hand did not move one bit lower. "Was there something you wanted?"

"Yes, yes," she panted, arching her hips up. "Touch me."

"But would that be romantic?"

She gave a frantic nod, for a nod was all she could manage between her panting breaths.

He eased his hand down between her legs, then slid his fingertip back up along the crease of her opening, and then, much to her frustration, he pulled his hand away.

"Sebastian!"

"Patience, my sweet." His hand glided upward, then slid along her hip, nudging gently as his other hand slid beneath her. "Roll onto your side," he ordered, moving her as he spoke.

She obeyed, and within moments, he was positioning himself behind her. His hard penis pushed between her legs at the curve of her bum, but he did not enter her. Instead, he began to move his hips, using the hard and aroused part of himself to arouse her as well.

As his penis slid back and forth along her opening from behind, he caressed her in front, murmuring things in her ear that heightened her arousal in the most delicious way.

"Do you like this?" he asked, rolling her nipple between his fingers. When she nodded, his hand drifted down over her stomach, brushed the curls at the apex of her thighs, and finally, eased between, parting her.

"And this?" He eased his finger into her opening, then back out, then back in deeper. "This doesn't hurt, does it?"

"N . . . n . . . no," she somehow managed to answer.

"It feels good?" Once again, his finger slid out of her opening, then along the crease of her sex to the nub at the top that seemed to be the center of all her sensations. "What about this?"

"Yes, yes. Oh, yes." Her body moved with the rhythm of his hand, a helpless slave to the sensations he was evoking. Her hips jerked, striving toward what she now knew would come. She felt it in the rising, thickening pleasure.

"Roll onto your stomach," he said, his own breathing ragged against her ear. As she obeyed, he slid his arm beneath her, lifting her hips and positioning her on her knees. "Open your legs," he ordered as he moved behind her. "I'm coming inside you now."

With that brief warning, he cupped her mound with his hand and pushed hard with his hips. She cried out as she felt his hard, hot shaft enter her, but it was a cry of surprise, for she felt no pain, only a wave of pure bliss. He began to move, caressing her from the front as he thrust into her from behind. Daisy pressed her hot cheek against the pillow, but she could not smother her own frantic, inarticulate sobs of pleasure. Her body pulsed with wave after wave of it, again and again, and yet again, until at last she was sated, and so was he. Slowly, he eased her down, moving with her, rolling them both to the side.

They lay there, cradled like two spoons in a drawer,

for a long time, the only sounds his breathing and hers, harsh, panting breaths that mingled in the quiet room, easing slowly back to normal.

"Better?" he asked at last, still inside her, his arms around her waist, his hand caressing her stomach.

She nodded. "Yes, but . . ." She paused, twisting her head to give him a doubtful look over her shoulder. "Sebastian?"

"Yes, petal?"

"I still don't think it's very romantic."

It wasn't romantic at all, but he couldn't bear to tell her that. Sebastian stared at his typewriter, unable to concentrate. He couldn't see the page before him; all he could see was her face, looking at him last night with all that adoration shining in her eyes. Her voice, so sincere, kept echoing in his ears, shouting past the rapid *rat-tat* of her new typewriting machine.

I love you.

He lifted his gaze to her, but unlike him, she seemed in a frame of mind to work this morning. She seemed happy with the Crandall, and she was quite skilled with it, for she was writing at her usual breakneck speed. He studied her face, remembering the radiance in it last night—the aftereffects of her first sexual experience. She'd looked utterly beautiful, with her hair all tumbled down around her shoulders like liquid fire in the candlelight.

I love you.

He tore his gaze away. He knew she didn't love him, not really. He knew what she felt wasn't anything deeper than infatuation and desire and the afterglow of lovemaking. And yet, for a moment, for one brief, shining moment, he'd wanted to believe what she felt for him was deeper than that. He'd looked into her shining eyes, and he'd wanted to believe that what she felt for him was real, that the way she saw him now was the way she'd see him forever. That love like that could last, that it could endure the inevitable disillusionments that came when passions cooled and reality set in.

I love you.

How many women had he said those words to in his life? Ten, perhaps more. But how many times had it been true? He didn't know. It had always *felt* true; every time he'd declared his love to a woman, he'd believed it to be true. But then, when the affair fell apart, he always came to understand it hadn't really been true after all. He couldn't pinpoint which love affair, which woman, had finally made him stop believing in love altogether, but he supposed it didn't matter. He had no romantic illusions left. In fact, he had no illusions left about anything.

Sebastian leaned back in his chair with a sigh, staring at the ceiling. *God*, he thought wearily, *when did I become such a cynical bastard?*

"Is something wrong?"

"Hmm?" Sebastian came out of his reverie with a start, realizing she had stopped typing and was watching him.

"No," he lied. "Nothing's wrong. Why do you ask?"

"You've been staring at your typewriter for at least an hour, but you haven't written a thing." She smiled, her face lit again with that radiant glow. "Having trouble concentrating this morning?"

It hurt to look at her and see that smile. She didn't understand, he thought with a hint of panic. She didn't understand that he was the same man he'd been before, but that for her, last night had changed everything. She was no longer innocent. She thought this was love, and when she found out it wasn't, the knowledge would break her heart.

He'd known that all along, known it ever since the day when she'd proposed exchanging kisses for pages. But he'd done it anyway, deliberately ratcheting up the stakes, knowing the result, knowing she hadn't a clue. And now, heaven bless her, the lamb was gazing at him as if he were king of the earth. Guilt slid through him, and he once again forced his gaze away, but he could feel her adoring gaze on him, and he knew he had to say something.

"I'm just . . . umm . . ." He paused and gave a cough, thinking hard. "I'm considering the . . . um . . . plot in light of . . . in light of . . ." Desperate, he reached for her revision letter and glanced at it, "The ending," he said, relieved to have a subject to discuss. "I'm reaching the halfway point, and I must start plotting out the ending. I'm rather at a loss."

"You'll work through it," she said with confidence. "You'll find a way."

With his abysmal inability to write for the past three years, he wondered how anyone could be so confident in his ability. He certainly wasn't.

"Perhaps," he allowed, "but I'm not sure what I come up with will satisfy you. After all, you are my staunchest critic."

"Whatever you write will be wonderful, I'm sure."

He was on the pedestal already, he realized with dismay. She'd never been inclined to put him there before. The feisty, impudent woman who loved to set him straight was giving way to a different sort—a woman who looked at everything he did and said in the most favorable light, who gave him more credit than he deserved, and who could no longer see his most glaring flaws.

How long before he fell off that pedestal? How long before he saw disillusionment in her eyes, and he wasn't wonderful anymore?

"Don't," he said with sudden savagery. "Don't gush, for the love of God!"

He looked at her, expecting to see hurt. But no, she was still smiling, looking at him with patient gravity. "Would you like to discuss your problem?" she asked.

He sighed and fell back in his chair. Talking about the book, he supposed, would at least be a productive use of his time. "You hate my ending."

"You're exaggerating. I don't hate it."

He leaned forward, tapping the appropriate paragraph of the letter on the desk with his finger as he read from it. "'The ending is unsatisfying, disappointing, even infuriating,'" he quoted, then he looked up. "That sounds like hate to me."

She made a grimace. "Did I really say that?" Without waiting for an answer, she rose from her seat and circled his desk to read her words over his shoulder. "Hmm," she murmured when she'd finished, "I was a bit harsh, wasn't I?"

"Just a bit, yes, but that's fine. I can take it on the chin. The problem is that I don't understand why you dislike it so much."

Daisy seemed surprised by that. "Amelie abandons him," she said as if that explained everything.

Sebastian remained unenlightened. "Yes, of course. Why is that a problem?"

"Why?" she echoed, sounding amazed he could even ask. "Because it's a crushing disappointment! When I read the end, it was so depressing, I didn't know whether to hurl the manuscript across the room or go leap off a bridge."

"Depressing?" His hand tightened around the letter, crumpling it. "Well, what were you hoping for?" he asked before he could stop himself. "True love and happy ever after?"

"Yes, damn it all, I was! I followed you through nearly five hundred pages of trials, tribulations, pain, and desire, and for what? For a heroine who goes off alone, being noble, giving up the man she loves because she's married and she can't bear to create a scandal for Samuel? Aren't you the one who's always saying people aren't that self-sacrificing?"

"But she has to abandon him."

Daisy folded her arms, leaned her hip against his desk, and set her jaw. "Why?"

That took him back, rather. "Well, because . . . because . . ." He paused, thinking how to explain. "Samuel has to learn that one can go on. That love isn't everything."

Daisy looked at him as if appalled. "But love *is* everything!"

He took a deep breath, tilted his chair back on two legs to look at her, and forced himself to say it. "I know women always want to think that, but it isn't true. There are other things in life, things more important than love."

She didn't seem impressed. "I can't think of any."

"Spoken by someone who's never been in love before."

The words were out of his mouth before he'd had the sense to stop them. He watched her stiffen. "Don't make fun of me."

Her hurt shimmered through him like a physical blow, and he couldn't bear it. He raked a hand through his hair with a heavy sigh. "I'm not making fun of you, petal," he said, thinking to explain, to let her down gently. "But I've been in love, and it doesn't last. And when it's over, it's hell for a while. And then one discovers that life goes on. Eventually, one falls in love again. This pattern repeats itself until one is too jaded to believe in it anymore, or too old for all the upheaval."

"How terribly depressing."

"Life is depressing a lot of the time."

"Which is why your book shouldn't be. No, listen to me," she added as he groaned and brought the chair back to the floor with a thud. "You're creating something wonderful here, a beautiful, moving love story." She pressed a hand to her heart. "Despite the flaws in the book, it was good because Samuel and Amelie seem real to me. I care about them as if they were my own family. When they suffer, I suffer. At the end, I want to put the book down knowing that these two people are going to spend their lives together, in love and happy."

"And all's right with the world?"

She lifted her chin a notch and that stubborn glint came into her eye, reminding him of the day they'd first met. "I like happy endings."

His artistic soul, colored no doubt by his cynical nature and the unhappy endings of his own love affairs, rebelled. "It's too neat," he complained. "It's too tidy, too pretty . . . too wrapped up with a ribbon and a bow and placed under the tree for Christmas. I can't write it."

She made a sound of impatience. "For heaven's sake, Sebastian, some people do fall in love and end up happy for life! It does happen, you know."

No, it doesn't.

The words hovered on his tongue, but he bit them back. He couldn't say that love's destiny was to die like everything else. He just couldn't say it. Not to her. He'd fall off the pedestal soon enough. It didn't have to be today.

He reached for her instead. "You've really thrown a spanner in the works with that one, you know," he murmured.

She smiled, cupping his face in her hands, her aggravation with him fading away at once. "How?"

"I've never written a happy ending before." His hand slid to her hip, and if there had been any doubt in his mind that he was an utter cad, it was gone now. He had to be a cad, because he'd just spent the entire morning thinking of all the reasons he should end this, and all the ways he was setting her up for heartbreak, and yet, the moment he touched her, any thought of ending their affair became unbearable. "To write it, I fear I'm going to need heaps of inspiration."

She cut him off by pressing two fingers to his mouth. "Oh, no, you don't," she said, laughing, and shoved his hand away from her hip. "No kisses for you. I've been softhearted enough as it is. You don't receive another kiss until I receive one hundred more pages of revised manuscript."

Undeterred, he kissed her fingers, and she pulled her hand down with a reproving look. "One hundred pages," she repeated firmly, then turned and started back toward her own desk.

He wrapped an arm around her waist and pulled her down to him. She laughed and started to rise, but he pulled her down again, turning her to sit across his lap, ignoring her indignant protests about playing the game fairly. "I'll write the hundred pages," he promised, "but I want a kiss now."

She shook her head, but even as she did so, she was pressing her lips together to stop her laughter from bubbling out. "No," she said, but not quite so firmly as before.

His hand slid up her back, sank into the coil of her hair. "C'mon, Daisy," he murmured and tilted her head back. "Just one."

"No." But her eyes closed and her lips parted even as spoke. "You always want more than one. You're greedy."

"Well, yes," he agreed and kissed her before she could make any more protests.

As always, she was luscious, her lips warm and soft, her kiss as heady and potent as any drug. He slid his free hand to her breast, and he closed his eyes, remembering the night before, feeling the thick heaviness of lust begin to overtake him.

He wasn't sure what made him open his eyes—a sound, the soft sound of a gasp, he fancied. His lips still locked with Daisy's, his hand still in her hair, he glanced up, and found Mathilda standing in the doorway, hand on the knob as if she'd just come in, an expression of utter shock on her face.

Their eyes met, and Sebastian felt her condemnation hit him with the force of a physical blow. She said nothing, however. Without a word, without a sound, she stepped backward out of the room and closed the door.

Chapter 18

Love is a misunderstanding between two friends.
Oscar Wilde

Mathilda wasted no time. Sebastian was dressing for dinner when the note from her arrived on a salver, brought by one of the footmen.

There was no need to read it, for he could already guess the contents, but he opened it anyway, and when he did, he found that the few lines written there confirmed his intuition. Lady Mathilda requested he join her in her private sitting room for a glass of Madeira before dinner.

The formality of the request did not escape him, and as Sebastian set the note aside, an image of his aunt's shocked face and the condemnation in her eyes came back with painful force. He'd lived away for so long, avoiding the condemnation of the people whose good opinion mattered to him, and the realization that he'd lost the good opinion that had always mattered most sickened him.

Still, he had to face his aunt some time. It might as well be now. He went to her boudoir at the requested time.

She reached for a crystal decanter as he came in. "Close the door, Avermore," she said as she poured Madeira into two glasses.

The use of his title was not a good sign. Nor was the fact that she did not invite him to sit down. She also remained standing, and she did not meet his gaze as she handed him his glass of Madeira. He knew he was about to be raked over the coals good and proper.

Surprisingly, however, she did not blister him with a scathing storm of criticism. Instead, it was herself she condemned. "I have never thought myself to be exceptionally dense," she said, staring meditatively into her glass, the chiffon draperies of the open balcony door behind her fluttering in the September breeze. "But today, I have been given cause to reassess my own character. All these weeks, I thought you and Miss Merrick were working in that library."

"We have been working."

Nothing in the world, he supposed, could make a grown man feel more like a fool than the reproving glance of a maiden aunt.

"I thought," she went on, "that having the library

doors closed was a wholly innocent thing—designed to allow two authors to write their prose undisturbed by the petty annoyances of the household." She gave a self-condemning laugh. "Now I see how stupid I have been. I'm no green girl. I should have known—a man and a woman thrown together all the day long with no one watching. I berate myself most bitterly for my obtuseness."

"It was just a kiss," he said, thankful that kiss was the only thing of which Mathilda could be aware. "Harmless enough, I dare say."

"Harmless?" Her gaze raked over him with disdain. "I thought I could trust you to behave like a gentleman."

Her words stung like a whiplash, flaying him with his own guilty conscience. Sebastian downed his Madeira in one swallow, grimacing at the sweetness. "Aunt," he began, but she cut him off.

"I heard about your exploits with women in Italy, Avermore, but I tried not to believe it. I believed you to be a better man than the scandal sheets had painted you. I couldn't bear to think the boy I had raised to have a proper consideration and regard for women could develop such a wild reputation, but today, I have been shown it is the scandal sheets which are correct, and I am the one who has been mistaken in regard to your character."

There was no way to explain Italy. "I'm not the same man I was. I've changed in the past three years—"

"Are you in love with the girl? Do you intend to marry her?"

The abrupt questions came out of nowhere, catching him by surprise. He stared at Mathilda, appalled. "God, no."

That blunt, emphatic answer made both of them wince.

Mathilda sank into a petit point chair as if her worst fears were now confirmed. "When Miss Merrick came here at Marlowe's request, I agreed to chaperoning her without a second thought, for despite your exploits with courtesans and married ladies, it never occurred to me that you would attempt a dalliance with an unmarried woman of respectable family in your own house under your own roof."

"I'm not dallying with the girl!"

"Indeed? What would you call it? You don't love her, you don't intend to marry her, yet I find her sitting on your lap. What were you doing? Discussing the next turn of your plot?"

Sebastian rubbed a hand over his face with a sigh. He knew he would have to attempt an explanation, but he was not sure there was one. "Mathilda, this is not merely a dalliance. For the first time in years, I'm writing again, and it's because of her. She has a way of inspiring me."

"Yes, I saw with my own eyes how inspired you were."

He made a sound of impatience. "It's not like that. It started out as a game, but—"

He stopped, but it was too late.

Mathilda was staring at him in horror. "A game? A young woman's virtue is not a game, Avermore! Have you compromised her?"

It occurred to him that protecting Daisy's virtue now was rather like locking the stable after the horses had been stolen, but there was nothing for it. "Of course not," he said, looking his beloved aunt straight in the eye as he gave her the lie. Too late, he remembered he'd never been able to lie to Mathilda.

Her disdainful expression deepened into contempt. "So you have. You have turned a respectable young woman into a strumpet."

That damnable guilt nudged him again, and he looked away, pressing his lips together.

"At least we can be grateful I am the only person who saw the pair of you this afternoon. Do the servants know? Never mind, servants always know, but I can manage them. If anyone else had seen you, the fat would be in the fire." She set aside her glass and rose, suddenly resolute, as if matters were now decided to her satisfaction. "If the girl proves to be with child as a result of this liaison, Avermore, you'll have to provide for it, and for her. If that happens, God knows what Marlowe will do. He'll probably want your head. Miss Merrick is a friend of his wife." She started for the door. "I will send her home to her sister at once, though what explanation I'll offer—"

"No!" Everything in Sebastian rebelled against that notion. "She isn't going home. She isn't going anywhere."

Mathilda stopped and turned to him in surprise. "I beg your pardon?"

The very idea of writing without her, of not having her near, sent panic coursing through his veins. "She can't go. Not yet. I have to finish the book."

"The book?" Mathilda was staring at him in disbelief.

"This book is good, Aunt," he said, desperate. "Damn good, the best thing I've written in a decade. I can't explain it, but she's the reason for that. She's given me back my purpose in life. I need her here. I must finish this book, and I can't finish it without her."

"Damn your book, sir!" his aunt interrupted, appalled. "That young woman has been under my supervision. I agreed to act as her chaperone, and when I did, I took on the sacred obligation to watch over her. It sickens me that I have so failed in my duty, that I have been so blinded by my affection for you that I have allowed a respectable young woman to be transformed into a strumpet under my very nose."

"She is not a strumpet!" he shouted, enraged by the description.

"She is what you have made her."

Sebastian clamped down on the rage, panic and guilt that were warring within him. "She is not leaving," he said through clenched teeth. He faced his aunt, ruthless in his determination. "I am the master of this house, and that girl isn't going anywhere. If the situation offends your delicate sensibilities, madam, you may move yourself to the summerhouse."

Mathilda was looking at him as if he were the lowest sort of cur imaginable, but he could not give Daisy up. Not yet, not now, not when he needed her so much.

Turning on his heel, he walked out of Mathilda's sitting room, slamming the door behind him.

God, no.

Sebastian's words echoed in her head like the beat of a kettledrum, the appalled sound of his voice tearing her heart apart. Daisy stared up at the balcony's open French windows, the conversation she'd overheard still echoing through her mind, and she realized she would always remember this particular view. The intricate ironwork of the balcony rail, the pale, straw color of the chiffon draperies, the dark red geraniums in their terra-cotta pots.

God, no.

In the wake of those words, the enchantment of last night came rushing back as if to mock her, and she realized she'd known the moment she'd told him she loved him that he didn't love her in return. She'd known it, felt it, and denied it. But there was no denying it now, and she wished she had been the last one down to dinner instead of the first, that she hadn't decided to take a stroll in the gardens while she waited, that curiosity hadn't impelled her to linger beneath the open window where she'd overheard her name mentioned. But wishes were pointless now.

Pain hit her squarely in the chest, then spread outward in waves that made her feel sick. She was a strumpet, she realized as Mathilda's words about a child echoed through her head, making her feel even more nauseous than before. She might be carrying a baby.

She thought of Mrs. Morris whispering to Mrs. Inkberry about strumpets who slept with men. Now she understood why. *Lucy, Lucy,* she thought with a hint of hysteria, *why didn't you tell me cabbage patches were a lie?*

Daisy pressed a hand to her mouth, stifling the sobs that rose up inside her, sobs of panic and fear. What would she do? If there was a baby, how would she ever face Lucy? Mrs. Morris? All her friends at Little Russell Street? She would be dispatched to the country for confinement, hidden away in shame.

She had probably ruined her life.

And for what? For a man who did not love her, who didn't want to marry her, who wanted only to finish his book. That was what mattered to him, not her. Never had she felt like a bigger fool.

Hand pressed to her mouth to stifle her sobs, she jumped to her feet. She raced along the side of the house and reentered the library, her only thought to be gone from here as soon as possible. She couldn't face him or his aunt. She couldn't. It would be too humiliating.

Inside the library, she scanned bookshelves in desperation, knowing there was a current Bradshaw along there somewhere. But her wits were so scattered, she couldn't remember quite where it was, and in her panic, it took her some minutes to find it.

With hands that shook, she opened it, and blinking back tears, she tried to read the railway schedule. There were two trains a week from Bovey Tracey to Exeter, she noted, but the next one wasn't for two days. There were, however, plenty of trains from Torquay, including one tomorrow, if she could arrive there in time to make it.

Daisy dropped the Bradshaw, and tugged the bell pull. She pulled a handkerchief from her pocket, dabbed at her eyes, and strove to regain her composure as she waited for a servant to appear.

A few moments later, one of the footmen entered the library, and Daisy shoved her handkerchief back in her pocket. "Have Miss Allyson pack my things at once, and fetch a carriage to take me to Torquay," she ordered, and even as the words came from her lips, she was remembering Mathilda's words about the servants always knowing. She felt her face turning scarlet.

Strumpet.

In desperation, she snatched up the letter from her sister that had come in the afternoon post and waved it in the air, adding, "I have received news which impels me to return to London immediately. Haste is vital."

With that, she turned toward the window. Behind her, she heard the footman depart, and she drew deep breaths, trying to steady her nerves.

It seemed like hours to Daisy before her trunk was brought downstairs, but in reality, it was only seventeen minutes. She knew this because she stood in the foyer, watching the enormous grandfather clock tick away each and every minute.

Dread seemed to make the time crawl by. Dread that at any moment, Lady Mathilda or, even worse, Sebastian, would appear. When her things had been loaded and the footman informed her that the carriage was ready to depart, Daisy felt an overwhelming relief. She would escape, it seemed, slipping away quietly without any fuss.

Her relief, however, was short-lived. She hadn't even stepped through the front door when an unmistakably male, very irate voice sounded behind her.

"Where are you going?"

Daisy halted, that feeling of dread returning to settle in her stomach like a stone. She nodded to the footman, and he went out, closing the front door behind him. She could hear Sebastian's footsteps coming toward her across the marble floor of the foyer, and she forced herself to turn around. "I'm leaving."

He halted, glancing over her tear-stained face. "What's wrong?"

"Wrong?" Daisy almost wanted to laugh. "Nothing's wrong. It's such a fine afternoon, in fact, I decided to take a stroll in the gardens. The south gardens."

He appreciated the vital point at once. "You overheard."

"Yes." The dinner gong sounded, and she felt a jolt of panic. "I have to go."

"No." He shook his head, denying it to her, seeming even to deny it to himself.

"I cannot stay here," Daisy whispered. "Lady Mathilda thinks I am a strumpet!"

"But you're not!"

"No?" she countered at once. "What am I, then? I'm not your wife, and as you so emphatically stated to your aunt, you have no intention of making me so. And even if you offered, I would refuse you, for I know you do not love me. Don't deny it," she added as he opened his mouth to interrupt. "I overheard your conversation, yes, but I knew the truth even before that. I saw it in your face last night. I tried not to believe it, but—" She broke off and gave a little laugh. "But reality is forced upon me. Since you do not love me and do not intend to marry me, we all know what I am. I'm your mistress. Nothing less, and certainly nothing more." She could hear her voice shaking. "God help me now."

"You've no need to worry." He closed the distance between them. Cupping her face, he looked straight into her eyes. "I'll take care of you."

Ah, yes. Shades of Mr. Pettigrew. "How?" she asked, hearing scorn enter her voice. "By giving me a tidy little income," she quoted her former employer, "and a house in a discreet neighborhood?"

He didn't answer, but she saw his lips tighten, and she feared that was exactly what his plan had been. Men, she realized with sudden, uncharacteristic cynicism, were very much alike, regardless of their age or station in life.

She refused the offer before he could confirm it. "No, thank you. It's very romantic of you," she couldn't help adding with heavy sarcasm, "wanting to take care of me and everything, but I fear I must decline your generosity." She pushed his wrists down and started to turn away, but he grabbed her by the arms.

"Don't go. Daisy, we have to talk about this. Make arrangements."

"I want nothing of your arrangements." She twisted in his hold, trying to free herself. "Let go of me."

He shook his head, and his hold did not slacken. "You can't leave me."

"I know the book's what's important, but you'll have to finish it without me."

"I can't! Daisy, I can't do this without you. If you

overheard my conversation with Mathilda, you know how much I need you." He gave her a little shake. "I can't let you go. I can't give you up."

"Need me?" she echoed, and desperate, she once again struggled in his grip, feeling her panic returning when he still didn't release her. "Can't do this without me?" she cried, frantic, twisting in his hold like a trapped animal. "Can't let me go, can't give me up? Listen to yourself. You make me sound like some sort of addiction!"

He went utterly still. "What did you say?" he asked in a whisper.

"You talk about me the same way my father always talked about his brandy," she went on, heedless of the sudden frozen stiffness of his face. "Medicine, he called it. Is that what I am, Sebastian? Your medicine?"

His hand shoved her away as if she burned, but his gray eyes were cold, like frozen lakes, and a shiver ran down her spine. "Go then," he said, taking a step back. "Go. Get the hell away from me."

Free at last, Daisy whirled around and left the house, feeling nothing but an overwhelming sense of relief. She raced down the front steps and climbed into the carriage that waited for her in the graveled drive. But when the footman closed the carriage door behind her, she made the mistake of glancing up through the window, and her relief died away into utter misery as she saw Sebastian standing in the doorway. Their eyes met for only a moment, and then he stepped back. When he shut the door, her heart fractured into pieces.

Her first love affair, it seemed, was now over.

Daisy secured a third-class ticket on the night train from Torquay to London, but as the train rushed through the countryside of Devonshire, Somerset, and Berkshire, she did not sleep. Instead, she stared out the darkened window and tried to think and decide what to do next.

What will you do now?

She'd asked Sebastian that question once, she remembered. And, as if it were an answer, his words came back to her.

There are other things in life, things that are more important than love. I've been in love, and it doesn't last. And when it's over, it's hell for a while. And then one discovers that life goes on.

Her life had to go on. Without him. She didn't have a manuscript to give Marlowe, so there would be no five hundred pounds, and she'd have to find another post. Typist, she expected, since that was the position for which she seemed most qualified. And she'd have to explain this latest debacle to Lucy. She leaned her head against the window, pressing her cheek to the cool glass with a sigh and wishing, not for the first time, that she was a more accomplished liar. The idea of facing her perfect older sister with the news that she had lost not only another job but her virtue as well was not something she could look forward to with enthusiasm. And she'd have to tell her; Daisy couldn't lie for toffee, and besides, there was the possibility of a child to consider.

A baby. Daisy's hand slid to her abdomen. What if there was a baby? Having a child out of wedlock was the worst shame a woman could suffer, and yet, curiously enough, Daisy couldn't summon her earlier panic and dismay. Lucy, she knew, would stand by her. She might lecture, she might berate, but Lucy would not abandon her. She wasn't alone, and that was a comforting thought.

Still, there was the fact that she would not be able to work if she was pregnant. No one would hire her. She could finish her novel, she supposed, try to sell it to a publisher. She'd have to go back to writing her books in longhand, since she hadn't taken the Crandall with her when she'd left Avermore. She couldn't. A mistress accepted expensive gifts. A respectable woman did not. Perhaps it was a bit late in the day to remember her morals, but nonetheless, she had left Sebastian's gift behind.

Daisy's heart clenched with pain, and she squeezed her eyes shut. Best not to think of Sebastian. Later, when she could stand it, she might think about him, but not now.

She didn't know she had fallen asleep until the train whistle woke her. She jerked upright, noting it was just coming on for dawn, and they were on the outskirts of London. Within an hour, she was at Victoria Station, arranging delivery of her trunk to the lodging house and hailing a taxi. Within two hours, she was in Holborn, standing at the door of Number 32 Little Russell Street.

Daisy paused on the sidewalk, studying the tidy brick building and its dark green shutters with affection. She'd missed the lodging house and all her friends. She'd even missed her sister, and that surprised her more than anything. Daisy took a deep breath and opened the front door.

It was breakfast time, she realized, hearing feminine voices, Lucy's among them, drifting to the foyer from the dining room. She set down her dispatch case by the coat tree, then crossed the foyer, went down a corridor, and entered the dining room.

Exclamations of surprise and delight greeted her as she paused in the doorway, but her sister's voice seemed to rise above them all.

"Daisy? What are you doing here?"

She tried to smile. "I've lost my post," she confessed. "Again."

Chapter 19

Away with your fictions of flimsy romance.
Lord Byron

Daisy's words began echoing in Sebastian's ears the moment she was out the door, and no matter how he tried, he could not silence them.

You make me sound like some sort of addiction.

She *was* an addiction. He knew it well enough. He recognized the symptoms. His need for her was a craving every bit as powerful as his craving for cocaine had been. But all addictions eventually required withdrawal, and in the days that followed Daisy's departure, he discovered that his withdrawal from her was just as painful.

He tried to distract himself with estate matters, but that did no good. There wasn't much activity on an estate that barely paid for itself, and he had a land agent.

Besides, everywhere he went, he found reminders of the woman he was trying to forget. The mill, the maze, the folly, the summerhouse, even his favorite fishing hole, all evoked memories of her, feeding his craving just enough to keep him from breaking free of it.

He tried distractions of a different sort. But the local pub, though friendly enough for the farm lads to share a pint, became quiet as a tomb the moment the local lord came in, and drinking alone to forget a woman was too pathetic to contemplate. Race meetings were all right for an afternoon, and the occasional country house party pleasant enough, but none of these activities could distract him for long.

A week went by, but he could find no relief. In desperation, he turned to the only thing he had left, the one thing that he'd taken so much trouble to avoid for so long. He turned to the book. For distraction and for solace, Sebastian tried to write.

The first time he tried after her departure was pure hell. He found himself looking up every few minutes, expecting to see her sitting at the desk opposite, always surprised for just a moment each time he stared at her empty chair. The second time was just as bad, and the third, and the fourth. After a week of trying, he was ready to hurl his typewriter through the window and give up.

He didn't. Something—he didn't know what— compelled him every morning to sit down and try again. Perhaps it was because he wanted to prove that he didn't need Daisy at all. Or perhaps to prove to himself that he had a purpose, that he was worth something beyond taking up space. Or to prove that he still had one more story worth telling left in him.

Another month went by, and then another. His deadline came and went. Through sheer force of will, pages somehow got written; but despite his persistence, writing seemed like harder work than ever before. Without Daisy, without being able to look up and see her face, without her to talk over the problems and reward him with kisses, there was no joy in it. Yes, he could do it alone. But without her, it wasn't any fun.

Sebastian typed another row of X's, crossing out the godawful sentence he'd just written. He was almost finished with the book, damn it, but he just couldn't make the ending work. No matter how he tried, the perfect finish eluded him.

The ending is unsatisfying, disappointing, even infuriating.

He muttered an oath as Daisy's revision letter came back to haunt him, and he ripped the sheet of crossed-out sentences from the roller of his Crandall, balled it up, and tossed it aside.

"Having trouble?"

Mathilda's voice caused him to look up. "No," he lied. "I'm not having trouble."

"I'm very glad to hear it." She came into the library

and walked over to a bookshelf. "I don't mean to disturb you," she added, "but I wanted something to read."

In furtherance of that goal, she wandered about the room, scanning bookshelves. When she finally decided upon a certain volume, however, she did not depart. Instead, she curled up in one of the leather chairs by the fireplace to read it while Sebastian resumed working.

He typed a sentence, crossed it out, typed another, and crossed it out. He set his jaw. In this book, he had something good, truly good, maybe the best thing he'd ever written. He was not—*was not*—going to ruin it with an unrealistic, sappy ending. He typed sentences with rapid-fire strokes, forcing Amelie to write the note, end the affair, and leave. But at the end of the page, he stopped, Daisy's voice once again echoing through his mind.

Aren't you the one who's always saying people aren't that self-sacrificing?

She was right. Having the heroine be so noble and unselfish made for an ending that deserved the criticism Daisy had given it.

He ripped the page he'd just written out of the typewriter, wadded it into a ball, and tossed it aside.

He looked up to find Mathilda watching him from the chair across the room. "All right, I am having trouble," he admitted. "The ending is giving me fits. It's not right."

"How is it supposed to end?"

"The heroine abandons the hero. She goes off alone, for his sake, but that doesn't work. It's too noble of her. It doesn't seem real." He paused to consider, drumming his fingers on the desk. "She could abandon him for another man, I suppose."

"That sounds quite depressing."

He groaned at yet another reminder of Daisy. Leaning forward, he plunked his elbows on the edge of his desk and rubbed his fingertips over his tired eyes. "Not you, too?" he muttered. "Why do women always want happy endings?" He lifted his head and scowled at his aunt. "This story is not getting a happy ending, damn it!"

"Why not?" Mathilda looked at him in bewilderment. "Why can't the story have a happy ending?"

He gave a violent start and stood up. "Because there is no such thing!" he snapped as he walked to one of the French windows. "Because happy endings don't happen. Because dogs die, love affairs end, and life goes on!"

Behind him, he heard Mathilda rise from her chair and cross the room to stand beside him. "Sebastian, love affairs don't always have to end, you know."

"Don't," he cut her off. "Don't even open the topic of Daisy Merrick. She's gone, and that's the end of it."

"If you say so."

"I do say so." Sebastian leaned one shoulder against the jamb and looked out the window, his gaze skipping past the terrace to the gardens beyond. He couldn't see the summerhouse from here, or the folly, but he could see the maze. He stared at the wall of tall green hedge, stared straight through it to the center. He could see her standing there, by the fountain of the Muses, with her brilliant hair falling like strands of fire through his fingers.

How? he thought with sudden despair. How was he ever going to conquer his need for her when memories of her were everywhere?

He could leave, he supposed. But where would he go? Africa no longer seemed to hold any charms for him. The Argentine didn't appeal much either. France, Italy, and Switzerland were out of the question for obvious reasons. America . . . He paused to consider America, the land of new beginnings. Going there had a certain irony about it, he supposed, but—

"It's odd," Mathilda's voice interrupted his thoughts, "but now that I think on it, I realize you've never written a story with a happy ending."

Sebastian paid no attention to this observation. America was all very well, he thought, and from what he'd heard, a magnificent country, but—

"Perhaps you should."

The sound of Mathilda's voice once again intruded. "I beg your pardon?" he asked without taking his gaze from his imagined view.

"I said, perhaps you should write a happy ending."

Lost in his thoughts, it took a few moments for Mathilda's words to sink in, but when they did, they brought to mind the words of another woman, the woman he was trying so hard to forget.

For heaven's sake, Sebastian, some people do fall in love and end up happy for life! It does happen, you know.

At the time, he hadn't paid Daisy's words much heed, but now, they struck him like an earthquake. Everything in the world cracked, shook, and shifted. And then, suddenly, he felt as if he was looking at things right side up instead of upside down. He didn't want to go away. He wanted to live right here at Avermore for the rest of his days, writing books in this library, fishing at Osbourne's Bend, and making a life. A life with the woman he loved.

"You're right." Sebastian started for the door, grabbing the manuscript as he went.

"Where are you going?" Mathilda called after him.

"In search of a happy ending," he answered, hoping fiction wasn't the only place to find one.

Daisy inserted a fresh sheet of notepaper into the typewriting machine and turned the roller. She pushed the metal lever three times to bring the sheet to its proper margin, then placed her fingers on the keys, found her place midway down the sheet of handwritten manuscript to her right and resumed work.

The novel, *Where Passion Flows Free*, by Rosamond Delacroix, was terrible, but Daisy was not working at Haughton's Typewriting and Secretarial Service to offer editorial opinions. She was a typist and stenographer, nothing more. She was paid five shillings per week to convert handwritten manuscripts to type, and to take shorthand dictation when required.

She hadn't obtained this post through Lucy's agency. She'd found it herself, and from the moment she had first sat down at this desk, she had vowed that no matter what, she was not going to lose it because of her rash tongue and impulsive nature. Over two months she'd been employed here, and she had not a single reprimand to her credit. Lucy was very proud of her.

He caught her up in his manly arms, she typed, but that was as far as she was able to go before her machine jammed, and she had to stop again. Daisy swung the undercarriage of the Remington upward, saw that the ribbon was caught, and proceeded to begin working it free.

In fact, Lucy had taken the entire situation rather well, much to Daisy's surprise. There had been no lectures. No recriminations, no censure of any kind. The fact that she'd lost her post in Devonshire had not come as any particular surprise to her sister, but the fact that she'd burst into tears right after announcing it had come as a bit of a shock. Lucy, however, had reacted with all her usual intrepid calm. She had jumped up from the breakfast table and guided her sobbing younger sister up to their rooms. There, with a tiny glass of Mrs. Morris's horrid damson gin, a stack of linen handkerchiefs, and Lucy's surprisingly tender sympathy to sustain her, Daisy had poured out the whole story, including a delicately phrased admission of her lost virtue.

When all had been revealed, once Daisy had regained control of her emotions and Lucy's fierce, protective anger had calmed, and after Daisy had dissuaded her sister from finding Papa's pistol and using it to shorten Avermore's lifespan, Daisy had outlined her future plans, including her intent to find her own next job and finish her novel.

In the ten weeks that had passed since then, Daisy had accomplished both goals. Her novel was with Marlowe, being considered, and she was the fastest, most accurate typist and stenographer at the bureau. It wasn't the exciting post she'd yearned for, but it was hers and she was good at it, and life went on. She tried to be content with that. But sometimes at night, when the lodging house was quiet and everyone else was in bed, Daisy would sit by her window, imagine a maze or a folly or a summerhouse, and remember what it was like to be in love.

All around her, the other typewriters made a raucous cacophony of sound. One of the clerks rushed past her desk and swung the green baize door wide as he entered the main reception area. He left the door open, as the clerks were always wont to do. Daisy, her hands occupied with handfuls of typewriter ribbon, could not get up to close it.

Because she sat nearest to the door, the haughty, female voice of Haughton's own secretary occasionally floated to her when the door was open. She could hear it now, speaking into the telephone.

"Oh, yes, madam. Haughton's Typewriting Bureau can send a stenographer to you straightaway. Your address, please?"

Daisy finally freed the jammed ribbon and began the painstaking process of rewinding it back onto the spool without removing it from the machine, but when she heard Miss Bateman say her name, she paused in her task, hopeful.

"Miss Merrick? She's done work for you before, you say?" There was a pause. "Quite so, your ladyship. She might have a previous engagement, but yes, of course I shall inquire of Mrs. Haughton. Shall I ring you back? Mayfair six—two—four—four? Yes, I have it."

Daisy wanted to jump for joy. Even on a cold, wet day in November, going out on a call was far better than being cooped up inside the bureau. But when Mrs. Haughton appeared a few moments later and paused before her desk, Daisy managed to contain her exuberance beneath a dignified, ladylike demeanor. "Yes, ma'am?" she said, rising to her feet.

"Six twenty-four Park Lane," Mrs. Haughton said.

"The Marchioness of Kayne requires a stenographer immediately. She asked for you."

Daisy blinked. Maria had rung up for a stenographer?

Mrs. Haughton held out sixpence. "Here's fare enough for a taxi to Mayfair and an omnibus back. Well, don't just stand there dawdling, miss," she added impatiently when Daisy failed to move. "Fetch your mackintosh, your notebook, and your pencils, and go. It won't do to keep a marchioness waiting!"

"Yes, ma'am." Daisy did as she was bid, but she was puzzled. Maria had formerly lived at Little Russell Street, but she had left the lodging house to open a bakery, and had subsequently married a marquess. It was quite a romantic story, worthy, in Daisy's mind, of a novel. But she couldn't understand why Maria would need a stenographer. The only thing she could conclude was that her friend was doing this as a favor to her, since being asked for specially by a marchioness would convey a most favorable impression upon Daisy's employer.

But when the butler at Park Lane had taken her cloak and led her into the gold and white drawing room of Lord Kayne's magnificent London residence, Daisy found that her friend was not the only one waiting for her.

Seated beside the fair-haired Maria on the sofa was a handsome, dark-haired man Daisy knew quite well.

She froze in the doorway as the butler announced her name, and she watched in dismay as Sebastian rose and turned toward her. His face was grave, without its usual ironic half smile, but he was still as handsome as ever, and he still looked much more like a venturing explorer than a writer. Pain twisted her heart at the sight of him, but she couldn't bear to look away.

"Daisy," Maria greeted her, stepping forward.

"Maria," she murmured absently, accepting her friend's kiss on the cheek without taking her gaze from Sebastian. "You sent for me?"

"I did," Sebastian corrected, answering for her. "But I had the marchioness place the call."

"You did? Why?"

That brought the smile. One corner of his mouth curved up a bit. "I thought she'd have better luck persuading you than I would."

Daisy recovered her surprise, lifting her chin to glare at him, trying to hide the prickle of alarm that ran up her spine. "What do you want?"

"I need a stenographer," he said simply.

Before she could ask any more questions, Maria spoke again. "I shall leave you to conduct business," the marchioness said. "I shall be in the library across the corridor if you need me," she added, and before Daisy could protest her departure, Maria was heading for the door.

"No, Maria, wait!" Daisy cried, but her friend seemed

to have gone deaf. She didn't even pause, walking out of the drawing room without another word and closing the door behind her.

Daisy turned toward Sebastian, hugging her notebook to her chest. "Why on earth do you need a stenographer?"

"Maybe I want to write something?" he suggested.

"I'm leaving," she said and turned to go, but when he spoke again, his words gave her reason to pause.

"I have something of yours."

Curiosity got the better of her, and she glanced back at him to find he was holding her copy of Byron, the one he'd given her in the maze.

"'Away with your fictions of flimsy romance,'" he quoted as he took a step toward her, "'those tissues of falsehood which Folly has wove. Give me the mild beam of the soul-breathing glance, or the rapture which dwells on the first kiss of love.'"

The memory of that day in the maze brought a wave of fresh pain ripping through her chest. "Stop it!" she cried. "Don't quote me poetry about love and kisses! I thought I made it clear there were no more kisses. You certainly made it clear there was no love!"

He held the small volume of poetry out to her. "The book is still yours."

Daisy bit her lip, staring at the copy of Byron in his outstretched hand. She'd left it behind on purpose, along with the Crandall. For the same reason. "I can't accept it," she said primly. "And now, I must return to work, Lord Avermore. Good day."

"I am your work, petal. At least for the next hour. I am paying Mrs. Haughton's establishment for one hour of your time, and I expect to receive it." At her sound of outrage, he gave her an apologetic look. "I fear if you leave before the hour is up, you might lose your post."

"This is ridiculous!" she cried, fighting the impulse to run for the door. "Why are you doing this?"

Since she had refused to accept the volume of Byron, he set it on the table beside the sofa, and it was then that she noticed that a sheaf of pages tied with twine was also on the table. He picked it up. "I've finished my book. Finished just this morning."

"Congratulations," she said, unimpressed. "But that has nothing to do with me."

"On the contrary. I'm sure Mrs. Haughton would be absolutely delighted to allow Miss Merrick to edit, type, and proof the latest Sebastian Grant novel before it goes to Marlowe Publishing."

Daisy stared at him, feeling rising dismay and a hint of panic. "You don't need your manuscript typed," she said. "You type your own."

"Since my editor deserted me over two hundred pages ago, at least one third of the book needs to be reviewed for content. Then it will have to be proofed and retyped. I want you to do it, my love. I won't let anyone else come near it until you've approved it. Not even Harry."

Daisy's panic deepened into stark fear. "I don't work for Marlowe Publishing, and I'm not your editor. Nor am I your proofreader, your assistant, your secretary, your writing partner, or your love. I'm nothing to you at all, and—" Her voice broke, much to her mortification, for she couldn't finish with the lie that hovered on her lips. She couldn't say he was nothing to her. "I'm nothing to you," she repeated to reinforce the point.

Once again, she started for the door, and this time, she had no intention of letting him stop her, no matter what he said.

"I had a cocaine habit."

Daisy froze. Slowly, she turned her head to look at him over her shoulder. "What?" she whispered in shock.

He set the manuscript back on the table. "It all started in Paris. Why, I don't know," he added with a shrug. "I was bored, I suppose. Like everything else, I thought it would give me a new experience, something to write about. And then, in Italy, I discovered how to write under the drug's influence, and it was like a godsend. Writing had always been hard for me, you see, and though I wanted to do it, and I was compelled to do it, and I made a great deal of money doing it, I had always wished there was a way to make it easier."

Daisy set her jaw and folded her arms. "Is any of this supposed to matter to me?"

If he noticed the hardness of her voice, he ignored it. "My father hated that I was a writer, and he could never understand why I cared about that more than I cared about Avermore. By the time I moved to Italy, I was earning enough to support the family estate. Being able to mete out a quarterly allowance to my father was sweet, but as I said, writing was never easy for me—not until I discovered cocaine. I learned that if I took the drug when I wrote, I could produce masses of work without any effort. Not very good work, you understand, but plenty of it. For the first time in my life, writing was *easy*. It was fun. I could write all day long, carouse all night long. I thought I'd found nirvana." He paused, and it seemed an eternity before he spoke again. "That nirvana lasted about three or four years. And then my life started falling apart."

Now she knew what he'd been referring to that day at the summerhouse—cocaine was his weakness. It was just like her father's brandy. Remembering the vulnerable thirteen-year-old girl who'd been so bitterly disillusioned was enough to keep her from softening, and Daisy turned her back on him. She started toward the door, but she got only as far as trying to open it.

"Don't go." Sebastian's voice spoke from right behind her, his hand flattening against the door to keep it closed. "Please, Daisy, don't go yet. Just let me finish what I have to say."

She didn't want to. She bit her lip, staring at the gold-and-white-painted panels of the door. She didn't want to hear this, she didn't want to know these things, she didn't want to understand or forgive. She wanted to leave, and yet, when his hand slid away from the door, she couldn't seem to make herself open it and walk out.

She stood there, hand on the knob, wavering, listening as he continued the story.

"Cocaine became more important than anything else," he went on behind her. "I stopped caring about the quality of my writing, and the critics began to shred me, but I didn't care. I spent lavishly, but my income began falling. I went into debt." The words were tumbling out of him as if he knew she was about to bolt and he wanted to explain everything first.

"Daisy, you asked me once why people ruin their lives for these things, and even though it happened to me, I can't give you an answer. Drugs blunt one's moral sense, I suppose. That's the only explanation I can offer."

"So the scandal sheets were right about you." She turned around to face him, wanting to use that fact against him, flay him with his past, but she couldn't. Despite everything, she still loved him, and she couldn't say cruel things to hurt him.

"Yes," he answered. "Wild parties, drink, reckless gambling—if it was a vice, I tried it. Nearly everything you've heard about me or read about me is true. But the cocaine—that was a secret. No one knows about that. No one except you, my friend St. Cyres, a British doctor living in Italy, and a few monks in Switzerland."

"Doctor? So you sought a cure?" Even as she asked, Daisy wanted to kick herself in the head. He was an addict. An addict was like a drunk. He would never be cured.

"I had to do something," he said. "One day, I took too much, and it nearly killed me. When I woke up, the doctor that had been sent for told me that if I continued to take cocaine, it would kill me, and having just come away a hair's breadth from death, I knew I had to stop. The doctor recommended a discreet place in the Swiss Alps for me to wean myself away from it—a monastery, of all places." He tried to smile. "Me, in a monastery. Can you imagine?"

She started to smile back, then stopped herself. "Go on," she said in a hard voice, closing her eyes. "Finish this, so I can leave."

"I spent three years there, overcoming my addiction. I've never told anyone about this, not even Mathilda, but your father drank, and I thought you had the right to know I have a similar weakness."

She forced herself to look into his eyes. When she did, the tenderness she saw there was almost her undoing. Hope began rising inside her—foolish, foolish hope. She could feel her old optimism coming back, cracking the new protective veneer she'd worked so hard to develop. "Do you still take the drug?"

"No, Daisy. I haven't taken it for three years. But it's only fair for me to tell you that the craving for it will always be with me. Once something like that happens to you, you can't go back. It's like losing your innocence," he murmured and reached out, his fingertips lightly brushing across her cheekbone.

She stiffened, pulling back from his touch, and he let his hand fall. "Once you've taken that step," he went on, "you're changed forever. But I swear to you, I won't ever take cocaine again."

"You might." Remembering her father, she tried to force hope back down, squash it before it could take hold.

"You have every right not to trust me, Daisy, but I know as surely as I know anything in life, that I will never take cocaine again. You see, that day in Italy when I took too much, I knew I was dying—I could feel it happening to me." He stirred, flattening his hand against his chest. "I felt as if I was being pulled in two directions at once—up and down—by two opposing forces."

"Heaven and hell?"

"I think so. I knew—don't ask me how, but I knew I was supposed to choose, surrender to one or to the other. But I refused to make that choice. I fought, Daisy, I fought hard for my life, but when I woke up, it was hard to understand why. Without cocaine, I couldn't seem to write anymore. I tried, but every time I sat down at my typewriter, I craved the drug so much, writing was unbearable. So I stopped altogether. I thought I'd never write again. My life had no purpose." He paused. "And then you came."

Daisy felt another crack in her armor at the tenderness in his voice. "I have to go."

She expected him to argue. He didn't.

"All right," he said quietly and stepped back. Disappointment stabbed at her, but she couldn't let him see that. She started to turn and reach for the doorknob, but his voice once again gave her pause. "I have one more thing to give you."

She glanced over her shoulder, watching as he turned away and walked to the sofa. He picked up the manuscript. As he came toward her with it in his hands, she shook her head. "Don't give it to me. I'm not helping you anymore."

He halted in front of her. "Daisy, writing had always been the most important thing in my life. The rest—the cocaine, the wild living—all that was only because I had become convinced I needed those things in order to write. They were the crutches, the tricks, if you will, that I used to convince myself I could do it. When I gave up cocaine, I gave up writing, sure I'd never be able to do it without the drug. But then, as I said, you came. You forced me to write. You pestered me and coerced me and bullied me into it."

She felt compelled to dispute that point. "I did not bully you!"

"Oh, yes, you did. And seduced me," he added, smiling, "and refused to give up on me when I'd long ago given up on myself. Somehow, with your optimism and your tenacity and your luscious incentives—" He broke off long enough to lean down and plant a kiss on her lips. "I began to believe that I could write again. But until you left, I still thought I needed outside forces to help me. I thought you were my latest drug, my crutch, my trick. When Mathilda found out about us and insisted you be sent home, it felt like I was giving up cocaine and writing all over again. I thought I needed you too much to let you go. But when you called me an addict, I knew I had to prove to myself that I could survive without any drugs, write without any help. When you left, I dredged up a strength I never thought I had, and I finished the book. I had to prove to myself at last that I don't need crutches of any kind in order to do it."

"Of course you could do it," she whispered. "It was always inside you. You didn't need cocaine. You didn't need crutches. You don't—" Her voice cracked. "You don't need me."

"That's where you're wrong. I need you more than you could possibly imagine. That's why I've dedicated this book to you."

"To me?"

"Yes, petal, to you."

"But . . . but you don't dedicate your books to anyone. That's just sappy sentiment, you said."

"Yes, well, for this book, I'm making an exception." He turned the manuscript around so she could read the first page.

> *To Daisy, my inspiration, my love,*
> *my reason for living.*

A sob tore from her throat.

"I know," he said cheerfully, nodding as if in agreement. "It's sappy, and it's sentimental. But I like it. And besides, it's the truth. For the first time, I'm grateful I fought so hard for my life. Because now I have a reason for living it." The manuscript was tossed aside, hitting the floor with a thud, and he caught her hands in his. "I love you, petal."

She found her voice. "You told Mathilda you didn't. I heard you."

"I didn't realize it, not until you were gone. Hell, I stopped believing in love so long ago, I couldn't even remember what it felt like. I thought you were just my latest addiction. But now I realize you are not that at all." His arms slid around her. "You are my love. You are my life. And I want you to marry me, and come back to Avermore with me, and write your books right across from where I write mine, so that whenever I'm working, I can look up and see your sweet, freckled face. And I'll help you any way I can to write yours."

"You won't give me the sack for speaking my mind?"

"No. And you won't ever have to worry about having your sister find you another job. All we'll have to worry about is making our deadlines. Publishers are sticklers for that sort of thing, you know." He kissed her nose. "And I want us to make love and have children and argue and kiss our way through each other's books for the rest of our lives. What do you think?"

Daisy looked up at him, her heart overflowing with joy. She loved this man, and what he'd just described sounded to her like heaven on earth.

"Well?" he asked when she didn't speak. "Is this love story going to have a happy ending?"

"I thought you didn't believe in happy endings. You never write them."

"Nonsense," he scoffed and nodded to the manuscript on the floor. "I just finished writing a book with a happy ending."

"You did?"

"Yes, I did. And I think I'm becoming addicted to them." He put his hands on her waist. "You haven't answered my question, by the way. Is our love story going to end happily or not?"

"Yes!" she cried, laughing. "Yes, yes, yes!"

"Thank God," he muttered. "There's nothing worse than reading a wonderful love story, only to reach the end and discover there's no happy ending. I hate it when that happens."

"Me, too." She slid her hands up his chest and wrapped her arms around his neck. "Oh, Sebastian, I love you so!"

"And I love you, my darling Daisy."

With those words, Sebastian Grant, the Earl of Avermore, swept Miss Daisy Merrick, girl-bachelor, off her feet and into his strong, manly arms, giving her a most passionate kiss.

THE END

P.S. Yes, they lived happily ever after.

RULES OF ENGAGEMENT

Rules . . . are made to be broken.

This fall, meet four ladies—who won't let a few wagging tongues stand in the way of happiness—and the handsome gents who are willing to help them break with convention.

Turn the page for a sneak preview at delicious new romances from Laura Lee Guhrke, Kathryn Caskie, and Anna Campbell, and a gorgeous repackaged classic from Rachel Gibson.

WITH SEDUCTION IN MIND

A Girl-Bachelor novel by
New York Times **Bestselling Author**
LAURA LEE GUHRKE

Infamous author Sebastian Grant, Earl of Avermore, has seen better days. His latest play opened
to crippling reviews, his next novel is years over-
due, and, to top it off, his editor assigned feisty,
fire-haired beauty Daisy Merrick as his writing
partner (never mind she's the critic who thrashed
his play)! And yet, as frustration turns to desire,
it seems the one place Sebastian can find relief is
in the beguiling Daisy's arms . . .

Sebastian rolled down his cuffs and fastened
them with his cuff links, then gave a tug to
the hem of his slate-blue waistcoat, raked his
fingers through his hair to put the unruly strands
in some sort of order, and smoothed his dark blue
necktie. He went down to the drawing room and
paused beside the open doorway.

Miss Merrick's appearance, he noted as he took
a peek around the doorjamb, was much the same
as before. The same sort of plain, starched white
shirtwaist, paired with a green skirt this time. Ribbons of darker green accented her collar and straw
boater. She was seated at one end of the long yellow

sofa, her hands resting on her thighs. Her fingers drummed against her knees and her toes tapped the floor in an agitated fashion, as if she was nervous. At her feet was a leather dispatch case.

He eyed the dispatch case, appalled. What if Harry wanted him to read her novel and give an endorsement? His publisher did have a perverse sense of humor. It would be just like Harry to pretend he was publishing the girl and blackmail Sebastian into reading eight hundred pages of bad prose before telling him it was all a joke. Or—and this was an even more nauseating possibility— she might actually be good, Harry did intend to publish her book, and they truly did want his endorsement.

Either way, he wasn't interested. Striving not to appear as grim as he felt, Sebastian pasted on a smile and entered the drawing room. "Miss Merrick, this is an unexpected pleasure."

She rose from the sofa as he crossed the room to greet her, and in response to his bow, she gave a curtsy. "Lord Avermore."

He glanced at the clock on the mantel, noting it was a quarter to five. Regardless of the fact that it was inappropriate for her to call upon a bachelor unchaperoned, the proper thing for any gentleman to do in these circumstances was to offer her tea. Sebastian's sense of civility, however, did not extend that far. "My butler tells me you have come at Lord Marlowe's request?"

"Yes. The viscount left London today for Torquay. He intends to spend the summer there with his family. Before he departed, however, he asked me to call upon you on his behalf regarding a matter of business."

So it was a request for an endorsement. "An author and his sternest critic meeting at the request of their mutual publisher to discuss business?" he murmured, keeping his smile in place even as he wondered how best to make the words "not a chance in hell" sound civil. "What an extraordinary notion."

"It is a bit unorthodox," she agreed.

He leaned closer to her, adopting a confidential, author-to-author sort of manner. "That's Marlowe all over. He's always been a bit eccentric. Perhaps he's gone off his onion at last."

"Lord Avermore, I know my review injured your feelings—"

"Your review and the seven others that came after it," he interrupted pleasantly. "They closed the play, you know."

"I heard that, yes." She bit her lip. "I'm sorry."

He shrugged as if the loss of at least ten thousand pounds was a thing of no consequence whatsoever. "It's quite all right, petal. I only contemplated hurling myself in front of a train once, before I came to my senses." He paused, but he couldn't resist adding, "Hauling you to Victoria Station, on the other hand, still holds a certain appeal, I must confess."

She gave a sigh, looking unhappy. As well she should. "I can appreciate that you are upset, but—"

"My dear girl, I am not in the least upset," he felt compelled to assure her. "I was being flippant. In all truth, I feel quite all right. You see, I have followed your advice."

"My advice?"

"Yes. I have chosen to be open-minded, to take your review in the proper spirit, and learn from your critique." He spread his hands, palms up in a gesture of goodwill. "After all," he added genially, "of what use to a writer is mere praise?"

She didn't seem to perceive the sarcasm. "Oh," she breathed and pressed one palm to her chest with a little laugh, "I am so relieved to hear you say that. When the viscount told me why he wanted me to come see you, I was concerned you would resent the situation, but your words give me hope that we will be able to work together in an amicable fashion."

Uneasiness flickered inside him. "Work together?" he echoed, his brows drawing together in bewilderment, though he forced himself to keep smiling.

"Yes. You see . . ." She paused, and her smile faded to a serious expression. She took a deep breath, as if readying herself to impart a difficult piece of news. "Lord Marlowe has employed me to assist you."

Sebastian's uneasiness deepened into dread as he stared into her upturned face, a face that shone with sincerity. He realized this was not one of Harry's jokes. He wanted to look away, but it was rather like watching a railway accident happen. One couldn't look away. "Assist me with what, in heaven's name?"

"With your work." She bent and grasped the handle of her dispatch case, and as she straightened, she met his astonishment with a rueful look. "I am here to help you write your next book."

THE MOST WICKED OF SINS

A Sinclair Family novel by
USA Today **Bestselling Author**
KATHRYN CASKIE

Lady Ivy Sinclair is used to getting her way. So
when an Irish beauty steals the attention of the
earl Ivy had claimed, she hatches a devious
plan: distract the chit with an irresistible actor
hired to impersonate a marquess. But can Ivy
resist Dominic Sheridan's sinful allure, or will she
fall victim to her own scheming?

D amn it all, answer me!" A deep voice cut
into her consciousness, rousing her from the
cocoon of darkness blanketing her. She could
feel herself being lifted, and then someone shouting
something about finding a physician.

She managed to flutter her lids open just as she felt
her back skim the seat cushion inside the carriage.

Blinking, she peered up at the dark silhouette of a
large man leaning over her.

"Oh, thank God, you are awake. I thought I killed
you when I coshed your head with the door." He
leaned back then, just enough that a flicker of light
touched his visage.

Ivy gasped at the sight of him.

He shoved his black hair away from eyes that

looked almost silver in the dimness. A cleft marked the center of his chin, and his angular jaw was defined by a dark sprinkling of stubble. His full lips parted in a relieved smile.

There was a distinct fluttering in Ivy's middle.

It was *him*. The perfect man . . . for the position.

"It's *you*," she whispered softly.

"I apologize, miss, but I didn't hear what you said." He leaned toward her. "Is there something more I can do to assist you?"

Ivy nodded and feebly beckoned him forward. He moved fully back inside the cab and sat next to her as she lay across the bench.

She gestured for him to come closer still.

It was wicked, what she was about to do, but she had to be sure. She had to know he was the right man. And there was only one way to truly know.

He turned his head so that his ear was just above her mouth. "Yes?"

"I assure you that I am quite well, sir," she whispered into his ear, "but there is indeed something you can do for me."

She didn't wait for him to respond. Ivy shoved her fingers through his thick hair and turned his face to her. Peering deeply into his eyes, she pressed her mouth to his, startling him. She immediately felt his fingers curl firmly around her wrist, and yet he didn't pull away.

Instead his lips moved over hers, making her yield to his own kiss. His mouth was warm and tasted faintly of brandy, and his lips parted slightly as he masterfully claimed her with his kiss.

Her heart pounded and her sudden breathlessness blocked out the sounds of carriages, whinnying horses, and theater patrons calling to their drivers on the street.

His tongue slid slowly along her top lip, somehow making her feel impossible things lower down. Then he nipped at her throbbing bottom lip, before urging her mouth wider and exploring the soft flesh inside with his probing tongue.

Hesitantly, she moved her tongue forward until it slid along his. At the moment their tongues touched, a soft groan welled up from the back of his throat and a surge of excitement shot through her.

Already she felt the tug of surrender. Of wanting to give herself over to the passion he somehow tapped within her.

And then—as if he knew what he made her feel, made her want—he suddenly pulled back from her.

She peered up at him through drowsy eyes.

"I fear, my lady, that you mistake me for someone else," he said, not looking the least bit disappointed or astounded by what she had done.

"No," Ivy replied, "no mistake." She wriggled, pulling herself to sit upright. "You are exactly who I thought you were." She straightened her back and looked quite earnestly into his eyes. "You are the Marquess Counterton . . . or rather you will be, if you accept my offer."

CAPTIVE OF SIN

**An eagerly anticipated new novel by
ANNA CAMPBELL**

Returning home to Cornwall after unspeakable tragedy, Sir Gideon Trevithick stumbles upon a defiant beauty in danger and vows to protect her—whatever the cost. Little does he know the waif is Lady Charis Weston, England's wealthiest heiress, and that to save her he must marry her himself! But can Charis accept a marriage of convenience, especially to a man who ignites her heart with a single touch?

Charis' eyes fastened on Sir Gideon, who waited outside. A cloud covered the moon, and the striking face became a mixture of shadows and light. Still beautiful but sinister.

She shivered. "Who are you?" she whispered, subsiding onto her seat.

"Who are you?" His dark gaze didn't waver from her as he resumed his place opposite, his back to the horses, as a gentleman would.

Charis wrapped the coat around her against the sharp early-morning chill and settled her injured arm more comfortably. "I asked first."

It was a childish response, and she knew he

Coming November 2009

recognized it as such from the twitch of his firm mouth. Like the rest of his face, his mouth was perfect. Sharply cut upper lip indicating character and integrity. A fuller lower lip indicating . . .

Something stirred and smoldered in her belly as she stared at him in the electric silence. What a time to realize she'd never before been alone with a man who wasn't a relative. The moment seemed dangerous in a way that had nothing to do with her quest to escape Felix and Hubert.

"My name is Gideon Trevithick." He paused as if expecting a response but the name meant nothing to her. "Of Penrhyn in Cornwall."

"Is that a famous house?" Perhaps that explained his watchful reaction.

Another wry smile. "No. That's two questions. My turn."

She stiffened although she should have expected this. And long before now.

"I'm tired." It was true, although a good meal and Akash's skills meant she didn't feel nearly as low as she had.

"It's a long journey to Portsmouth. Surely you can stay awake a few moments to entertain your fellow traveler."

She sighed. Her deceit made her sick with self-loathing. But what could she do? If she told the truth, he'd hand her over to the nearest magistrate.

"I've told you my name and where I live. I've told you the disaster that befell me today. I seek my aunt in Portsmouth." Her uninjured hand fiddled at the sling and betrayed her nervousness. With a shuddering breath, she pressed her palm flat on her lap. "We're chance-met travelers. What else can you need to know?" She knew she sounded churlish, but she hated telling lies.

In the uncertain light, his face was a gorgeous mask. She had no idea if he believed her or not. He paused as if winnowing her answers, then spoke in a somber voice. "I need to know why you're so frightened."

"The footpads . . ."

He made a slashing gesture with his gloved hand, silencing her. "If you truly had been set upon by thieves, you wouldn't have hidden in the stable. Won't you trust me, Sarah?" His soft request vibrated deep in her bones, and for one yearning moment, she almost told him the truth. Before she remembered what was at stake.

"I . . . I have trusted you," she said huskily. She swallowed nervously. His use of her Christian name, even a false one, established a new intimacy. It made her lies more heinous.

Disappointment shadowed his face as he sat back against the worn leather. "I can't help you if I don't know what trouble you flee."

"You are helping me." Charis blinked back the mist that appeared in front of her eyes. He deserved better return for his generosity than deceit.

She tried to tell herself he was a man, and, for that reason alone, she couldn't trust him. The insistence rang hollow. Her father had been a good man. Everything told her Sir Gideon Trevithick was a good man too.

She forced a stronger tone. "It's my turn for a question."

He folded his arms across his powerful chest and surveyed her from under lowered black brows. "Ask away."

TRUE CONFESSIONS

The classic novel by
New York Times Bestselling Author
RACHEL GIBSON

Tabloid reporter Hope Spencer is in a rut. But when she flees her same-old LA life for the respite of Gospel, Idaho—she gets oh-so-much more than she bargained for. Sticking out like a sore thumb in her silver Porsche and designer duds, Hope isn't looking for any entanglements. But when a years-old murder mystery throws her together with Gospel's sexy sheriff Dylan Taber—she might not want to avoid this snag in her plan.

W hat in the hell is that?"
    Dylan glanced across the top of the Chevy at Lewis, then turned his attention to the silver sports car driving toward him.

"He must have taken a wrong turn before he hit Sun Valley," Lewis guessed. "Must be lost."

In Gospel, where the color of a man's neck favored the color red and where pickup trucks and power rigs ruled the roads, a Porsche was about as inconspicuous as a gay rights parade marching toward the pearly gates.

"If he's lost, someone will tell him," Dylan said as

he shoved his hand into his pants pocket once more and found his keys. "Sooner or later," he added. In the resort town of Sun Valley, a Porsche wasn't that rare a sight, but in the wilderness area, it was damn unusual. A lot of the roads in Gospel weren't even paved. And some of those that weren't had potholes the size of basketballs. If that little car took a wrong turn, it was bound to lose an oil pan or an axle.

The car rolled slowly past, its tinted windows concealing whoever was inside. Dylan dropped his gaze to the iridescent vanity license plate with the seven blue letters spelling out MZBHAVN. If that wasn't bad enough, splashed across the top of the plate like a neon kick-me sign was the word "California" painted in red. Dylan hoped like hell the car pulled an illegal U and headed right back out of town.

Instead, the Porsche pulled into a space in front of the Blazer and the engine died. The driver's door swung open. One turquoise silver-toed Tony Lama hit the pavement and a slender bare arm reached out to grasp the top of the doorframe. Glimmers of light caught on a thin gold watch wrapped around a slim wrist. Then MZBHAVN stood, looking for all the world like she was stepping out of one of those women's glamour magazines that gave beauty tips.

"Holy shit," Lewis uttered.

Like her watch, sunlight shimmered like gold in her straight blond hair. From a side part, her glossy hair fell to her shoulders without so much as one unruly wave or curl. The ends so blunt they might have been cut with a carpenter's level. A pair of black cat's-eye sunglasses covered her eyes, but couldn't conceal the arch of her blond brows or her smooth, creamy complexion.

The car door shut, and Dylan watched MZBHAVN walk toward him. There was absolutely no overlooking those full lips. Her dewy red mouth drew his attenion like a bee to the brightest flower in the garden, and he wondered if she'd had fat injected into her lips.

The last time Dylan had seen his son's mother, Julie, she'd had that done, and her lips had just sort of lain there on her face when she talked. Real spooky.

Even if he hadn't seen the woman's California plates, and if she were dressed in a potato sack, he'd know she was big-city. It was all in the way she moved, straight forward, with purpose, and in a hurry. Big-city women were always in such a hurry. She looked like she belonged strolling down Rodeo Drive instead of in the Idaho wilderness. A stretchy white tank top covered the full curves of her breasts and a pair of equally tight jeans bonded to her like she was a seal-a-meal.

"Excuse me," she said as she came to stand by the hood of the Blazer. "I was hoping you might be able to help me." Her voice was as smooth as the rest of her, but impatient as hell.

"Are you lost, ma'am?" Lewis asked.

At Avon Books, we know your passion for romance—once you finish one of our novels, you find yourself wanting more.

May we tempt you with . . .

- **Excerpts** from our upcoming releases.

- Entertaining **extras**, including authors' personal photo albums and book lists.

- Behind-the-scenes **scoop** on your favorite characters and series.

- **Sweepstakes** for the chance to win free books, romantic getaways, and other fun prizes.

- Writing **tips** from our authors and editors.

- **Blog** with our authors and find out why they love to write romance.

- **Exclusive content** that's not contained within the pages of our novels.

Join us at
www.avonbooks.com

AVON *An Imprint of* HarperCollins*Publishers*
www.avonromance.com